DATE DUE

AVON PUBLIC LIBRARY
BOX 977 / 200 BENCHMARK RD.
AVON, COLORADO 81620

Here Lies Linc

Here Lies Linc

DELIA RAY

Alfred A. Knopf New York

Aven $19.99 8/12 BoT

THIS IS A BORZOI BOOK PUBLISHED BY ALFRED A. KNOPF

This is a work of fiction. Names, characters, places, and incidents either are the product of the author's imagination or are used fictitiously. Any resemblance to actual persons, living or dead, events, or locales is entirely coincidental.

Text copyright © 2011 by Delia Ray
Jacket art copyright © 2011 by Tim Jessell
Map art copyright © 2011 by Fred van Deelen

All rights reserved. Published in the United States by Alfred A. Knopf, an imprint of Random House Children's Books, a division of Random House, Inc., New York.

Knopf, Borzoi Books, and the colophon are registered trademarks of Random House, Inc.

Visit us on the Web! www.randomhouse.com/kids

Educators and librarians, for a variety of teaching tools, visit us at
www.randomhouse.com/teachers

Library of Congress Cataloging-in-Publication Data
Ray, Delia.
Here lies Linc / by Delia Ray.—1st ed.
p.   cm.
Summary: While researching a rumored-to-be-haunted grave for a local history project, twelve-year-old Lincoln Crenshaw unearths some startling truths about his own family.
ISBN 978-0-375-86757-6 (trade) — ISBN 978-0-375-96756-6 (lib. bdg.) —
ISBN 978-0-375-89844-0 (ebook)
[1. Cemeteries—Fiction. 2. Families—Fiction. 3. Death—Fiction. 4. Junior high schools—Fiction. 5. Schools—Fiction. 6. Iowa—Fiction.] I. Title.
PZ7.R2101315He 2011
[Fic]—dc22   2010030004

The text of this book is set in 12-point Goudy.

Printed in the United States of America
August 2011
10 9 8 7 6 5 4 3 2 1

First Edition

Random House Children's Books supports the First Amendment
and celebrates the right to read.

For Lily,
who's always there to fill in my blanks

Prologue

Most people end their lives in a graveyard. Sometimes I think my life began there.

My First Memory: Crouching behind a crooked headstone, playing hide-and-go-seek with my dad.

My First Best Friend: Jeeter, the groundskeeper at Oakland Cemetery, who used to let me ride along on his big mower for hours whenever he trimmed graves.

My First Vacation: To Smith's Burying Ground in Franklin County, Ohio, so my mother could study the inscriptions on the pioneers' tombstones.

I could go on. This is the kind of life you get when you grow up next to graveyards and your mother happens to be a history professor who studies burial customs.

When I was little, this didn't seem so weird. I was used to my mom slamming on the brakes on country roads all across the Midwest, swerving onto the shoulder whenever she spotted even the tiniest cemetery set back in the trees. Once in a while I would whine, "Do we have to, Lottie?" (Lottie was Dad's nickname for my mother, and people tell me I used to copy my father whenever possible.)

But whining never worked with Lottie. She didn't even seem to hear it as she hid her car keys under the mat and turned to squint at the spots of stone in the distance. So I'd tag along, over guardrails and barbed wire fences, past cows and horses, through plowed farm fields and weeds and brambles. Lottie would bring her camera and notebook. I'd bring the ratty quilt from the backseat in case I got sleepy while she was wandering around taking notes.

"Some people might think this is disrespectful, Linc," I remember Lottie saying as she settled me in for one of those naps, spreading the quilt over a grave so that the headstone looked more like the headboard of a bed. "But not me. You know, the word 'cemetery' comes from a Greek term that means 'a large dormitory where lots of people are sleeping.'" She laughed as she bent down to kiss me on the cheek.

I would wake up from my naps and stare at the writing on the gravestones above me, trying to sound out the words and figure out how old the people were when they died. Lottie swears I taught myself to read deciphering headstones.

As I got older, I entertained myself during Lottie's cemetery trips by keeping a journal of my favorite epitaphs written on the stones. And in her office my mother had books full of interesting inscriptions—from ancient tombs in Europe or the headstones of well-known authors and actors and leaders buried around the world—so I added some of those to my journal too. It was like collecting autographs, but more interesting.

I got one of my best ones when Lottie and I took a research trip through Missouri, from the grave of the outlaw Jesse James:

MURDERED
APR. 3, 1882
BY A TRAITOR
AND COWARD
WHOSE NAME
IS NOT WORTHY
TO APPEAR HERE

But most of the epitaphs in my journal weren't from the graves of famous people. Most I scribbled down because they were strange or sad or just plain funny, like Number 42 in my notebook:

I Told You I Was Sick

Number 79 came from the grave of someone named Elizabeth Rich, buried in Eufaula, Alabama:

36–33–01–24–17
Honey, you don't know what you did for me,
Always playing the lottery.
The numbers you picked came in to play
Two days after you passed away.

For this, a huge monument I do erect
For now I get a yearly check
How I wish you were alive,
For now we are worth 8.5

I liked the fact that epitaphs didn't have any rules, that headstones could be etched with whatever crazy thing people needed to help them remember the one who died—a winning lottery number, a portrait of a favorite pet, the name of a Cub Scout troop, or lyrics to a song.

That's why I've never been happy with what Lottie decided to do for Dad. Even though I was only seven when he died, I still remember exactly how I felt when she took me out to Oakland to see his grave for the first time.

Gipped.

For one thing, there wasn't even a headstone. Instead of leading me across the cemetery to one of the newer graves scattered on the fringe like I expected, Lottie stopped at a long wall made of shiny black granite. I had asked Jeeter about the wall when we rode past it on the riding mower one day. A columbarium, he called it, pronouncing the syllables as if they left a bad taste on his tongue.

"That's where they store ashes of cremated people," he said. "Call me old-fashioned, but when I go, I'd rather be laid out in a nice roomy burial plot 'stead of getting sealed up in a hole no bigger than a post office box."

Lottie had walked about halfway down the wall and gently placed her fingertips on one of the black compartments in the third row from the top. I had to take a few steps closer to read the small writing. This is what it said:

Lincoln Raintree Crenshaw
1965–2005

That's it, the end.

"That's it?" I remember asking. "*That's* Dad's grave?"

Lottie turned toward me. "Well, yes. . . . Yes, honey," she said. "You know your father. He liked to keep things simple. This is what he would have wanted." But her voice didn't sound so sure.

She reached out to touch my face then, with that same hand she had pressed on the wall. I didn't let her. I yanked back as if her fingers were on fire, and ran crying through the graveyard, all the way home.

Like I said, I felt gipped. Gipped by only two lines of writing on a tiny little square of stone. Gipped by the heart attack that took my father, out of the blue—my dad, of all people, who never got sick and used to swing me up on his shoulders and had climbed more than fourteen thousand feet to the top of Mount Rainier in Washington State. Dad, who the ambulance guys said was riding his bike to work at eight o'clock one morning and then lying on the sidewalk on River Street by 8:05.

"Hearts can be tricky," they told my mom.

The only thing that made me feel better back then was writing in my epitaph journal, scribbling down all the epitaphs

I might have put on a real headstone for Dad if Lottie had bothered to ask me. I liked my rhyming ones the best:

> Here lies Lincoln Crenshaw
> Geologist, Husband, Pa
> He liked climbing and black-bottom pie.
> We were going to build a tree house three stories high.

LINCOLN RAINTREE CRENSHAW
We had the same name
Father and Son
First there were two, now there's one

I wrote lots more over the next year or so, all about how he liked to make us blueberry pancakes and never skipped the funnies in the newspaper, and how he wore long johns to bed and won the gold plaque on our mantel that said GEOLOGY RESEARCH PRIZE, 1999. But I never showed Lottie. Talking about him only made her sadder. Actually, it seemed like she didn't even want to think about him anymore. One day while I was at school, she took his clothes to Goodwill and packed everything else—his books and his favorite coffee mug and the gold plaque and their wedding picture—into boxes and hid them away in the attic. At least she saved one picture out for me. I still have it by my bed—a photo of me with Dad when I was two. We've got our tongues out, sharing a drippy chocolate ice cream cone.

But the truth is the last few years haven't been nearly as dismal as they sound. My mother and I have gotten on with things. After Dad died, we adopted one of the world's funniest-looking dogs from the animal shelter. Lottie went straight back to her cemetery research and teaching classes at the university. I've kept busy going to school down the street and helping around the house—basically trying to be a normal kid.

Once I turned twelve this past June, I decided it wasn't normal for someone my age to be spending so much time in graveyards anymore. So lately I've been making up excuses to stay behind on Lottie's research trips. All summer I pretended to be too busy to hang out with Jeeter at the cemetery. And while I can't quite bring myself to toss out my epitaph journal yet, I haven't added a single new listing in weeks.

But then along comes September and my first taste of junior high, and suddenly I've found myself right back where I started.

My First Field Trip of the Seventh Grade: Not to the state capital or to a show at the performing arts center or to the science museum in Cedar Rapids. My American Studies teacher just announced that our entire class is going to Oakland Cemetery to study graves.

In memory of
Deacon Ezekiel Pease . . .
What lies here is
only the pod;
He shelled out his Pease
and went to his God.

ENFIELD, CONNECTICUT

CHAPTER 1

PLAINVIEW JUNIOR HIGH WAS supposed to be a fresh start for me. But it's hard to start fresh when kids keep asking you questions about your past. During the first week of school at least ten kids had tried to strike up conversations.

They always started the same way.

"You're new, right? Where're you from?"

"I'm from around here."

"Then how come I've never seen you before? Which elementary school did you go to?"

"Uh . . . you've probably never heard of it," I'd say. "It's really small."

"Oh, you mean Washington Elementary? Or Kennedy?"

"No. . . ."

"Well, which one?"

"Uh—"

"*Which one?*"

"Well, it's called the Home-Away-from-Homeschool. A retired professor runs it out of her basement. It's sort of like a homeschool . . . but, you know, away from home. There were only a few of us. . . ."

That's about the time their ten pairs of eyes would cloud over and their ten pairs of feet would find an excuse to shuffle away.

And that's about the time I started to think that maybe I had made a big mistake switching to public school. Part of me wished I was back in Dr. Lindstrom's stuffy basement with the other oddball university professors' kids who made up the Ho-Hos. That's what Dr. Lindstrom had called us—the Ho-Hos, short for Home-Away-from-Homeschoolers.

Next to the typical Ho-Ho—like Sebastian, who could list every ancient Egyptian ruler back to King Khufu and wrote his name in hieroglyphics on the top of all his papers, or Vladka, who came from Russia and hardly ever spoke above a whisper and could multiply five-digit numbers in her head—I felt downright ordinary. I had transferred to Plainview hoping to find more regular kids like me. Lottie had always said if I *really* wanted, I could switch schools once junior high rolled around. But after just a few days at Plainview, I began to realize that I must be a full-fledged Ho-Ho after all, with extra cream filling on the side.

Still, I kept trying to fit in, and I was doing a pretty good job of it until the end of September, when Mr. Oliver made his surprise announcement in American Studies class.

That afternoon's lecture on the settlement of the Midwest territories hadn't exactly been riveting. So to entertain myself, I had grabbed a Kleenex from the box on the window-sill beside my desk and, like a surgeon, gotten busy dissecting the tissue into two see-through layers. Once the dissection was complete, I tuned back in, just in time to hear Mr. Oliver say, "And listen up, people! I've got some good news. Next week you'll actually have a chance to see where some of our city's most famous settlers are buried, because we're all going on a field trip to Oakland Cemetery."

While the rest of the kids whooped and high-fived over the prospect of missing class for a day, I froze in my seat, trying to make sense of the weird coincidence.

But Mr. Oliver wasn't finished.

"And, people . . . ," he said, pausing for effect while We the People waited, "here's the best part. I've managed to convince one of the nation's premier cemetery experts to come over from the university and lead our tour. Her name is Professor Charlotte Landers."

Lottie.

Why didn't she tell me?

If the sport of blushing could be an Olympic event, I'd win the gold medal. I've always turned beet red without a second's notice, even over dumb stuff like having to answer "Here" during attendance or if a halfway-decent girl happens to look in my direction or if Lottie sends me to the grocery store for something embarrassing like diarrhea medicine or dandruff shampoo.

So obviously, as soon as Mr. Oliver called out my mother's name, I felt my cheeks start to turn the color of raw hamburger. I grabbed a dissected tissue from my desk and pretended to blow my nose, bracing myself for the next part of the announcement, the part when Mr. Oliver would tell everyone that the graveyard expert's son was, in fact, a member of our very own fifth-period class. I waited with my face buried in the wad of Kleenex, praying for the blood to hurry up and drain back to where it belonged, into my overactive arteries and capillaries and veins.

A few more long seconds passed, and when I didn't hear my name called, I lifted my face out of the tissues, inch by inch, and looked around the room. But Mr. Oliver had already turned back to the blackboard, and the kids in the next row were busy copying down details of a new assignment. I slumped back in my desk with relief. . . . Nobody knew. For some reason Lottie must not have told Mr. Oliver that she was my mother. And since we had different last names, no one had any idea that we were even related.

Still, by the time school ended that day, the upcoming field trip had lodged itself like a splinter in my brain. The timing couldn't have been worse. Right when the Ho-Ho questions were starting to die down, now this—Lottie leading my class on a tour of the graveyard. It's not that I didn't love my mother. I loved her more than anything. It's just that she was kind of . . . kind of unusual. The way she thought and talked and dressed, everything about her was different from other moms. I knew the kids in my class weren't prepared for the likes of Lottie Landers.

She called home that night to check on me—from some tiny town on the coast of Rhode Island where she was spending a week of research in an old slave cemetery. This would be the longest Lottie had ever been gone, and she had insisted on hiring one of her graduate students to "take care of" me while she was away, even though I had become pretty good at running things around the house over the past few years. Luckily I had barely seen the guy since he'd shown up on our doorstep with his four bags of laundry the day before.

I wanted to interrogate Lottie about the field trip the minute I picked up the phone, but I forced myself to hold back until she had finished telling me about how her research was going. I couldn't remember the last time she had sounded so excited.

"Oh, Linc," she said. "I wish you could see this place. They call it God's Little Acre, and the stones are amazing. So artful and *poignant*. A lot of them list just a slave name and then who the slave belonged to. 'In memory of Cato. Servant to Mr. Brinley.' 'Peter. Servant of Captain John Browning.' Can you imagine? Linc? Are you there?"

"I'm here."

"Well, you're so quiet. Are you all right? Is Rick helping to fix dinner like he promised?"

"Uh-huh," I lied, looking down at the dregs of Rice Krispies floating in my bowl on the kitchen table. I couldn't complain. I was the one who had convinced her that I'd be fine staying home while she went to Rhode Island. I clamped the phone under my chin and started flipping through the stack of mail that had been piling up next to Lottie's spot at the table for the past month. "There's an overdue notice here, Lottie." I said. My mother had a habit of avoiding bill paying until the envelopes arrived with bright red alert messages and exclamation points stamped across the front. "It's from that plumber who came to fix our toilet back in July."

"Oh, shoot," Lottie muttered. "I meant to pay that one before I left. Can you take care of it for me, Linc? I signed a couple checks for you in case something came up. They're on the desk in my office . . . I think." She hurried to change the subject. "How's C.B.?"

"Fine," I said, trying not to sound too testy as I turned in my chair to look at C.B. He was sprawled on his hairy dog bed by the back door. As usual there was mud caked on the top of his big nose and dirt clods trapped in his mustache. "He's been busy," I told Lottie, "working on a new hole by the front porch."

She groaned. "Not the front yard too? Pretty soon we're going to look like we're living on top of an archaeological dig."

I plunked my bowl of soggy cereal on the floor for C.B. Even with the cranky mood I was in, I couldn't help smiling as I watched him roust himself from his bed and wander over to investigate. C.B. caused the same reaction in most people. I could never get very far in the park without someone stopping to ask me, "What kind of breed *is* that?" C.B. looked like some sort of canine mutant with his sheepdog head, basset-hound body, and long rat tail. And just to make his pedigree even more of a mystery, he was the color of a chocolate lab, all except for the blond eyebrows that sprang from his head like furry antennae.

I slid down to the floor so I could sit next to C.B. while he licked out my cereal bowl. He smelled like a swamp, but I hugged him anyway.

"Well, how was school today?"

I sat up, dodging C.B.'s tongue. *Finally.* Time to let the logjam loose. "Pretty good until fifth period," I said. "Why didn't you tell me that Mr. Oliver asked you to give our class a tour of the cemetery?"

"Mr. Oliver?" Lottie repeated in bewilderment. Then she gasped. "Oh, shoot! I almost forgot. Did I miss it? Wait a minute, that's *your* class going to Oakland?"

"Mom!" I barked into the phone. We both knew I only called her Mom when I was mad. And we both knew that she had a habit of forgetting things, but this was bordering on amnesia territory. "No, you didn't miss it. The field trip's not till *next* Tuesday . . . and yes, it's *my* American Studies class that you're supposed to lead on the tour." C.B. scooted out of the way as I grabbed the bowl he had licked clean and clambered to my feet in frustration.

"I'm sorry, Linc," Lottie said helplessly. "Before, there was just Dr. Lindstrom to keep track of, but now you have . . . is it six? Seven different teachers? And you know I get called to do lots of tours and special lectures. It's hard to keep everything straight."

I had started toward the sink with the bowl, but the phone cord was too short and tangled for me to get very far. I gave it a hard yank. Maybe if I broke it, Lottie would join the rest of the modern world and buy us a portable phone.

"Well, you can't do it anyway, can you?" I asked, standing motionless for a hopeful second at the end of my phone-cord tether. "You're not even getting home till the day of the field trip."

"What time does your class go to Oakland?"

"Around one o'clock."

"Piece of cake," she said. "I think my plane gets in around noon. See there? Everything's going to work out fine."

I didn't answer. It was so quiet in the house, I could hear C.B.'s long toenails clicking on the linoleum as he headed back to his bed.

"Linc?"

"I'm here," I said, taking a deep breath as I set the cereal bowl on top of the scattered mail on the table. "Listen, Lottie, do you think we could pretend . . . for this field trip that . . . you know . . . that we're not related?"

There was another pause. "Why?" she asked, the cheeriness suddenly draining out of her voice. "Why would we do that?"

I breezed ahead, trying to sound casual. "Well, you have to admit that you've got a pretty weird job, you know, spending your whole life studying dead people and symbols on headstones and why graves face east to west instead of north to south . . . and it's just that I'm . . . I'm new at Plainview and . . ." My words started to lose some of their steam.

"Ohhhhh. So *that's* what this is about," she said shrewdly. "Now that you're in *junior high*, you're embarrassed. You know, you never used to think twice about my job when you were with the Ho-Hos."

"I know," I said, holding back a sigh. "It's hard to explain. But I think I'd get a lot more out of the day if I could blend in with the other kids."

"Don't any of your friends already know what I do?"

I let my pent-up sigh whoosh out as I sank down in my place at the table again. *What friends?* Ever since I had switched to Plainview, Lottie kept referring to this mysterious group of "your friends," even though I had never mentioned meeting anyone new. "What are your friends up to this weekend?" she would ask. "Do any of your friends ride the bus?" As if I had a fresh crop of buddies lined up like rows of corn, just waiting for the pleasure of my company.

"Nope," I said quietly. "We don't really talk about our parents that much." I couldn't bring myself to admit to Lottie that so far, I was running on empty in the friends department. I gave myself a little shake and tried to make a joke. "Somehow I haven't gotten around to telling them my mom is Charlotte Landers, *Dr. Death*."

Lottie's soft chuckle came drifting over the phone lines. "Dr. Death, huh?"

"Please, Lottie?"

"Fine," she finally said. "I'll play along just this once, for the field trip. Even though it might be difficult, considering I won't have seen you for a whole week." Then she started to wobble, ready to change her mind. "But what if I go to a PTA meeting sometime, or what if I have a parent-teacher conference with Mr. What's-His-Name? He's bound to make the connection sooner or later."

I rolled my eyes around in their sockets. "His name is Mr. Oliver. And c'mon, Lottie, *PTA meeting*? You?"

"Oh, all right," she said. "You win."

"Thank you," I breathed.

Then I let my mind race ahead. "Lottie? There's one more thing."

"What is it?"

"Are we going anywhere near Dad's wall?" I needed to prepare myself. I couldn't even remember the last time I had felt like visiting my father's little block of stone.

Even from a thousand miles away, I could see Lottie sitting on the bed in her hotel room, blinking her silvery gray eyes closed, the way she always does whenever she's forced to think about Dad.

"No," she said after a few seconds. "We'll be staying in the old part of the cemetery."

"Okay." I found myself nodding into the phone. So far, so good.

I MADE A
LOT OF DEALS
IN MY LIFE
BUT I WENT
IN THE HOLE
ON THIS ONE

ZACHARY, LOUISIANA

CHAPTER 2

WHEN THE HO-HOS FOUND OUT I was transferring to public school, they tried to stage an intervention. Sebastian and Vladka showed up at my house one afternoon at the beginning of September, right before classes started. I sat between them on my front porch steps, looking back and forth while they told me how terrible Plainview would be.

"I came from that place, remember?" Sebastian said. His face was so sweaty, his glasses kept sliding down his nose. "I know what I'm talking about. It's just like life in ancient Egypt. You'll know who the pharaoh is right off the bat. Then you've got the high priests and nobles—all the jocks and the good-looking people. And under them there're the slaves and peasants—everybody else."

"You will be a peasant," Vladka whispered in her leftover Russian accent. She sounded just like a fortune-teller.

Of course Vladka's prediction turned out to be right. I was a peasant—a fact that became clearer with each passing day of junior high. So, on the day of the field trip, on a crisp afternoon in early October, I took my place in the front of the bus with the rest of the peasants while the high priests and nobles held court in the back. They yelled jokes across the aisle and laughed and shoved into one another whenever the bus took a sharp corner. Anybody listening would have thought we were headed to Disney World instead of some sleepy old cemetery barely four miles away from school.

I didn't feel like chatting during the bus ride. I was too nervous thinking about what was in store for me during the next hour. But a kid named Cliff from the robot fighting club had slid into the seat next to me when we got on the bus, and he kept trying to start up conversations. Cliff had the palest skin and the brightest orange hair I had ever seen—exactly the same color as sweet potatoes. I had met him on the first day of school when I couldn't figure out where to sit at lunch and ended up at his table with the rest of the BattleBots. "So how's cross-country going?" Cliff asked me.

"Oh. I didn't make it," I told him.

"I thought everybody made cross-country."

I shrugged. "Not me." Actually, I hadn't stayed past the first ten minutes of tryouts. Once I saw all the guys in their cool running gear and heard how far we were supposed to go that day, I chickened out and slipped around the corner of the gym when no one was looking. How was I supposed to run two miles in my blown-out sneakers and baggy shorts when I'd hardly ever jogged around my block before?

Cliff's pale face brightened. "So now you can come to BattleBots. Since you're not doing cross-country, I mean."

"Yeah, maybe." I hesitated. "I'll have to see. I have a job walking my neighbor's dog in the afternoons. . . ."

"We meet on Tuesdays and Thursdays," Cliff added quietly. I felt bad. Cliff was nice and all, but the BattleBots reminded me an awful lot of the Ho-Hos. They spent their whole lunchtime arguing about stuff like whether they should build their robot with a overhead pickax or kinetic spike weapon, or whether their bot should be called the Vladiator or Dr. DeathBlow. The thought of spending four more hours a week in the midst of all that geeky bickering just made me feel tired.

My ears pricked up. I could hear Sylvie Rothaker in the seat ahead of me babbling on about Professor Landers. "I hope Professor Landers tells us more about the Curse of the Black Angel," she was saying to her friend Rosa. "People say the statue used to be white, but the marble turned black because the man who's buried there was so evil."

I saw Rosa's dark eyes widen as she swiveled sideways to listen to Sylvie. "What did he do, this man?"

"My uncle told me that he was a preacher who murdered his son," Sylvie said. "He got away with it in court, but a lot of bad things happened to him after that. We'll have to ask the professor."

I slumped down further in my seat. Everybody was fascinated with the Black Angel—a creepy monument that towered over one of the graves in the middle of Oakland Cemetery. Everybody except my mother, that is. Whenever anyone even mentioned the subject, Lottie would shake her head in disgust. She thought the kind of superstitious legends that swirled around the Angel were ridiculous, and anyone silly enough to believe them, she'd say, must not be very smart.

"We're here," Cliff murmured. I sat up and took a shaky breath as we rattled between the brick pillars at the entrance gates to Oakland, past the tall trees and waves of headstones spread out on either side. My palms felt slick.

"Vel-come, children," someone crooned from the back of the bus. "Mua-ha-ha-HA-HA!" It was a terrible Dracula impersonation, but a bunch of kids thought it was hilarious and started chipping in with their own scary sound effects. A werewolf howl. Ghost noises. More shrieks and moans.

"Quiet down, people!" Mr. Oliver bellowed from up front as the bus rumbled to a stop. "Has everybody got what they need for taking notes?"

"Yep!" Sylvie called back. She waved her hot-pink binder in the air.

I pressed my face to the window, searching the small parking area for Lottie. There was no sign of her. A last flicker of hope sprang up inside me. Maybe her flight had been delayed. Even if her plane was only an hour late, she wouldn't make it back to town in time to give us a tour. I rubbed my damp palms on my jeans, resisting the urge to cross my fingers for good luck.

Cliff leaned in beside me. "My grandma Hunnicutt is

buried over there," he whispered, pointing toward the newer area of the cemetery where Dad's wall stood. "We all went to see her before she died. Her feet were swollen up like watermelons."

"Huh," I said, trying not to flinch. I didn't want to think about Cliff's grandmother with her watermelon feet being anywhere near my father's ashes.

When it was my turn to file off the bus, I shuffled along behind the other kids, keeping my head down. I knew if Jeeter spotted me, he'd come rushing over with that lopsided grin and bouncy walk of his. "Hey there, Lincoln Log!" he'd say. "Where you been hidin'?" I sneaked a quick glance toward the cemetery office as I stepped into the parking lot and let out another sigh of relief. Jeeter's old truck was missing from its usual spot outside the toolshed. Hopefully, he had decided to take an extra-long lunch break.

Mr. Oliver stood on the bottom step of the bus, checking his watch. "Professor Landers is running a little late, kids," he called out. "But she should be here soon, so don't wander off anywhere." I imagined my poor mother stuck on some runway in Rhode Island, wringing her hands over missing my field trip. *That's okay, Lottie!* I wanted to yell into the airspace above me. *We'll manage somehow!*

I tried to stay hidden in the middle of the pack in the parking lot, in case Jeeter came driving up. But soon our class was dividing into its usual clusters. Cliff had drifted over to tell Mr. Oliver about his grandma Hunnicutt, so I found myself alone at the edge of the crowd, watching a guy named

Mellecker joke around with his buddies from the back of the bus.

I might as well admit it. I had been watching Mellecker a lot since school started. He was the type of kid Sebastian had warned me about—the pharaoh of seventh grade. I knew it the first time I saw him sauntering through the halls at orientation, greeting his flock of admiring friends. But I never caught his name until he turned up in my American Studies class and Mr. Oliver had to say it twice during roll call. "Blair?" he repeated as he scanned the room, waiting for someone to answer "Here." A long second passed before Mellecker raised his hand and told Mr. Oliver that he preferred going by his last name.

That's when it hit me. Blair Mellecker used to be a Ho-Ho.

I couldn't believe I hadn't recognized him sooner. Blair and I had spent a few months of "free-choice" periods playing together in Dr. Lindstrom's yard. But he had looked so different back when we were eight-year-olds—kind of short and pudgy, and I remembered he couldn't say his y sounds. "Lello," he would say instead of "yellow." "Can ya pass me that lello Magic Marker?" I also remembered him telling me that the kids at his old elementary school used to make fun of him whenever the teacher wasn't looking. They kept calling him "Teddy Blair," he said, which drove him absolutely bananas, and that's why he had transferred to the Home-Away-from-Homeschool.

But a few months later, just when we were starting to be

good friends, he disappeared. There was no warning. I came to school one Monday and he was gone. I was kind of sad about it for a while, especially after losing my dad so unexpectedly the year before. And Dr. Lindstrom didn't really explain much about why Blair left. All she said was his parents had found a public elementary school that they thought would suit their son better.

I guess they were right. Mellecker had completely transformed from the roly-poly little kid he had been four years ago. He must have grown a foot, and now it seemed like he was good at everything, including his *y* sounds. The Battle-Bots informed me that the high school coaches were already dropping by football practices at Plainview, sizing him up to play varsity quarterback in a couple of years. And supposedly Mellecker was smart too. He and Cliff had both tested out of junior high math, and they got to come to school late every morning, since they were taking Algebra II over at City High.

I kept waiting for Mellecker to recognize *me* during those first weeks of school. I didn't see why he wouldn't. Unfortunately, I hadn't changed much at all since I was eight. I was still on the short side, still skinny, with the same little chip in my front tooth, the same shaggy hair because Lottie didn't believe in getting haircuts more than once a year. But so far I hadn't seen the slightest glimmer of recognition in Mellecker's eyes. Maybe he was just embarrassed, too mortified to let the word out that he had ever been a Ho-Ho and associated with somebody like me.

I watched glumly as a cute girl named Amy, who always wore lots of eye makeup and clothes that showed off her permanent tan, reached out and gave Mellecker a playful little shove. That was another thing about Mellecker. Girls. He had them swarming around him like bees on a Coke can.

"Excuse me. Mr. Oliver?" I heard Sylvie say. My heart jumped. Sylvie was pointing to something across the graveyard. "Is that Professor Landers over there?"

Everybody turned to look.

"Uh . . . I'm not sure," Mr. Oliver said as he stepped down to the pavement and squinted past a row of shrubbery at the strange figure heading toward us. The woman was hurrying from the middle of the cemetery, as if she might have floated up from one of the graves.

I swallowed. It was Lottie, all right. There was no mistaking that long purple skirt and determined stride of hers. I started to edge back in the crowd as Lottie moved closer. Maybe because I hadn't seen her for a week or maybe just because she hadn't remembered to brush her hair when she got off the airplane, my mother looked more eccentric than ever—sort of like a jigsaw puzzle whose pieces didn't fit together quite right. Her face (smooth and pale without a single freckle or age spot) didn't match her hair (wild and curly and streaked with gray). Her clothes (an extra-large pullover sweater and a droopy skirt) didn't match her size (extra small). Then there were those clunky brown boots with muddy shoelaces that she always wore for her graveyard work.

I could see the other kids giving Lottie the once-over as

she rushed up and stood panting in front of us, trying to catch her breath. "All *righty*!" she gasped. "Which one of you is Mr. Oliver?"

I felt my face go hot. Was she trying to be funny? Who'd she think the bald guy was, the one with the mustache, standing right in front of her? I stared down at my tennis shoes. I couldn't stand to watch.

"That's me," I heard Mr. Oliver say. "Hey, you caught us a little off guard there, Professor Landers. . . . Where exactly did you park your car?"

"Oh, I didn't drive here," Lottie told him. "I walked. We live—"

I felt my head pop up. For a half second Lottie's eyes found mine. She started to smile; then her gaze skimmed away. "I mean, *I* live on Claiborne Street, right on the other side of Oakland. My yard borders the cemetery."

Mr. Oliver's mustache twitched with amusement. "Wow. That makes it a little difficult to leave your work at the office, doesn't it?"

A few kids laughed. When Lottie didn't join in, Mr. Oliver looked embarrassed and started again. "I only meant, isn't that interesting? You study cemeteries, and you happen to live next to a graveyard. . . ."

"Oh, it's not a coincidence," Lottie said with a little flip of her hand. "I've always made a point of living close to graveyards. We lived next to a cemetery in Wisconsin too. It's like having your own private park—more peaceful than a park, actually. So when we moved here a few years ago and I spotted a FOR SALE sign right next door to Oakland, I knew it was the perfect house for us . . . I mean, for me." Lottie spun around to survey the acres of stone crosses and urns and monuments spread out like a mixed-up chess set in front of us. "Well, Mr. Oliver, shall we get started?" she said, rubbing her hands together. "Let's see . . . where to begin?"

Sylvie chimed in before Mr. Oliver could say anything. "How about the Black Angel?"

"Yeah!" a few others agreed.

Oh boy. I held my breath, bracing for what might happen next.

Lottie turned back to the group, closing her eyes for a second as if a volt of pain were passing through her body. "W-e-l-l-l," she said slowly, working to keep her voice patient, "we *could* start with the Black Angel . . . but not if we want to do justice to the rich history Oakland Cemetery has to offer. Those kinds of silly ghost stories and myths that surround the Angel are what give people the wrong idea about cemeteries—that they're scary, sinister places."

The excited smile on Sylvie's face started to fade.

But Lottie was just getting warmed up. She shook her head hard, sending her hair swirling around her face like a tornado. "Visitors from all over just flock to the Black Angel, thrilled by all those legends—about why the statue turned black and what happens if you touch her under the moonlight. *Nonsense!* All that sort of ghost-story mumbo jumbo prevents us from understanding the real stories these gravestones have to tell."

Lottie had been waving her hands, and now without any warning she turned and set off across the old section of the graveyard, still lecturing and making a stubborn beeline away from the direction of the Black Angel. We all looked at Mr. Oliver, wondering what to do next.

"Professor?" he called after Lottie. "Weren't we going to start with Governor Lucas's grave?" Lottie kept walking.

Somebody piped up with that high-pitched tune from *The Twilight Zone*—"doo-doo-doo-doo, doo-doo-doo-doo"—the one people always sing whenever anything weird happens.

Mr. Oliver pretended not to hear. "C'mon, people," he said, turning gruff. He motioned for us to hurry and catch up with the professor. "You're supposed to be taking notes, remember?"

I hung behind as my class straggled after Lottie. But bits and pieces of her lesson kept floating back to me. I had heard most of it before, though I couldn't remember exactly when. She was talking about the carvings on old headstones and what they meant. A carving of a broken chain represented a life cut short. A cedar tree symbolized strong faith. A willow tree—grief and mourning. An arch—victory over death.

I watched a couple of squirrels zip through the yellow maple leaves over my head and tried to let Lottie's lecture melt into the sound of traffic out on Dodge Street. But Mr. Oliver had spotted me lagging, and even from nine or ten graves away I could see his mustache jerk down at the corners as he turned to scowl and jab his finger at my unopened notebook. I shuffled closer and found a place at the edge of the group, on the opposite side of where he was snooping around for field trip violations.

"Now let's talk about lambs," Lottie was saying. "A lamb is one of the three or four most common symbols found in cemeteries throughout the United States. Can anyone guess what a lamb is meant to symbolize? Anyone?"

Nobody even tried to make a guess.

"Innocence!" she flung out at our circle of blank faces. "Purity! The lamb often marks the death of an infant or a child. Over in Babyland, you'll find dozens of small sculptures or carvings of lambs on the headstones."

"*Babyland?*" Sylvie sounded offended. "Ewww. Isn't that kind of creepy?"

Lottie nodded, trying to look sympathetic. "I know it seems morbid. But lots of older cemeteries have sections designated for the burial of children. And it's been traditional, not only in the Midwest but all across the country, to name those sections Babyland."

"That's so sad," a girl standing near me said, almost to herself. Actually, she said "say-ad," drawing out the word into two syllables. It was a surprise to hear her voice at all. Just like me, she was new that year and kept quiet most of the time. All I knew about her was that her name was Delaney Baldwin, and with her accent and the way she said "Yes, ma'am" and "No, ma'am" to the cafeteria ladies in the lunch line, I figured she had come from down south somewhere.

I was still sneaking looks at Delaney, who seemed hypnotized by whatever my mother was saying about Babyland, when I noticed Mellecker standing right in front of me. He was bent over his notebook and scribbling so hard, you would

29

have thought Lottie was feeding him plays for the football game on Thursday. I rocked up on my toes so I could get a look over his shoulder and see what he was writing.

He was drawing, actually . . . a picture of my mother.

"I HAD A
LOVER'S QUARREL
WITH THE WORLD."

ROBERT FROST
BENNINGTON, VERMONT

CHAPTER 3

ALTHOUGH MELLECKER WASN'T MUCH of an artist, there was no mistaking his subject matter. He had drawn a stick figure, then added a triangle skirt, combat boots, and wild curlicues for hair. For my mother's eyes Mellecker had drawn X marks, making her look like somebody had just punched her lights out. Then, at the top of the page, he sketched a big headstone and labeled it with the words "Professor" and "R.I.P." in big block letters. Rest in Peace.

For a few seconds my ears filled up with a rush of white noise like TV static. I wanted to flatten him. I wanted to grab the back of his head and shove that handsome, magazine-ad face of his into the nearest grave plot. But I couldn't seem to move. All I could do was watch while Mellecker sketched more and more details on his dead-Lottie cartoon.

Now he was adding doodles to her headstone—first a bat

with stretched-out wings and then something that looked like a big peanut.

He held out his notebook so that one of his sidekicks from the football team—Jake Beasley—could see. I didn't like what I had seen of Beez so far. He was big and loud, always swaggering around trying to be funny. But I figured he had to be one of Mellecker's best friends, since all the guys in that circle went by their last names. Apparently Mellecker had started a trend.

"What do you think, Beez?" I heard him whisper. "Like my symbols for the professor's grave?"

Beez stared blankly down at Mellecker's bat and peanut doodles. "I don't get it."

Mellecker rolled his eyes at him. "She's bats!" he hissed. "Nuts!"

"Oh, *yeah*," Beez said, not even trying to muffle his guffaw. "Now I get it." I glared at the back of his meaty head.

Mellecker must have felt me breathing down his neck. All of a sudden he glanced at me over his shoulder and then turned with his notebook to give me a better view.

"Pretty good, huh, Linc?" he said softly.

So he knew my name after all. I felt my mouth stretch into a sickly Halloween-pumpkin smile as I searched his face for some sort of clue. Did he know it was *me*—his old Ho-Ho playmate? Or did he only remember my name from Mr. Oliver's annoying roll call every afternoon? Whatever it was, Mellecker didn't let on. He just stood there, grinning at me, waiting for me to laugh at his nasty cartoon.

I could feel my pumpkin smile caving in. But before I could decide whether to force out a fake laugh or walk away in a huff, we were interrupted by the sound of Lottie's voice rising in frustration. Someone must have asked her about the Black Angel again. "Look," she was saying. "The only reason that angel is black is because the statue is made of bronze, not marble, and when bronze is exposed to the elements, oxidation occurs and the metal turns dark."

She paused.

"BUT!" she almost shouted, making everybody, even Mellecker, jump. "If you don't believe me, you should come out here at midnight tonight and see for yourself. Climb up on the pedestal and give that angel a *big—fat—wet* kiss right on her lips. If you're dead tomorrow morning, we'll all know the legends are true."

From the startled expressions on everyone's faces, Lottie had to know her little speech had gone too far. But I guess something about the awkward pause that followed struck her as funny, because all at once she started to laugh. First it was only a little laugh that bubbled out. But then her giggle turned into a cackle, and I watched in growing horror as she pressed her knuckles to her mouth and spun away from us with her shoulders shaking, struggling to regain control. If we had been anywhere else, I probably would have burst out laughing too. But not here. Not on my junior high field trip, with my whole class staring at my mother like she was a lunatic.

"Okay, everybody," Mr. Oliver broke in nervously, giving

Lottie a chance to compose herself. "I think the professor is saying that's *enough* questions about the Black Angel. We're not focusing on legends today. We're focusing on historical facts and what this graveyard can tell us about our town's early citizens. Agreed?"

Mr. Oliver shot a warning glance around our group. Then he cautiously turned back to Lottie. "Shall we continue, Professor?"

Lottie finished wiping the tears from under her eyes. "Certainly," she said with a businesslike little sniff. "You had asked about Governor Lucas's grave. Why don't we head over there?"

Mellecker fell into step beside me as we all set off behind Lottie. He nudged my arm, tapping his cartoon with the point of his pencil. "See what I mean?"

"Yeah," I muttered before I could stop myself. "Definitely. You should draw a fruitcake next to that peanut. And while you're at it, add a rocking chair."

"Whoa," Mellecker exclaimed under his breath. "Nutty as a fruitcake . . . off her rocker. You're good." He hunched over his drawing again, more eager than ever.

I let myself be herded along, wishing I could sink down into the ground with the corpses for a while. How could I have said those things about Lottie? I was a traitor. A mother backstabber. And then another thought dawned on me—an idea that made me feel even worse. What if Mellecker really *did* remember me from four years ago? And what if he remembered my mother too and was just taunting me, waiting for me to spill my stupid secret? I racked my brain trying to recall when he might have met Lottie at Dr. Lindstrom's. Even when I was eight, I had always walked back and forth to school by myself. But we Ho-Hos used to put on all sorts of special plays and performances for our parents. Maybe Lottie had come to one of them and Mellecker had seen her then.

"Hey, look at this, Linc," Mellecker said in my ear. "I got another one. Cuckoo clock."

I didn't answer. Beez had shoved his way closer to see the latest additions to Mellecker's cartoon, and now Amy and a couple of other kids were drifting over to find out what was so interesting. I started to edge away from them. Our class had strayed off the paved walkway, and we were zigzagging around family plots and through rows of headstones. When I looked around to get my bearings, I realized with a jolt where we were headed. Lottie was taking us on a shortcut to Governor Lucas's grave—a shortcut that happened to lead straight past our house.

Ours was the last one in a block of old bungalows that dead-ended at a side entrance to Oakland. There weren't any important graves close by. So even with all my worrying the past few days, I hadn't considered the fact that my entire class might be walking right past our run-down backyard, with its ugly stretch of C.B.'s digging holes and my old Big Wheel covered in vines and the vegetable patch I had tried to start that was too shady to grow anything besides weeds. It was all too close for comfort.

But up ahead, Lottie seemed to have completely lost track of her surroundings. She kept marching along, sweeping her hands back and forth as she explained some point to Mr. Oliver and Sylvie and Delaney, the only ones in the group who appeared halfway interested in what she had to say.

I dropped a few steps behind Mellecker and his crew, keeping my gaze pinned on the ground. By now we were coming up on the stretch of graves that ran alongside my house. I could even smell the leaves from our maple thick on the ground and the mossy pile of tree house boards that Dad had stacked in the backyard before he died.

I held my breath as Lottie kept lecturing and moving along. We were almost past the woodpile, past our rusted barbecue grill, past my upstairs bedroom window.

Then I heard it. A yip rang out across the cemetery. I knew right away it was C.B. But what was he doing *outside*? I had left him asleep on his dog bed when I took off for school that morning. My stomach turned queasy as I realized what had happened. Sometimes during nice weather we left C.B. tied to the clothesline pole in the backyard. Lottie must have come home from the airport and put him outside before she rushed over to meet us.

I clenched my fists and plowed forward, praying C.B. wouldn't notice me in the crowd. But the sound of his whimper obviously caught Lottie by surprise. She stopped and whipped around, her lecture about graves cut off midstream.

"Awww, look at the poor doggie!" Sylvie cried out. I stole a glance over my shoulder and got a quick glimpse of C.B. straining on his rope, leaping higher and higher as if his stubby legs were mounted on pogo sticks. Lottie tried to shoot me a look of apology as I stalked past her, staring straight ahead.

"Come on, everybody!" she called, sounding just as frantic as C.B. "Mr. Oliver, we've got to keep the class moving if we want to stay on schedule!"

Then I heard Beez shout. "Hey, look! Pooch on the loose!"

I stopped and turned around just in time to see C.B. streak into the graveyard, trailing a long piece of frayed rope from his collar. He flung himself against Lottie's legs, covering her purple skirt with muddy paw prints.

"Hey there, boy," she said, bending down to bury her hands in his scraggly fur. "How'd you get loose, huh? C'mon, buddy, calm down."

Everybody crowded around to watch the reunion. "Is that *your* dog?" Mr. Oliver asked.

"Yep," Lottie said, and sighed, taking hold of his frayed rope and scratching his favorite spot under the collar. "It sure is."

"Awww, he's so cute," Sylvie said. "What kind of dog *is* that?"

"Nobody's quite sure," Lottie told her. "Even the people at the animal shelter didn't know what to call him. But we call him C.B. It's short for Cerberus."

"Cerb-rus?" Beez scoffed out of the side of his mouth. "What kind of a name for a dog is that?" Beez probably thought he was being quiet. He didn't know my mother had ears like a bat.

She stood up in surprise. "You kids haven't heard of Cerberus?" She swiveled around to face Mr. Oliver. "Don't you-all teach Greek mythology in that school of yours?"

I squeezed my eyes shut. I knew what was coming.

Before Mr. Oliver could reply, Lottie was already rattling off an explanation of our dog's unusual name. "So Hades was the god of the dead," she said briskly. "Otherwise known as king of the underworld. And Cerberus was the three-headed dog that guarded Hades's house on the River Styx." She reached down to give C.B. another rub. "And since this guy absolutely *loves* to dig and bury things underground, especially dead stuff, we decided to call him Cerberus."

Mellecker poked me in the ribs with his elbow. Somehow he had ended up standing next to me again. I felt a tight ball of anger growing red-hot in my chest. I wasn't sure who made me madder—Mellecker with that smirk on his face or my mother for acting like she had just been let out of the psych ward on a day pass. All I knew was that I would explode if I had to stand in that spot, stuck between the two of them, for much longer. I decided to risk it. A tiny step backward.

Right away, C.B. started to squirm.

Lottie crouched down to soothe him. "Easy, boy. It's okay!"

But she was too late. The rope slipped out of her hands, and in two seconds C.B. was all over me. Licking and panting and smearing gummy black dirt on my jeans. My notebook flopped to the ground as I hunched over, trying to decide whether I should pet C.B. or push him away.

"Hey, look, Linc. Devil Dog likes you," Mellecker teased

in a whispery voice. "You and the professor must have a lot in common."

I stood up to face him with that ball of anger turning to lava rising in my chest.

"That's real funny, *Teddy Blair*," I burst out, sending a shock wave across the small space between us. "Why don't you go ahead and tell everybody? Go on. I don't care anymore." I whirled around, shouting the news to my entire class. "She's my mother, okay? *She's my mother!*"

GO AWAY—
I'M ASLEEP

HOLLYWOOD, CALIFORNIA

CHAPTER 4

AFTER THAT, THERE WAS ONLY ONE THING TO DO.

Run.

While everybody watched with their jaws hanging open, I shoved past Mellecker and tore across the hundred yards that separated the graveyard from my back door. I didn't stop running until I'd made it upstairs to my room, where I dove for my bed like it was a foxhole. C.B. was right on my heels. He settled into his usual nest next to my hip while I buried my face in my pillow, waiting for the worst attacks of anger and embarrassment to pass. Finally, once I was certain no one was coming to try and coax me back down to the graveyard, I turned over and scowled up at the posters plastered across the walls and the ceiling above me.

It had taken me years to collect them. But now I had pictures of all Seven Summits—representing the highest mountains in the world, one from each continent. Mount Everest towered over my head at night. Kilimanjaro and Mount McKinley reared up in the distance on either side of my window. The Carstensz Pyramid on the continent of Australia bordered my closet door. Dad used to marvel over the Seven Summits. My father had climbed a few impressive mountains during his time. But Mount Rainier was an anthill, he would tell me, compared to a killer peak like the Aconcagua in South America. I hung my first poster not too long after Dad died, promising myself to live out his dream and conquer a mountain like the ice-capped Elbrus in Russia someday. But who was I fooling? Here I was stuck on the plains of Iowa, hiding in my room like a scared rabbit in its hole. How did I think I could ever scale one of the Seven Summits when I couldn't even keep up with my junior high cross-country team?

C.B. must have sensed I was feeling bad. He rested his chin on my stomach and watched me through his eyebrows. "This is all your fault, you old mutt," I whispered. Then I lay there awhile longer, scratching his favorite spot on his neck, until the hands on my alarm clock scraped their way to two-thirty.

My class had to be on its way back to Plainview by now. But just to make sure, I swung my feet to the floor and crept over to the window to sneak a look down. Sure enough, the graveyard was completely quiet, all except for my noisy neighbors—Winslow, Dobbins, York & McNutt.

Okay, so they weren't real neighbors, but it sure felt like it sometimes. Whenever I glanced out my bedroom window, there they were—those names etched in big, bold letters in stone. Most likely the folks buried in the short row underneath my window never had a thing in common besides the fact that their tombstones were placed in an odd direction, facing south instead of west like most of the other graves in Oakland. But somehow, along the way, I had started to think of them as a club, a foursome of cranky old men who had been fishing buddies once or played poker together on Saturday nights or maybe worked as partners in a law office downtown.

I couldn't help imagining they were watching me all the time, commenting to one another about my latest slew of troubles.

Look at that sorry excuse for a garden, I'd hear Winslow say whenever I watered my yellow vegetable plants that summer.

Pitiful! McNutt would agree. *That boy couldn't grow mold on a piece of year-old bread!*

The four of them must have had a field day watching me humiliate myself in front of my entire class.

Winslow: *Look at Mr. Tomato Head! Too bad the ones in his garden never managed to turn that nice red color. Hey, where does he think he's going?*

Dobbins: *Awww, he's running home to hide. At least he's taking that yappy pile of fur with him. Maybe now we can get some rest around here.*

York: *Isn't his teacher going to stop him and make him go back to school like he's supposed to? Times have changed, fellas. Can you imagine teachers in our day letting us get away with those kinds of shenanigans?*

McNutt: *Not a chance. But wait till that wise guy Mellecker and his friends get ahold of him tomorrow—*

I jerked the cord by the window, and the metal blinds came rattling down. C.B. scrambled off my bed. At first I thought he was just startled by the noisy blinds, but then he sat in front of my closed bedroom door with his tail thumping the floorboards, and in the next instant I heard Lottie's soft knock.

I sank down into my desk chair, feeling grateful for the shadowy light in the room as Lottie carefully entered. Once she had given C.B. a wan smile and he had gone *click-click*ing downstairs, she took a few steps closer and peered at me as if she were a scientist discovering something new under her microscope.

"What in the world happened out there?" she asked. "Why'd you run off like that?"

"I don't know." I shrugged. "It was stupid."

Lottie went over to sit on my rumpled bed. "That's not much of an explanation."

I closed my eyes and shook my head, not wanting to re-member. "It was embarrassing, that's all. All of it. That laughing fit of yours and walking past our backyard and C.B. getting loose and jumping all over me, and the way you kept . . ." My voice dwindled away.

Lottie blinked. "The way I kept what?"

"Well, you were acting kind of wacky, Lottie. Kind of . . . wound up."

"What do you mean, *wound up*? You mean I'm not sup-posed to show that I'm excited about what I do?"

"That's not it," I told her with a sigh.

"Then what, Linc? *What?* First you want me to pretend I'm not your mother because you're embarrassed about what I do, and I actually agree to play along even though I haven't seen you for a whole week. Then, from what I could tell, things are going fine until for some unknown reason you start shouting at the other kids in your class. And the next thing I know, you disappear."

"Things were not going fine, Mom," I blurted out. "Mellecker was making fun of you! They all were!"

Even in the dim light I could see her flinch. "What do you mean making fun of me?" she asked in disbelief. "And who's this Mellecker person? Is he the one who had never even heard of Cerberus before?" She gave a dismissive snort.

Typical, I thought. Obviously Lottie didn't have the faintest recollection of Blair Mellecker, even though I must have talked about him a lot back when I was eight.

"Listen, Lottie," I said, scrubbing my hand across my face in exasperation. "It's just that sometimes I wish you could act a little more like a regular mom."

Lottie hugged her arms over her chest and lifted her chin. "And what does a regular mom act like, pray tell?" she snipped.

"Well, for one thing, a regular mom doesn't forget to brush her hair in the morning," I fired back. "Especially when she has to lead a bunch of kids on a field trip."

I faltered for a second as Lottie reached up to touch her disheveled hair. I never talked this way to my mother. But suddenly I couldn't help it. I had to let it out, every stupid

44

little thing that had been building up since school started. "Look, I don't want to hurt your feelings, Lottie," I flung out, "but you need to know. Other moms, they do stuff like . . . like they make real dinners once in a while, you know? Like pot roast and mashed potatoes. And they make friends with other ladies and go out for coffee sometimes or the movies. Don't you ever want to do that sort of stuff, Lottie? Go out for coffee instead of working on your cemetery research eighteen hours a day?"

I didn't give Lottie a chance to answer. I didn't even look at her as I stood up and stalked back and forth in the narrow alleyway of space between the bed and my desk, between the jagged peaks rising up along my walls.

"Sometimes I hear kids talking at school, and I feel like—like we're back in the Dark Ages or something, with the way we've been living in our own little bubble, just the two of us for so long. I mean, nobody can believe it when I tell them we don't have a TV. Sure, I understand how you thought it might be a bad influence on me when I was little. But I'm almost in high school now, and I'm still having to ask for permission to use *your* computer!"

I flailed my hands up at Mount Everest on my ceiling. "It's not that I want a bunch of stuff. Heck, I'd be happy if we had a vacuum cleaner that works." I coughed out a bitter laugh. "I mean, that's the kind of thing I'm talking about, Lottie. We've been sweeping our rugs with a broom for a *whole year*, ever since the vacuum broke down. Don't you ever want to get it fixed so we can really clean this place up once in a while?" My voice rose higher. "Don't you?"

I whipped around and stood over my mother like a prosecutor in a courtroom, breathing hard, ready to hear some answers at last. But Lottie didn't say a word. She just kept staring down at her palms, open in her lap. She looked like a rag doll, perched there on the edge of my bed with her shoulders slumped and her sock feet barely touching the floor.

I lowered myself into the chair at my desk again, feeling weak and sick to my stomach. The afternoon had been horrible enough already, and now I had gone and made things a hundred times worse. There was another heavy stretch of quiet before Lottie finally raised her head. She lifted her arms a little and let them flop back to her sides. "This is just who I am," she whispered. But then I realized: Lottie wasn't looking at me. She was gazing at the picture on my nightstand. And her eyes were round and moist, as if she were trying to explain something to Dad, who grinned back at her from the photo, holding that drippy chocolate ice cream cone.

I opened my mouth to apologize. But before I could think of what to say, anything to make her feel better, Lottie was rising to her feet and heading toward the door. She turned in the hallway, her face carved by the slivers of light seeping through the blinds. "I need to go in to work for a while and catch up on a few things," she said quietly.

I nodded as she disappeared down the stairs. By now I had learned to recognize that frozen tone in her voice and the way she stiffened her shoulders before getting on with things.

I rushed to the doorway. "What time will you be home?" I called.

But Lottie was already down in the kitchen, grabbing her keys, letting the screen door slam behind her. I stood still for a while longer, listening to the chug of the Dodge Dart's tired engine as she pulled out of our driveway. Then my bedroom went silent.

I shouldn't have glanced toward the window. Suddenly the old geezers down in the graveyard were at it again, all grumbling and scolding me at once, trying to get their digs in edgewise.

Shame on you, boy. How could you treat your own mother that way?

Have you got any idea how tough it is being a single parent these days?

You know she's never gotten over losing your dad.

And here you go rubbing salt in the wounds. And where does that get you?

They were right, of course. I wished I could take it all back. Without Lottie, all there was . . . was me.

I AM A BUSY MAN
I DON'T HAVE
TIME FOR THIS

PRAIRIE GROVE, ARKANSAS

CHAPTER 5

The ADOPT-a-GRAVE Project

At the conclusion of our tour in Oakland Cemetery, please choose one of the headstones in the old section for further study. Choose your site wisely, people! Select a stone with markings that are clearly visible. The more clues on the stone, the better. Throughout October, our class will be visiting the State Historical Society of Iowa and the school library to learn as much as we can about the individuals buried at our sites.

Be ready to present a ten-minute oral report on your findings by November 17.

DUE IN CLASS TOMORROW: A sketch of your gravestone selection in the space below, including the name, dates of birth and death, and any other important clues.

The assignment sheet, along with my muddy notebook, was propped against the pile of mail in the middle of the kitchen table. I had almost forgotten. Mr. Oliver had warned us that he'd be giving out details of a new project during the field trip. He must have asked Lottie to deliver my copy of the instructions. I spotted the words "DUE IN CLASS TOMORROW" and felt my shoulders sag. The last thing I wanted to do that afternoon was go back into the cemetery.

C.B. cocked his head and let out one of his grumbly moans, waiting for me to unglue my feet from the kitchen floor and take him on his afternoon outing. My neighbor Mr. Krasny would be waiting too. He had hired me to exercise his Boston terrier every afternoon. He paid only ten dollars a week, averaging me a measly $1.42 per day. But I hadn't been able to say no that summer when he stopped me on one of my walks with C.B. to ask if I'd mind taking Spunky along. Mr. Krasny told me he was ninety-three and his joints weren't cooperating like they used to. *Obviously*. I had seen him hobbling past our house to visit his wife's grave in Oakland. There was no way he could handle a leash-yanker like Spunky.

Lately, though, I had started to appreciate my job a little more—ever since I'd decided to kill two birds with one stone and use my sessions with Spunky as a way to get better at running. When I jogged, Spunky never had a chance to yank on his leash, and maybe if I kept it up, I'd be ready to join the cross-country team by the time eighth grade rolled around. I was glad I had eleven more months to prepare. So far I could hardly run five blocks without getting winded.

I sighed and bent down to tighten up my shoelaces. Of course my year-old sneakers and baggy sweatpants weren't doing much to improve my stamina. But I had promised myself I wouldn't ask Lottie for new running shoes or any other gear until I could jog for at least twenty minutes without stopping.

C.B. gnawed impatiently at an itch between his long toenails. I folded up Mr. Oliver's project assignment sheet and tucked it into the front pocket of my sweatshirt, along with a stubby pencil. "Come on, buddy," I said, grabbing C.B.'s leash from the hook by the back door. "Time for another field trip."

Just as I expected, Mr. Krasny was on his front porch waiting for me. Even though it was only October, with barely a chill in the air, he looked like he was ready for a snowstorm in his wool overcoat, rubber boots, and plaid hat with dangling earflaps. Spunky darted back and forth around his toothpick legs while Mr. Krasny fumbled with the leash, trying to keep his feet from being tangled in the snare.

"Excellent, Linc," he said when I came hurrying up his walkway with C.B. "You're here. Spunky's getting restless." Mr. Krasny always talked like that—in urgent little bursts as if he were calling out answers on a game show with only two seconds left before the buzzer went off.

"We might be gone a little longer today," I said, reaching for Spunky's leash. "I'd like to take the dogs a different way than usual, if it's okay with you."

"Certainly!" he said. "My land, he needs a good romp. Been standing at the window all afternoon. Waiting for his fine friend C.B."

That's another thing Mr. Krasny always did, talked about our pets as if they were old buddies who couldn't wait to share each other's company every day. The truth was that C.B. couldn't stand Spunky. Spunky was one of those pesky kinds of dogs, constantly trotting over to bump noses with C.B. or sniff whatever he sniffed or pee wherever he peed. Even when C.B. showed his teeth or let out a little growl, Spunky didn't get the hint. He just wagged his backside with its nub of a tail and shoved his smushed-up nose in for another good whiff.

We said goodbye to Mr. Krasny and backtracked along Claiborne Street toward the side gate of Oakland, just past my house. I was planning on starting out at a slow jog. But Spunky was so excited to be heading in a new direction, opposite of our normal route to the neighborhood park around the corner, that he dragged C.B. and me at a dead run into the cemetery—straight past the ALL PETS MUST BE CONFINED IN VEHICLE sign. Luckily, Jeeter and his boss, old Mr.

Nicknish, the cemetery superintendent, had never seemed to mind people walking their dogs through the grounds, especially if they were regulars from the neighborhood. Plus, visitors to Oakland were scarce on weekday afternoons. Most people waited for Sundays and holidays to pay their respects. So after scanning the distance to make sure we were alone, I unclipped the dogs' leashes and stuffed them into the pocket of my sweatshirt.

With C.B. and Spunky darting in and out of the rows of graves nearby, I jogged along the driveway for a while. Whenever I came to a hill and felt like stopping, I just thought of the wicked smile on Mellecker's face as he added another flourish to his Lottie cartoon, and a new burst of angry energy carried me to the top of the next rise. As I circled back to the old part of the cemetery, I was surprised at how much better I felt. Although I was heaving for breath, with drips of sweat sliding down my temples, even the Adopt-a-Grave Project didn't seem quite so terrible anymore.

Soon I was wandering among the tall oaks and leaning headstones, waiting for a grave to grab my attention, to send me some sort of message—*Pick me. Pick me.* But like Mr. Oliver had warned, lots of the epitaphs were too hard to read, with the letters covered in moss or worn smooth through the years. Hundreds of other stones had clear markings, but they were too plain to be special—nothing besides names and dates carved in gray granite. I was standing there, wishing I could find an epitaph nearly half as interesting as some of the ones I had collected in my journal, when I heard a rustle of leaves behind me.

I swung around to find Jeeter grinning at me with his arms crossed over his chest. "Well, well, well, Lincoln Log. I was beginning to take this personally. You been avoidin' me?"

"Hey there, Jeeter!" I cried. I almost hugged him. I had forgotten how much I missed Jeeter. "Wow, I like your beard. Or whatever that is."

He rubbed his hand across the short scruff of reddish whiskers on his chin. "This here's a goatee, Lincoln Log!" He shook his head, chuckling at himself. "I thought it might make me look sophisticated. Help with the ladies."

I laughed. I couldn't imagine any lady thinking Jeeter was *sophisticated*. When I was little, Lottie had taken me to a special showing of *The Wizard of Oz* over at the university, and as soon as the Scarecrow came on, I had shouted, "It's Jeeter!" The way the Scarecrow listened to Dorothy's troubles and wrinkled his brow when he thought hard and loped along that Yellow Brick Road—that was Jeeter to a T.

"Well, you still haven't answered my question yet," Jeeter said. "Where you been? I haven't seen hide nor hair of you since the beginning of the summer. You got yourself a girlfriend or something?"

I rolled my eyes. Huh. Fat chance. "No, it's nothing like that," I said. "I haven't had much free time lately. I go to Plainview now. You know, the junior high?"

Jeeter's eyebrows flew up. "Junior high, huh? That must be pretty different from your old school. What was that one kid's name who you used to pal around with? The one who used to wear knee pads whenever he rode his bike?"

I smiled forlornly. "You mean Sebastian. He's still with

the Ho-Hos. I don't see him much anymore." It was sad. I had called Sebastian to hang out with me a couple of times since school started, but things hadn't gone so well. He kept interrogating me about what we were studying at Plainview.

"What about science?" he had demanded the last time we got together.

"Um, I think we're starting a unit on levers and pulleys soon," I told him.

"You're kidding," he had said, eyeing me with disdain. "Vladka and I are designing our own microchips."

Now Jeeter was the one giving me the eye. "I think you've grown an inch or two over the summer. You're starting to look a lot like your father, you know."

"You think so?"

Jeeter nodded as he finished sizing me up. "You got your mom's eyes, but the rest of you? Looks like your dad's genes got the upper hand." I smiled. Jeeter and my father hadn't had a chance to be friends for very long, but they had liked each other from the start. Since Jeeter was about ten years younger, Dad had treated him like the little brother he never had, showering him with lots of teasing and advice. A few days after Dad's heart attack, Jeeter had shown up at our front door with a huge mayonnaise jar full of wildflowers for Lottie and a bag of bite-size Hershey bars for me.

"Are you here to visit your dad?"

I shook my head with a twinge of guilt rising in my chest. With his ashes buried so close by, there was no excuse for not visiting. But somehow it always seemed too depressing, the thought of standing in front of that big black wall, with all those other names of dead people crowding in.

"So you were looking for *me?*" Jeeter asked hopefully.

For half a second I was tempted to say yes. But Jeeter wasn't the kind of person you could tell lies to, even little white lies.

"I'm actually here for an assignment," I admitted sheepishly. "For school." And pretty soon I was pouring out the whole pathetic story—all about the field trip and Lottie and Mellecker and C.B. getting loose and the Adopt-a-Grave Project. Most guys would have interrupted after the first five minutes and made up some excuse about having to get back to hedge clipping or tree trimming or grave digging, but Jeeter was different. He just stood there and listened to me dump my troubles like heavy rocks at his feet, nodding and thinking hard in that Scarecrow way of his.

The next thing I knew, Jeeter was leading me a few graves down and a couple rows across to show me what he thought would be a perfect Adopt-a-Grave pick. "I always wondered about old Hannah here. She lived a good long life. And you said you needed details. That's what I call dee-tails." He pointed down at the impressive amount of information stacked up on the tombstone:

Hannah Marshall Dalton
Born at
Sheffield England
April 2 1822

Died Dec. 20 1909
Aged 87 yrs. 8 Mos.
18 Ds.

"Yeah, that one's pretty good," I agreed. "She's an immigrant. Immigrants are interesting. But I don't know. . . ." A picture of Hannah Dalton popped into my mind. Nothing but a shriveled old lady in a rocker, sipping a cup of tea.

But Jeeter wasn't a bit put off by my lack of enthusiasm. "Okay," he said quickly, rubbing his palms together. "I got another idea. C'mon over this way."

He headed across the paved driveway, swinging his loose arms back and forth as he strode along. I almost had to run to keep up with him. Then he stopped suddenly in front of a group of matching bleached-white headstones. "Civil War veterans," he announced proudly. "Can't get much better than that. Look. There's Corporal Randolph Phinney. A member of the cavalry."

"Uh-huh, those are good too, but . . ." I shot Jeeter an apologetic look.

"But what?"

"I bet you anything Mellecker and all the rest of the guys in the class are picking veterans. I'd kind of like to do something different."

"Well, sure. You don't want a heehaw like that thinking you copied him."

I smiled at the thought of Mellecker with donkey ears and a bristly tail swishing at flies. Jeeter always had the best expressions.

56

He was ready to lead me over to another potential gravesite when I felt the leashes in my front pocket and remembered the dogs. I hadn't seen them in a while. "Hey," I said, glancing around. "I wonder where C.B. and Spunky went."

"Who?"

"The dogs. . . . Oh, I guess I forgot to tell you. I got a job walking Mr. Krasny's terrier. But lately we've been running more than walking."

Jeeter's head snapped up. "You let the dogs loose in *here?*"

"Well, I had to. My assignment's due tomorrow, and Mr. Krasny gets upset if Spunky doesn't get his walk. . . ."

I let my voice trail off. Jeeter was spinning around, searching the cemetery with a worried look in his eyes.

"What's wrong?" I asked.

"Dogs aren't allowed in here anymore, Linc, especially if they're not on a leash."

"But you and Mr. Nicknish always let—"

"Old Nick's gone. Retired. We got a new boss a few weeks ago, and oh man, he can be ornery as a snake on a stick. Get this. He likes being called Warden instead of Superintendent, and the name sure suits him." Jeeter glanced over his shoulder again. "So which way do you think those dogs went?"

I stood on my toes, trying to get a look over the hill, back toward Claiborne Street. "Uh, I'm not sure. I didn't think they'd run off like this. But maybe C.B. found a rabbit or something."

Jeeter pressed his hand on my shoulder. "Look, Linc, you gotta find them quick and hightail it out of here. I'll run over to the office and see if I can keep the warden occupied till you're gone."

"Okay," I said with a nervous little gulp. Jeeter wasn't exactly the anxious type. He would never act this way unless he had a good reason.

I'D RATHER BE
AT THE MALL

EAST GREENBUSH, NEW YORK

CHAPTER 6

"C.B.!" I squawked as I ran through the graveyard. "Spunk!"
I knew the dogs might come if I whistled and called louder,
but I didn't want to bring the warden running too, in case he
happened to be nearby.

I slowed down when I got near the gate at the end of my
street, hoping that C.B. had led Spunky home for a rest in our
yard. But there was no sign of them on the front porch or
around back, so I stalked into the graveyard again, past Winslow, Dobbins, York & McNutt.

"C.B.!" I yelled a little louder.

What are you tryin' to do? Raise the dead? I heard Winslow
croak.

Oh, leave him alone. He's having a bad day.

*Ew-weeee, is he ever! Those mutts have probably been carted
off to the pound by now. He might as well give up and go home.*

"Shut up," I muttered before McNutt could chime in.

The light was already turning, throwing stretchy shadows of trees and tombstones across the ground. Mr. Krasny would start getting worried soon. What if I had to go back and tell him I had lost Spunky? Another chill shivered through me as I searched the distance and the dark line of forest on the edge of the graveyard. What if the dogs had headed into Hickory Hill Park? The park spanned hundreds of brambly acres and trails. It would take me all night to track them down there.

But with all those rabbits and squirrels waiting to be chased, Hickory Hill was the obvious place to look. So I set off toward the shadowy fringe of trees, calling the dogs in a strained voice as I trotted along through row after row of graves. I was so distracted, checking over my shoulder to make sure the warden wasn't on my trail, that I almost ran right into it—the columbarium wall, rising up in the dusk. I veered around and broke into a jog again. But a fresh stab of guilt made me turn back. I couldn't run right by without at least checking on Dad's stone.

At first I couldn't find it. Lots more names had filled in during the last few years. I could hear myself huffing for breath as I searched the rows of compartments. Where was he? It wasn't until I swallowed and forced myself to start back at the edge of the wall that I remembered—third row from the top, halfway across. Then I found him right away. "Lincoln Rain-tree Crenshaw," I whispered as I stood gazing at the stone. I was tall enough now to reach up and touch it if I wanted.

I squeezed my eyes shut trying to recall the exact sound of my father's voice, but it kept drifting in and out like a bad phone connection. Instead, all I could hear was Dad's Elmer

Fudd impression in my head. He used to be good at all kinds of voices—Pepé Le Pew, the Three Stooges, Muhammad Ali. But his Elmer Fudd was the best. Dad would chase me around the house before bedtime—my least favorite time of the day—calling, "Come back, you wascally wabbit! Wockabye babe-eeee, in the tweeeeeee-tops!"

I shook my head, smiling to myself as I stood there remembering, and for one crazy second it occurred to me: *Here's the grave I should adopt.* Other than scraps of memories from when I was little, I barely knew anything about my father.

I was still standing there when I heard the whimper. I must have jumped a foot. "C.B.!" I cried, and whirled around in relief. Then I stopped. It was the dogs, all right. But a man with a crew cut and a jaggedy face stood behind them, hauling back on lengths of rope that he had tied onto their collars. He wore a short-sleeved work shirt buttoned up tight around his skinny neck.

The warden. I had no idea how he had managed to come so close without me noticing sooner. "You missing something?" he asked. His voice was cold and quiet.

"Yes, sir," I said. "Those are my dogs. I've been looking for them."

I could hear C.B.'s toenails scratch against the stone paving as he tried to scrabble closer to greet me. I reached my hand out to take the dogs, but the warden didn't budge. I dropped my arm to my side.

"Sure didn't appear as though you were looking too hard just now," he said. His eyes were glittery, and he had a peculiar way of chewing on his words, like there was grit between his teeth. He looked me up and down. "Didn't you read that big sign out front that says NO DOGS ALLOWED?"

"No, sir," I fibbed. "I didn't." I let my gaze flick down to the writing sewn across his breast pocket: R. KILGORE—OAKLAND CEMETERY. Where was Jeeter? I stole a look past Kilgore's shoulder, hoping I would see him come loping around the corner to rescue me at any second.

"You must think this is some kind of a park where you get to run your dogs and play fetch."

I shook my head. "No, sir. I just—"

The dogs had worked themselves into a frenzy by now. I could see the whites of their scared eyes as they strained toward me, whining louder. "Listen, Mr. Kilgore. I'm really sorry. I won't ever bring my dogs in here again. So . . . do you think I could just take them now and . . . leave?"

He glanced down at the embroidered writing above his pocket, and his lips curled up in a slow smile. "So you *can* read after all."

I blinked back a little shock of surprise. I was used to fending off sarcastic comments from kids, but no adult had ever talked to me that way. What was it Jeeter had called him? Ornery as a snake on a stick? He wasn't kidding.

"Here," Kilgore finally said. "Take 'em." I held my breath and stepped forward to grab the ropes. C.B. and Spunky were all over me in a second, a blur of paws and tongues and tails. Kilgore crossed his arms over his chest and watched without a word while I struggled to untangle myself and herd the dogs toward home. But he wasn't done with me yet. We had made it only a few yards when I heard his voice again behind me, still oddly quiet. "Where you think you're going?" he asked, sounding amused.

I reined in the dogs and turned around. Maybe he only wanted his ropes back.

"I'm going home," I said as I fished for the leashes in the pocket of my sweatshirt. "My house is right over—"

"I don't care where you live," he cut in. "You can't cross the cemetery with those dogs. You'll have to go through there." He jerked his head toward the direction of the woods.

"You mean Hickory Hill?"

"Bingo."

Was he crazy? It was getting dark, and going home through the park would take three times as long. Kilgore's mouth twitched with laughter. "You better get a move on. You could lose your way in those woods around nightfall."

What was the *deal* with this guy? I took my time leading the dogs toward the park, determined not to give him the satisfaction of seeing me run. Then, once we were a few steps into the cover of the woods, I pulled C.B. and Spunky behind a thick mound of brush. I couldn't resist looking back. I hunched down and peered through the branches as the dogs sat beside me with their tongues hanging sideways. Kilgore was still there, at his post beside the wall. I watched him reach into his front pocket for something. Suddenly the sharp hollows of his face were lit up as he held a match to the cigarette clamped in his mouth. I ducked lower and froze while he stood smoking, scanning the edge of the woods where I hid.

When Kilgore finally finished his cigarette and turned to go, I sank down into the layer of rotten leaves at my feet. My knees felt spongy from crouching for so long. But even with Kilgore gone, I was too scared to risk taking the short-cut home. The dogs snuffled closer, and for a minute I stared out at the night descending over Oakland, my mind spinning through all the lousy things that had happened to me that day.

Everyone at school thought I was a loser.

My mother wasn't speaking to me anymore.

And to make matters worse, I still didn't have a decent idea for my Adopt-a-Grave Project.

I was beginning to think I was cursed, just like that Black Angel.

The Black Angel.

I smiled into the shadows.

Maybe I had an idea after all.

Here I lie bereft of breath
Because a cough
carried me off;
Then a coffin
they carried me off in.

BOSTON, MASSACHUSETTS

CHAPTER 7

I SHOULD HAVE KNOWN. Instead of letting us quietly hand in our work sheets the next day, Mr. Oliver wanted us to announce our picks for the Adopt-a-Grave Project. Out loud. To the whole class.

Sylvie went first. She sounded like she was running for Miss America. "I chose Lenora S. Cadwaller, MD, born 1840, died 1910," she told us loudly, "because I'd like to be a doctor too someday and Lenora must have been one of the first female physicians in our state."

I rolled my eyes along with everybody else.

Pretty soon it was Mellecker's turn. All day long I had been waiting for him to pounce, to tap my shoulder at my locker or stop by the BattleBots table, ready to teach me a lesson for daring to call him Teddy Blair. But so far nothing. Obviously, he was saving his revenge for fifth period, when the entire class would be watching.

"All right, Mellecker," Mr. Oliver called out. "Who'd you pick?"

Mellecker leaned back in his desk with his fingers laced behind his head. "Is it okay if I pick more than one person?"

"What do you mean?" Mr. Oliver asked.

"I mean I picked a whole family. The Ransom family."

"That might be all right. Why'd you choose the Ransoms?"

"Because they were *rich*," Mellecker said, sending a ripple of laughter through the room.

Mr. Oliver was trying not to smile. That's how it was for Mellecker. Even teachers let him get away with being a smart aleck. "And how did you reach that conclusion?" Mr. Oliver asked.

"Well, they're all buried in one of those giant, creepy-looking vaults with columns and fancy carvings. So they must have been pretty important, right?"

"It's a good possibility," Mr. Oliver said. "I guess you'll need to get started on your research and find out if your theory is true."

Then Mr. Oliver moved on. Although Mellecker hadn't chosen a war veteran like I expected, Beez and some other guys in our class made up for it. Corporals, captains, cadets. I stopped listening. There were only five kids to go before my turn.

No blushing, I chanted to myself. *No blushing*.

I could feel the air in the classroom turning thick with suspense. Of course everyone had been waiting to see what I would say.

Two more kids to go.

One more . . .

I took a deep breath and licked my lips and squirmed in my seat.

"Linc?" Mr. Oliver called.

That's all it took. In a split second my face felt hot enough to melt.

"I'm hoping you were able to complete yesterday's assignment?"

I gave a quick nod. Out of the corner of my eye, I could see Mellecker and Beez angling to get a better view.

"Well?" Mr. Oliver asked, shifting his weight impatiently. "Would you care to share with us who you chose?"

I nodded again and then made my announcement, but the words didn't come out the way I had planned. I had thought maybe if I said my answer loud enough, no one would notice the quiver in my voice. So I ended up bellowing by mistake. "The Black Angel!" I practically shouted.

The room went still.

Sylvie was the first one to recover from her surprise. "Wait!" she called out, flapping her hand at Mr. Oliver. "I thought you said the Black Angel was off-limits!"

"Well, not exactly," Mr. Oliver said carefully. "I remember saying that I wasn't going to allow any more discussion about superstitions and legends. But maybe Linc has a different approach."

"I do," I insisted, forgetting to be nervous for a few seconds. "I want to find out the facts, like who's really buried there and what happened to them, so I can prove there's no such thing as the Curse of the Black Angel."

"Sounds intriguing," Mr. Oliver said. "But do you mind my asking what the professor thinks of your plan?"

I pretended not to notice all the whispering and kids trading looks across the aisles. "She really likes the idea," I lied. "She told me I'd be doing this town a big favor if I could show, once and for all, that the Black Angel legends are nothing but a bunch of bull."

Mr. Oliver's bushy eyebrows climbed higher on his forehead.

The truth was I hadn't even told Lottie yet. I had wanted to tell her last night—right after I apologized for that tirade up in my room. But she didn't get home from work until after dinnertime, and when I had wandered downstairs to talk, she said she was exhausted from her trip and needed to go straight to bed.

Sylvie was still complaining. "It's not fair," she grumbled to no one in particular. "I bet you anything he's gonna get his mom to help him."

"What's wrong with that?" somebody across the room shot back. I stared in confusion. It was Mellecker, and it sounded like he was taking my side. "She's an expert on graveyards," he said to Sylvie. "Wouldn't you ask her for help if she were *your* mother?"

Sylvie slouched back in her seat with her arms crossed over her chest. I kept gawking at Mellecker, wondering whether I had heard him right. But before I could figure out for sure, Mr. Oliver raised his hand for quiet. "I'm sure Linc will rely on his mother for advice and nothing more," he said, turning to me with a pointed glance. "We'll look forward to hearing the truth about the Black Angel when you deliver your report in November."

Cliff flashed me a quick thumbs-up sign from the next row. I smiled back at him, feeling a tiny surge of triumph and relief. My turn was over, and so far American Studies class was going a lot better than I had expected.

Then I snapped back to attention. Mr. Oliver had just called on the new girl, Delaney, and she was talking in that dreamy, sipping-lemonade-on-the-front-porch voice of hers. "I'm not too sure why I picked the one I did," I heard her say. "I just had a feelin'."

"Feelin'," she said, without the *g* on the end.

"And I thought the name on the headstone had a nice ring to it," Delaney added.

Mr. Oliver closed his eyes and kneaded the heel of his hand into his brow bone as if he were fighting off a headache. "All right," he said. "I wouldn't exactly say your reason for your choice is very strong. But now you've got me curious. What's the name with the nice ring to it?"

"Raintree," Delaney announced. "Robert Raintree."

Raintree? I whipped around in my desk and stared at Delaney, hard. She stared right back with her clever cat eyes. I had never heard of anybody else with that name before. Nobody except for me and my dad.

ELLEN SHANNON
Who was fatally burned
March 21, 1870
By the explosion of a lamp
Filled with "R.E. Danforth's
Non-Explosive
Burning Fluid"

GIRARD, PENNSYLVANIA

CHAPTER 8

ONCE THE BELL RANG, I waited for Delaney to collect her books and leave the classroom first. We were supposed to turn in our Adopt-a-Grave work sheets on the way out. I dropped mine in the basket on Mr. Oliver's desk and hurried to catch up with Delaney in the hall. I had just gathered up enough courage to tap her on the shoulder when I heard Mr. Oliver call me back. "Linc, can I have a word with you?"

Delaney turned around with her green eyes wide. I snatched looks back and forth, from her to the classroom, like I was watching a Ping-Pong match. "I'll be right there," I called to Mr. Oliver.

"Did you want something?" Delaney asked.

By now the hallway had started to fill up with kids, and a few of them bumped me with their backpacks as I stood planted in the middle of traffic.

My face was heating up. "Yeah. Or . . . I mean, that's okay, it can wait till later. Never mind." A group of girls bulldozed between us as I tried to give her one of those don't-worry-about-it waves. "Well, I'll see ya," I spluttered. Then I lurched back toward the classroom. Jeeter's term for a big loser landed on the tip of my tongue. "Heehaw," I muttered. That was me. A total heehaw.

Mr. Oliver had no idea his timing had been so rotten. He led me into the empty classroom and lazily settled himself on the edge of his desk. "Listen, Linc," he finally started, "I'm not sure exactly what happened yesterday. . . ." He paused, waiting for me to jump in with an explanation.

"It's kind of complicated," I said.

Mr. Oliver nodded. "Can you at least fill me in on why you didn't tell me before the field trip that Professor Landers is your mother?"

I winced. "Um. I guess I just thought it would make things easier. But it was dumb not to tell you. I'm really sorry."

Another nod. He reached over and retrieved my work sheet from the basket beside him. I followed his gaze down to my drawing at the bottom of the page. It was terrible. Last night, after Kilgore had run me out of the graveyard, I had had to resort to sketching the Black Angel from memory. Under the bright lights of the classroom, my scribbly drawing looked like a third grader's—like a lamppost with wings instead of a statue.

"You didn't follow my instructions," Mr. Oliver said. "You've got a sketch, but where's the name and the dates? Isn't there an epitaph on the Black Angel?"

"I guess I forgot to check," I mumbled.

Mr. Oliver sighed and handed me a new work sheet from a stack on his desk. "Listen, Linc, I gave you permission to do this monument because from what you said in class, I thought you were serious about this project. If you *are* serious, you're going to need to start over and pay a lot more attention to detail."

"I will, Mr. Oliver. I promise." I grabbed the work sheet, thanked him, and bolted for the hallway. I needed to find Delaney, but there were only three minutes until the next bell. Maybe she'd still be at her locker. I always passed her there on my way to French. A few times I had caught a glimpse of a little calendar that she had hung on the inside of her locker door. She had x'd off in red Magic Marker each day since school started. I couldn't help wondering about the countdown. What was she waiting for? Her birthday? Summer vacation?

I took the stairs two at a time. My backpack banged against my shoulder as I cut in and out of stragglers on their way to class. But by the time I made it to the east wing, there was no sign of Delaney.

I checked back at her locker after sixth period. Nope.

After seventh period—the last one of the day. *Still* no. She'd probably left for a dentist's appointment or something. I stayed a few more minutes, searching for her in the river of faces flooding down the hall. But soon the crowds dwindled down, and when some kids chatting by their lockers started to give me funny looks for lurking, I gave up and set off for my own locker downstairs.

I almost ran into Mellecker coming out of the boys' bathroom. He looked startled to see me. "Oh, hey," he said, wobbling for a second.

"Hi," I mumbled, and kept heading for the stairwell.

"Wait," he called after me.

I stopped. *Here it comes,* I thought as I slowly turned around. At least there weren't a lot of kids nearby to witness whatever happened next.

Mellecker sauntered toward me. He started to smile. "Remember when we used to climb up that huge dirt pile in the Ho-Hos' backyard and you kept saying we were climbing Mount Everest?"

I blinked up at Mellecker, speechless with surprise. "Yeah," I finally answered softly. "And I brought that rope from home, and we tied ourselves together in case one of us fell in a crevasse. . . ."

Mellecker laughed and looked at the floor, shaking his head. "Yeah. What dopes." Then his expression suddenly shifted, and he glanced at me with a pained light in his dark eyes. "Listen," he said, "I had no idea that lady on the field trip was your mother. If I had remembered, I never would have drawn that stupid cartoon. You know that, right?"

I founded myself nodding. He actually looked sincere.

Mellecker's face cleared. "I recognized you right off, though, as soon as I saw you coming down the hall. You still do that same little move with your head." Mellecker imitated me flipping my hair out of my eyes. "I used to think it was so cool back when I first met you. I kept trying to do it too, but my hair was never long enough."

73

I smiled in amazement. Mellecker thought my "little move" was cool? I never even knew I had a "little move."

"So if you recognized me," I asked, "why didn't you say anything?"

Mellecker shrugged. "Why didn't *you*?"

I paused and let out a big breath of air. "I don't know. You weren't a Ho-Ho very long. I guess I figured you didn't want to be reminded."

"Yeah," Mellecker confessed. He shoved his hands into his pockets with an embarrassed grin. "I kinda thought my Teddy Blair days were behind me."

"Sorry about that," I said sheepishly.

Mellecker shrugged again. "It's okay. Let's call it even." He glanced toward the clock on the wall. "Well, I better be getting to practice," he said, starting to walk backward down the hall. "But I'll see ya tomorrow, Crenshaw. Okay?"

"Yep." I lifted my hand in a wave as he turned and disappeared around the corner. Then I stood there with my heart swelling like the Grinch's on Christmas morning when he hears all those Whos singing down in Whoville. So Mellecker wasn't such a jerk after all. He remembered everything—the dirt pile, even the dumb way I flipped my hair out of my eyes. And he had called me Crenshaw, just like he called the rest of his buddies by their last names. Suddenly the idea that we could ever be friends again didn't seem so far-fetched anymore.

I headed downstairs, humming, still thinking about all the possibilities. I was so preoccupied that I didn't even notice Delaney until I was halfway down the hall. She was leaning against one of the lockers toward the end of the corridor. Not just any locker. It was *mine*.

I strolled closer, trying to act calm and collected, but Delaney didn't even attempt to hide her happy smile when she looked up and saw me. "Golly day," she said, sounding more southern than ever. "You don't use your locker much, do you?"

"I guess not," I said. I was too self-conscious to admit I'd been circling hers like a buzzard all afternoon.

"Didn't you want to talk to me about something. After American Studies?"

"Oh, yeah," I said, pretending it had almost slipped my mind. I reached for the dial on my locker and spun it round and round. Was it 6–12–21? Or 6–21–12? "I wanted to ask you about the last name on the grave you picked. It's kind of different, right?"

She nodded. "That's one of the reasons why I picked it."

"Well, the funny thing is that's my middle name. Raintree."

She let out a soft gasp. "Really? So you're related to him? Robert Raintree?"

I stopped spinning the dial. "No. . . . I don't think so. I mean, that's why I was surprised. If we have any relatives in town, my parents never mentioned them."

Delaney tucked a stray piece of blond hair behind her ear, thinking hard. "Well, where'd the name Raintree come from? Who were you named after?"

"My father. Raintree was his middle name too. But Dad didn't grow up around here. He grew up in Wisconsin. We only moved here because my parents got jobs teaching at the university."

The little crease between Delaney's eyebrows deepened. "Well, who was your father named after?"

I banged my locker with my fist and tried the combination again, stalling for time. It was strange. All these years I had walked around with a funny middle name like Raintree, but I'd never thought to track down exactly where it came from.

"I think it's just an old family name that kept getting passed down," I said with a little shrug.

Delaney hesitated. "Well, would it be all right if I talked to your father?" she asked shyly. "Maybe he knows more."

My locker finally decided to clank open. I stuck my head inside for a second and pretended to hunt for books. "I wish you could," I said. "But he's not around anymore. He died when I was seven." I pulled my head out and slammed the locker shut.

Delaney stared at me with her mouth open, as if I had reached out and pinched her. "Oh," she breathed. "I'm sorry."

"That's okay," I told her. "I don't even know why I brought all this up. It's probably just a coincidence."

"Maybe so," Delaney agreed. Her shoulders sank a little.

"But I'd still like to see it anyway," I said, just to keep the conversation going. "That grave you picked. Where is it exactly?"

Delaney told me she wasn't sure how to give me directions, but then her face lit up. "I could show you, though," she offered.

"Great!" My answer popped out so fast, I started to blush for the fifth time that day. "I mean, that would be good. When?"

"How about tomorrow? I'll have to go home for a little while after school. But maybe we could meet in the graveyard after that."

"Sure."

The corners of Delaney's mouth twitched up in a mysterious smile. "Then I can show you the real reason I picked Robert Raintree's grave."

"The *real* reason?" I asked. "What do you mean?"

"You'll see," she said. "Tomorrow."

If Tears Could Build A
Stairway, and Memories
A Lane, I'd Walk Right Up
To Heaven and Bring
You Home Again.

OAKLAND CEMETERY
IOWA CITY, IOWA

CHAPTER 9

WHEN I CAME HOME from jogging with the dogs that afternoon, our old Electrolux was parked in the middle of the kitchen floor with a repair tag attached to the hose. I found Lottie lodged behind the giant oak desk in her study, sorting through a pile of musty-looking books. She barely glanced up when I came into the room and moved a stack of papers off the tattered swivel chair in the corner.

I sat down and spun in a slow circle, waiting for Lottie to say something. Her office had been a sunporch before we moved in. But with all the filing cabinets and crowded shelves of books blocking the smeared windows, you could hardly tell anymore. I had always thought about how nice the room would look if we cleared away the clutter and let the light shine through all those hidden panes of glass.

I stopped swiveling long enough to study Lottie's rubbing wall. The walls on either side of the door to her office were papered, floor to ceiling, with charcoal impressions from tombstones all over the world—an imprint of a famous French poet's grave, an English knight in full armor, an epitaph for a sea captain who had been lost somewhere in the Atlantic. A few of the rubbings on the wall were mine. I still remembered the first one Lottie had let me do on my own. We were at a little graveyard somewhere out in the country in Massachusetts, and even when my hand had locked up in a cramp, I wouldn't quit rubbing—not until the name Thankfull Parsons and the year 1758 and a shadowy skull with wings had appeared underneath the side of my black crayon.

I spun around to face Lottie again. "Thanks, Thankfull," I said.

She stopped what she was doing, thumbing through a heavy leather-bound book, and her face softened as she looked up at me. I *knew* she'd remember. We used to say that all the time after our cemetery trip to Massachusetts together, whenever one of us passed the salt or did something nice. *Thanks, Thankfull.*

"Thanks for what?" Lottie asked.

"For getting the vacuum cleaner fixed."

"It only took the repairman two minutes," she confessed. "Turns out it was only a sock stuck in the hose."

I gulped back an incredulous laugh and wheeled myself closer. "I'm sorry about all that stuff I said yesterday."

"No," Lottie said slowly. "You were right about a lot of it. I know I get lost in my work sometimes. And I forget what it's like to be your age." Her brow furrowed, and then a puzzled expression wandered across her face. "Wait a minute. I guess I have no idea what it's like to be you. I wasn't exactly the typical teenager, you know."

"No kidding!" I said with a laugh bubbling out of my throat. "What *were* you like, anyway?"

"A bookworm mostly. Happiest when I had the old sofa on the second floor of the public library all to myself . . . with a stack of fresh books waiting at my feet."

I winced, thinking of Lottie spending all her weekends in the tiny library in New Hope, Wisconsin, coming home to her prim and proper parents. Every other year we went to visit Grandma Dee and Grandad at their quiet retirement village in Florida. I could never wait to escape the way they watched my every move at dinnertime in the dining hall, waiting to see whether I would pick vanilla pudding or chocolate cake for dessert, or their funny rules about no baseball caps indoors or no swimming in the pool until at least two hours after eating.

"Weren't you ever lonely?" I asked.

"Not really. I guess I was used to being by myself."

With Lottie in such a talkative mood, I decided to push my luck. "It's kinda funny. You didn't have any brothers and sisters, and neither did Dad, and then you guys decided to have just one kid too."

Lottie smiled wistfully, and I held my breath waiting for her to answer. "We used to tease each other about that," she said at last. "About being spoiled only children. We called ourselves the Onlies. And we always talked about wanting to have another child, but . . ." Her voice faded on the last word.

I knew what she was thinking. Life didn't go according to plan.

"I've been wondering," I said, rushing to change the subject. "Who were we named after? Dad and I?"

Lottie gazed toward the rubbing wall. "The name Lincoln came from your dad's uncle. And Raintree was a family name from way back on his mother's side. When I asked Ellen about it once, she told me she had found the name Raintree recorded in her family's old Bible, and she liked it well enough to pass it on to her son. I've always loved it too. Lincoln and Crenshaw are such strong, sturdy names, and Raintree seems to balance everything out. It sounds so clean and peaceful."

"Whatever happened to that Bible?"

"It's packed away up in the attic," Lottie told me. "Your father came across it in his parents' basement after his mother passed away."

"I can't even remember her."

"I know. It's a shame." Lottie shook her head. "You were only three when Ellen was diagnosed with cancer. And your grandfather died just before you were born. He would have been smitten with you, just like she was."

She let her sad gaze linger on me a little longer before she reached for one of the stacks of paper on her desk, ready to get back to work. But then she stopped. "Wait a minute. Why are you asking all these questions?"

"You know that Adopt-a-Grave Project that Mr. Oliver assigned us? There's a girl in my class who picked a grave with the name Robert Raintree on it. Maybe he's a long-lost relative," I said, trying to sound mysterious.

I was halfway kidding, but Lottie tilted her head to one side. "Huh, that's funny. Your father used to joke about having some sort of family connection in Iowa City."

"Really?" I leaned forward. "Why would he have joked about something like that?"

Lottie eyed her waiting pile of papers. "Please, Lottie," I said quietly. "I want to hear everything."

She tipped her head back with a resigned sigh and stared at the ceiling. "Well," she finally began, "I used to tease your father about his so-called *signs*. Sometimes he would make big decisions based on what he thought were little omens— silly things like a black cat in his path, or it could be a coincidence like a report on the radio that mentioned whatever he had been stewing over."

"Oh, I bet you loved *that*," I interrupted, thinking back to her rants about the Black Angel yesterday.

"Oh, it drove me crazy. Here was this very science-minded geologist crossing the street so he wouldn't have to walk under a ladder." Lottie shook her head as if she were feeling the exasperation all over again. "Ridiculous!"

She pushed her curls away from her face and went on. "When we decided we wanted to find new jobs, your dad and I interviewed at four universities around the country, and we ended up with four sets of job offers." She gave me a smug little nod. "But we had a terrible time deciding which offer to accept. Then about this same time, your father was cleaning out his parents' house, getting it ready to sell. We had been renting it out ever since his mother died. One day he came home and announced that he knew where we should move. Without a doubt! He had seen one of his signs." She rolled her eyes.

"What was it?" I asked.

"He said he had been going through a crate of old mail that had been left behind over the last few years. The renters were always terrible about telling the post office where their mail should be forwarded. Anyway, your father found a letter in the pile that was addressed to his mother. Of course Ellen had been dead for quite a while by that time, so he opened it."

Lottie squinted, trying to remember. "He showed the letter to me. It was very odd, just one or two lines long, and it said something like 'I apologize for writing, but I've been worried about you. Please let me know if you're well.' That was it. But here's the mysterious part. There was no name on the letter—just some initials." She frowned in thought for a second. "Now I can't even remember what they were. The only real clue was a return address from Iowa City."

Lottie threw up her hands. "Anyway, you see how crazy your father was? *That* was his sign for us to move here, that this was the offer we had to accept. I tried to argue with him about it at first, but he would just laugh and say *obviously* his mother had a long-lost lover in Iowa City, and that was as good a reason as any to move here. Then we came for another visit, fell in love with the town, found this house . . . and there was no turning back."

I sat there with my mouth hanging open, waiting for

the punch line of the story. "So Dad never figured out who wrote the letter?"

"Not that I know of," Lottie said with a shrug. "I'm not even sure what happened to it. Your father talked about tracking down the address as soon as he got a chance. But we were so swamped with work and getting you settled and fixing up the house when we first moved here. And then . . ." Something in her face shifted, and when she spoke again, all the oomph had drained from her voice. "He ran out of time. We only had a few months here before he died."

I couldn't help myself. Even though I could see Lottie wanted to be done with the subject, I had to ask. "What about Dad's omens? Do you think he had any warning about what would happen to him?"

"No," Lottie said flatly. "He left for work that day humming a Beatles song." Her mouth twisted with bitterness. "So you see why I'm not exactly a big believer in signs and superstitions."

I nodded. Lottie pressed her fingertips to her eyelids for a long second. She startled me when she suddenly blinked her eyes open and demanded, "So who'd *you* pick?"

"What?"

"Whose grave did you pick for your project?"

I shifted uneasily in my seat. "Well, I—"

"Don't tell me you haven't done it yet? Didn't you see that work sheet I left for you on the table last night?"

"Yes, I saw it."

"Then who . . . did . . . you . . . pick?" Lottie asked again, rapping out each word on her desk with her knuckles.

My answer came out sort of whispery and scared.

Lottie leaned forward and squinted as if she couldn't possibly have heard me correctly. *"What?"* Then she flopped back in her chair with an amazed cackle. "Oh, that's too much," she said as she sat massaging her forehead for a few seconds. When she spoke again, she sounded like a psychiatrist, clinical and calm. "Linc, is this your way of proving something to the other kids in your class?" she asked. "That you're nothing like your crazy mother who led them on the graveyard tour?"

"No," I told her. "I'm just interested in who's actually buried there, that's all. Nobody really knows, right?"

"Of course people know, Linc. Didn't I explain this well enough yesterday? Every crackpot ghost chaser within three hundred miles has ransacked the records at the historical society, trying to dig up information about the Black Angel. But once they find out the real story isn't very exciting, they either lose interest or make things up to keep the legends alive."

"So what's the real story?"

"No murder. No mayhem. Just some poor woman who spent her life's savings on a statue to honor her dead husband and son."

"So there's no preacher buried there who murdered his kid?"

"Nope," she said.

"And you've seen all those records yourself?"

She waited a beat too long. "Well, no. But I've had colleagues who've looked into them."

"Then how do you know *for sure* whether all their information is right?"

Lottie didn't answer.

"Huh?" I asked again. "Huh?"

She sniffed. "I guess I don't know, for sure."

"Aha!" But I wasn't finished. "Aren't you the one who's always told me, 'Secondhand information makes second-rate historians'? How are all the kids in my class supposed to believe there's no Curse of the Black Angel unless somebody shows them some cold, hard proof? Somebody like me."

At last Lottie's pursed lips slipped into a smile. "You might have a point there."

I flung my arms up and did two victory spins in the swivel chair. "I won't even ask you for help," I insisted once I had stopped spinning. Sylvie's whiny protests were still drifting through my head. "I want to see if I can do this all on my own."

"Be my guest," Lottie replied. "I wouldn't help even if you asked. I'd like to see whether all those years of dragging you around on my research trips actually paid off."

"Thanks a lot, Thankfull," I said drily, and hurried off to start my detective work.

CHAPTER 10

Good friend for Jesus
sake forbeare,
To digg the dust
encloased heare!
Blese be the man that
spares thes stones,
And curst be he that
moves my bones.

WILLIAM SHAKESPEARE
STRATFORD-UPON-AVON, ENGLAND

THE NEXT AFTERNOON I got to the Black Angel fifteen minutes before I was supposed to meet Delaney there. I had come early to find Jeeter. I wanted to tell him about my run-in with his boss. But as soon as I started for the cemetery, I heard the buzz of hedge clippers off in the distance, which meant Jeeter was trimming the row of yews way over on the north side. There wasn't time to track him down.

So I headed straight for the Angel, keeping my eye out for Kilgore along the way. I couldn't figure out why I felt so jittery. I wasn't doing anything wrong. I hadn't even considered bringing the dogs along.

Maybe I was just nervous about finally meeting up with Delaney. Once we'd decided on our plan at my locker that morning, the day had seemed to drag on forever. We didn't talk again, even when we passed each other in the halls. But it was obvious we were both counting down the hours. I had caught Delaney's eye on her way into Mr. Oliver's class that afternoon just in time to see her smile and bite down on her lower lip like she was holding back a secret.

But I forgot all about Kilgore and Delaney and everything else as soon as I arrived at the foot of the Black Angel. When I gazed up at the statue, a chill immediately prickled up my spine, and I found myself pulling the zipper of my jacket up to my chin. Of all the angels in cemeteries I had seen over the years, this one was the strangest. Most others looked the way you would expect, carved from white stone with their dainty wings and their kind faces raised up to heaven. You were supposed to feel comforted in the presence of those angels, protected and hopeful. But the Black Angel was anything but comforting. First off, her color was all wrong. She was dark as tar, and she was *huge*, with wings that looked way too heavy to fly. One wing shielded her shadowy face from the world, while the other drooped around her like a thick cape. How were you supposed to feel anything but depressed with a gloomy statue like that towering over you?

When I was little, I used to beg Jeeter to tell me stories about the Curse. He always told the one about the three university students who had pulled a midnight prank and chopped off some of the Angel's bronze fingers. It didn't take long for each of them to be struck down by some kind of horrible accident. The first lost his hand working at a sawmill that summer. The next one fell over with a stroke on his twenty-first birthday and woke up with a paralyzed arm. The last student thought he was home free until he happened to nick his hand with his pocketknife on graduation day. His tiny cut became infected and slowly got worse. There wasn't a single doctor at the university hospital who could figure out how to stop the raging gangrene. The only solution was to amputate.

I always pretended to be fearless when Jeeter told me those stories as he puttered around the toolshed. But later, riding my bicycle home at dusk, I could barely stand to glance up at the Black Angel as I rode past. I'd steal one peek at those dark wings or the hand with its three missing fingers, and suddenly I was clenching my handlebars like they were life ropes, with my feet pedaling fast enough to launch a rocket.

After all the time I had spent avoiding the Angel when I was little, it felt almost forbidden to step so close—close enough to read the names chiseled into the base of the statue.

Eddie Dolezal
Born
March 10 1873
Died
Jan 14 1891

Nicholas Feldevert 1825–1911
Theresa Feldevert 1836–

According to those dates, Eddie Dolezal died when he was only seventeen. So from what Lottie had told me, I knew

Eddie must have been Theresa's son. But what had happened to Eddie's father—Mr. Dolezal? And why wasn't there a date of death filled in for Theresa?

I had brought along my notebook and the new work sheet from Mr. Oliver. I quickly copied down the details of the inscription, and I was almost finished with my sketch when Delaney arrived.

"Hey there," she said shyly, dropping her backpack on the ground beside me. Most of her wispy blond hair had worked its way out of her ponytail, and her face looked sort of splotchy, like she might have been crying.

"So you found your way okay?"

"Uh-huh. Sylvie showed some of us how to get here on the field trip." She let out a long, shaky breath of air. "I'm just a little late on account of my mother. She didn't feel so good this afternoon, and I was worried about asking her to drive me over here."

"Oh."

"But Mama swears she's feeling fine now," she added quickly, glancing at her watch. "She went to run a couple errands, and I'm supposed to meet her back in the parking lot in half an hour."

I nodded, and Delaney's gaze drifted up to the Black Angel. "Lordy," she said softly. "She really is spooky, isn't she? But she's kind of beautiful too."

I raised one eyebrow. "Beautiful?"

Delaney circled around the statue, sizing her up from different angles. "Well, her face isn't the prettiest, but her arms are so graceful under those wings. And look at her gown. You can just tell it's silk, can't you? The way it flows around her feet?"

She crouched down. "What's this?" she asked. I hurried over to see. There was an inscription carved into the granite on the other side of the pedestal—several lines in old-fashioned, slanty type.

"What's it say?" Delaney asked. "It's in another language, isn't it?"

I knelt down and swiped my palm back and forth across the rough stone, hoping the words might come clear. But the epitaph was so worn and fuzzy with moss that I could only make out parts of the lines.

"Yeah, definitely not English," I said, getting to my feet. And it didn't look like any of the languages Dr. Lindstrom had introduced during my Ho-Ho days either—not French or German or Spanish or Latin.

I had my work cut out for me, but I'd have to come back later to finish my sketch and copy down the weird jumble of consonants and vowels in the epitaph. Delaney was checking her watch again, so I scribbled a few final notes, and we set out for the Raintree grave.

The marker stood off by itself, in a far corner of the cemetery where an ancient oak tree loomed. Since the oak still had most of its leaves, the space under the thick canopy of branches looked dim and shadowy—except for a bright splash of yellow on the ground that we could see from all the way at the top of the hill overlooking the tree.

Delaney led the way, and soon we were standing side by side staring down at a huge bunch of sunflowers propped against Robert Raintree's tombstone. The bouquet was tied with a piece of lace, and against the weathered marble the gold petals blazed like a neon sign. The flowers looked pretty fresh, other than a few petals that had started to curl and turn brown at the edges.

"See why I picked this one?" Delaney asked in a hushed voice. "I thought it was so romantic, this big bouquet for somebody who died almost fifty years ago."

I nodded, following her gaze to the dates etched beneath the name: 1900–1965.

"He died the same year my dad was born," I murmured.

But there was something else—the edge of a carving peeking from behind the sunflowers. I reached down and nudged the bouquet out of the way.

It was a torch, fallen on its side, with its flames dying to a flicker.

Delaney knelt next to the stone. "I can't believe I didn't notice this before," she said. "It's one of those symbols we learned about, isn't it?"

"Yeah, a torch is a pretty common one. It's just another symbol for life."

Delaney looked so impressed, I couldn't help adding more. "The ones I've seen before are always inverted . . . upside down, I mean . . . which makes sense because the person's dead, obviously." I started to blush, suddenly feeling like a show-off. "But I've never seen a torch on its side before. I'm not exactly sure what this one means."

Delaney hesitated. "Maybe you could ask your mom," she said gently.

"I could." I sighed. "But I've decided it might be best if I try to keep my mother out of this project as much as possible."

Delaney was dusting off her knees and heading over to sit on a gnarled tree root. "How come?" she asked. "She's an expert."

So far I had been dodging the subject of my mother and the field trip like a prizefighter. But now that Delaney was asking, it was a relief to try and explain why I had acted the way I did when Lottie led our class on the tour. I went over to find a spot in the roots beside her. "It's kind of complicated," I started, recycling my line from the conversation with Mr. Oliver. "Ever since my dad died, it's always been just me and my mom. I don't have any brothers and sisters."

"Me neither," Delaney said.

"So you know what it's like being an only child. And as you might have noticed . . . Lottie's a little different from your run-of-the-mill mom."

Delaney tried not to smile. "You call your mother by her first name?" she asked.

I shrugged. "Like I said, things are different at my house. For instance, Lottie didn't really want me to go to Plainview. She says the education there is *mainstream*. Says it's *for the masses*." I drew the words out, rolling my eyes. "Lottie likes to keep to herself. But the truth is I kind of *want* to be mainstream . . . part of the masses for a change. That's why I switched schools."

I ended up telling Delaney all about the Ho-Hos—the good parts and the bad. Then I broke the news that Mellecker used to be one too. "You might not want to spread that around, though," I warned after I had described how different he was a few years ago. "I don't think Mellecker wants a lot of people knowing about his former life."

Delaney's face had gone still while I had been blabbering away. "You're so lucky," she said once I let her get a word in edgewise. "You've only had to switch schools once, and you've lived on the same street since you were little."

"How many places have you lived?"

Delaney gazed up at the patchwork of leaves and branches over our heads, softly listing the places. I could hardly hear. Montgomery, Alabama, I think she said. Knoxville, Tennessee, and a couple others. She stopped and held up one hand with her fingers outstretched.

"Five?"

She nodded. "My father's a factory manager, and he keeps getting transferred or promoted. Half the time I don't know which."

"Where'd you start out?"

"South Carolina. That's where my grandma and most of my cousins live. I miss them a lot. But we keep getting farther and farther away from everybody back home. Sometimes I think Daddy's gonna get us all the way to California before we turn around and start back again. The last place, in Indiana? We were only there a hundred and seventy-four days."

A memory of her red Magic Marker X's flashed through my head. My question rushed out before I realized how nosy it sounded. "Is that what you're keeping track of on that calendar in your locker? How many days you stay in one place?"

Delaney's mouth opened a little in surprise. A few more strands of her ponytail came loose when she shook her head. "No," she said, busying herself with gathering up her hair again. "That's something different. . . ." Her hands froze at the back of her neck. "Oh, my gosh!" she gasped, and checked her watch. "I forgot all about Mama. I was supposed to be in the parking lot fifteen minutes ago." Delaney scrambled to her feet, grabbing her backpack. I jumped up with my notebook, uncertain what to do.

"Wait a minute!" I said. "I think I can get us a ride." Out of the corner of my eye, I had spotted Jeeter zipping along the narrow drive in the little golf cart that he used for his rounds in the cemetery. His hedge clippers and rakes were piled in the back. I ran toward him waving my arms.

As soon as I had made the introductions and we had squeezed in next to him, Jeeter waited until Delaney looked away and then wiggled his eyebrows at me. I could almost see the thought bubble blossoming over his head: "Ol' Lincoln Log's got himself a girlfriend." I gave him one of my death glares, and he chuckled to himself as he shifted the cart into gear.

"We've been working on that project I was telling you about," I explained before Jeeter could say anything embarrassing.

"Oh, yeah?" He nodded. "You finally figure out which grave you're gonna pick?"

"Yep." I grinned. I couldn't wait to see Jeeter's reaction. "I'm adopting the Black Angel."

Jeeter's goatee sagged as he shook his head. "You're a braver man than me, Lincoln Crenshaw."

I scanned the distance and checked over my shoulder as we rounded a bend in the driveway. "Hey, the Black Angel doesn't scare me half as much as that new boss of yours. What's the deal with that guy?"

"Yeah, I heard you had the pleasure of making Captain Kilgore's acquaintance the other day," Jeeter said with a snort. "Don't worry. He's just one of these fellas who need to make sure everybody knows exactly who's in charge. You say, 'Yes, sir . . . no, sir,' do things his way, you'll be fine."

Jeeter glanced over at Delaney. "So you've got the same assignment as my buddy Linc here?"

"Yes, sir," she said. Jeeter's goatee twitched, and I rubbed my hand over my mouth to keep from laughing. I don't think Jeeter had ever been called "sir" before. Delaney tried to describe which grave she had picked. "It's under that giant oak tree back there," she said, "near the place where you stopped to give us a ride."

"You mean the grave with the sunflowers?" Jeeter asked.

Delaney perked up. "That's right. Do you know anything about it?"

Jeeter took his eyes off the driveway long enough to give her one of his wise nods. "For as long as I been here, that old lady's been coming to visit that grave every single Monday, rain or shine, right around two o'clock. If it's summer or early fall, she always leaves a big bunch of flowers behind. Always the same kind. Sunflowers."

Delaney leaned across me. "So you've talked with her?"

"Oh, no," he said. "I like to respect visitors' privacy. And she doesn't seem to want to talk to anybody much. Except herself, that is."

"What do you mean?" I asked.

"Well, she kinda whispers to herself. Old people do that sometimes."

Of course we had a lot more questions, but we were coming up on the cemetery office already, and there was a woman with her arms crossed standing by a blue car on the far side of the parking lot. I knew it had to be Delaney's mother. She was pretty, with wispy blond hair just like Delaney's.

The only surprise was that she was pregnant. As Jeeter pulled the golf cart into its parking place, I noticed her wincing and moving her hand to the small of her back as if she had a sore spot there. I wondered why Delaney hadn't told me, especially after we had been talking about what it was like to be only children.

Delaney jumped out of the cart before Jeeter had even set the parking brake. "I'll see you tomorrow, Linc," she called over her shoulder. "Thanks for helping with my project." She made a beeline straight for the passenger side of the blue car. "Sorry I'm late, Mama," I heard her say breathlessly as she disappeared inside.

Her mother hesitated, staring back at Jeeter and me with a searching gaze. Her lips moved, on the edge of a smile. But when Delaney's car door slammed shut behind her, she turned away and carefully lowered herself into the driver's seat.

"Why's your girlfriend in such a big hurry?" Jeeter asked as we watched them pull out of the cemetery.

"Beats me," I said. I didn't bother trying to set him straight on the girlfriend part.

Why not let him think what he wanted for a while?

Once I wasn't
Then I was
Now I ain't again.

CLEVELAND, OHIO

CHAPTER 11

I BARELY HAD A CHANCE to talk to Delaney over the next few days. Except for American Studies, we didn't have any classes together or even the same lunch period, and she seemed to disappear as soon as the bell rang each afternoon. So the week after we met in the graveyard, when a team of parents came to drive everyone in our class downtown to the historical society, I kept hoping that Delaney and I would be assigned to the same van. No such luck. I ended up in the back of a station wagon squeezed between Queen of Annoying Sylvie and a moody kid named Douglas Spratt, who decided it would be a good time to dig into his backpack and finish off the leftovers of his bologna sandwich from lunch.

I tried to catch up to Delaney when we arrived at the historical society. But I was at the back of the pack shuffling through the entryway. The minute I stepped inside, that old familiar smell hit me like a sleeping potion. I remembered it from tagging along with Lottie through the years. It's exactly what you would smell if you cracked open an old encyclopedia and buried your nose down in the middle of the musty pages.

We filed past the portraits of the city's first settlers—a bunch of dead-eyed men with high collars and bushy sideburns—and as our class gathered in a subdued semicircle in the reading room, I gave up trying to catch Delaney's eye. Ms. Beckett, the head archivist, was one of those no-nonsense librarian types. She had a pointy face and straight black hair cut into sharp angles at her chin, and she gave a curt speech about proper etiquette in the archives. (No chatting; no backpacks allowed; pencils only; no pens.) Then she explained some of the reference materials that would help us find out more about our "deceased."

"Your deceased," she kept saying. "Those of you who found an exact date of death on the headstone for your deceased are quite fortunate," she told us. "You can go to our collection of old newspapers on microfilm and look through issues published around the same date. Chances are you'll be able to find an obituary or death notice for your deceased."

I brightened up a little. I had an exact date of death for Eddie Dolezal—the one buried under the Black Angel who had died when he was only seventeen.

"Any questions?" Ms. Beckett asked pertly. No one spoke up.

"Off you go, then," she said with a tight smile. She flicked her hands like she was shooing flies.

I paused, waiting to see where Delaney was going. She hurried straight for the row of computers where Ms. Beckett had said we could search the database for any mention of the names on our graves. I was tempted to follow her, but there were only three terminals, and when I saw that Mellecker was already sitting at one of them, I spun on my heel and headed for the microfilm viewers in the far corner of the research room. Although Mellecker and I had nodded to each other and waved a few times during the past week, we hadn't had a real conversation since our heart-to-heart outside the boys' bathroom. So I still felt awkward around him, wondering if he really might want to be friends again or if he'd rather keep our brief acquaintance as a thing of the past.

I quickly flipped through my notebook as I walked back to the microfilm area. I found the epitaph I had copied down from the base of the Black Angel and made a note of the exact date when Eddie died.

January 14, 1891.

The reels of film were stored in several extra-wide filing cabinets, in row after row of small cardboard boxes lining the shallow drawers. But since there was only one newspaper published in town at the time of Eddie's death, it didn't take me long to find what I needed—the *Daily Republican*, 1890–1892.

No one else had ventured back to the microfilm area yet, so I had my pick of the viewers. And threading the film through the machine seemed easy after watching Lottie so many times. I clicked on the light, and soon I was scrolling through months of old-timey news.

I felt a little rush of curiosity as I wound my way closer and closer to the date of Eddie's death. I scanned the pages of the January 14 issue, then the next day's paper and the next, and the day after. Nothing. I had to close my eyes for a few seconds and blow out a big breath of air. All those waves of words were starting to make me seasick, so I forced myself to slow down and roll the film backward inch by inch. And suddenly, there it was! On page three, buried in between advertisements for Dr. Bull's Cough Syrup and J. A. Pickering's Traveling Musical Show. The obituary was so small, I had to squint to read the skinny column of print frozen on the screen:

Eddie Dolezal, the only son of Madame Theresa Dolezal, died yesterday afternoon of inflammation of the brain at the age of 17 years. He had been sick only a few days, having left Boerner Bros.' Pharmacy (where he was a faithful employee) last Friday, complaining of illness.

The departed was a bright young man who planned to study medicine at the university. He and his mother have resided on the north side of town since making their voyage to America when Eddie was just a young boy of four. Eddie was preceded into the hereafter by his father and an infant brother, who both died earlier in the family's native village of Strmilov, Bohemia. Madame Dolezal has the sympathy of everyone for the loss of her only remaining son.

I sat back in my chair, staring at the screen. Poor Theresa. She had lost her whole family, one by one, like falling dominoes. How unlucky could you get?

Then I remembered those weird foreign words that Delaney had spotted on the back of the Angel's base, the ones that had been too faded to read. The obituary said the Dolezal family had come from a place called Bohemia. So that would explain it! Maybe the epitaph was written in Bohemian.

"But where in the heck is Bohemia?" I muttered to myself.

I reached for my notebook so I could double-check the names that had been engraved under Eddie's on the front of the statue's base.

Nicholas Feldevert 1825–1911
Theresa Feldevert 1836–

So at least Theresa had managed to find a new husband after Eddie died. But what happened to her after that? Questions slithered in and out of my brain. I opened my notebook to a clean page, figuring I might as well try the Lottie approach. Whenever my mother was stumped in her research, she would hunch over one of her yellow legal pads and scribble and scratch and scribble some more until she had a list of her most burning questions. My list was about ten times shorter than most of Lottie's.

—*Where's Bohemia?*
—*Who was Nicholas Feldevert?*
—*Did Theresa's luck turn around once she married him?*
—*Is Theresa dead yet?*

I smiled down at my notebook, thinking of how Lottie would be rolling her eyes at the idea of Theresa still wandering the earth more than a hundred and seventy years after she was born. But even Professor Landers would have to admit that the missing death date was too mysterious to ignore.

I was ready to switch off the light on the viewing machine when I heard someone behind me. It was Amy, the one who was always following Mellecker around. Her lip gloss had worn off and she had a dazed look in her eyes. She swooped into the seat next to mine, clutching a box of microfilm. "You actually know how to work that thing?" she whispered frantically. "Can you show me? Pleeeeeease? I can't stand to ask that Ms. Beckett. She's a witch! Know what she did? She snatched my purse right off my shoulder and stuffed it in one of those grimy lockers in the hall. Can you believe that? I've got a lot of important stuff in there."

I showed Amy how to thread the slippery film through the maze of slots and spools in the viewer, then how to enlarge the picture and fast-forward and reverse. "Oh, thank you, thank you," she breathed. "You're the best." She squeezed my arm and looked so amazed, you would have thought I had just scrubbed out of open-heart surgery.

But I wasn't done. Rosa came along begging for help. Then Cliff corralled me into showing him where to find the right boxes of microfilm. By the time I finally managed to break away, Mr. Oliver was already starting to round people up to head back to school.

I found Delaney out on the sidewalk, where everyone was waiting for the parents to pick us up. "Guess what," she said excitedly, as if no time at all had passed since we'd last talked. "I know who Robert Raintree was."

"You're kidding. Already?"

Delaney proudly told me about her findings. "He used to be head of the law school at the university. I guess he was kind of famous back then. There was a whole bunch of stuff about him on the Internet."

"So what about that woman Jeeter told us about? The one who puts the sunflowers on his grave. Who do you think she is?"

Delaney frowned. "I'm still not sure. It can't be his wife. She would have died a long time ago. Maybe it's his daughter." Delaney stood there thinking, gnawing her bottom lip. "I've already looked online and checked the phone book, but there's not a single listing for anyone named Raintree. Of course, that doesn't mean much. His daughter could have gotten married and changed her name, or maybe the Raintrees have an unlisted phone number." Delaney's shoulders drooped. "I just wish there was a way I could talk to that lady from the graveyard."

"Well, why can't you?" I asked. "Jeeter said she's come every single Monday for as long as he can remember."

"Uh-huh, but he also said she comes around two o'clock. I'd have to skip school to talk to her. I doubt Mama's gonna like that idea."

"But wait," I said. "Don't we have a Monday off coming up?"

"Oh, you're right." Delaney gasped. "There's one of those teacher conference days week after next. It's on that Monday right before Halloween. We could go then!"

My heart gave a little jolt when she said the word "we." "Yeah, we can stake out the graveyard all afternoon and be waiting for her when she gets there."

But then Delaney's face clouded over.

"What's wrong?" I asked.

"Oh, nothing. I was just thinking about Mama." Delaney snatched a nervous look in my direction. "Didn't you notice the other day? My mother's expecting a baby."

I nodded. "So . . . I should say congratulations, right? Aren't you happy about it?"

"Oh, I'm happy," Delaney said quickly. "It's just that the baby's due in a month. But you never know. So it's been kind of hard to plan ahead about things."

Before I could ask more questions, I felt a hand clamp down on my shoulder. I turned to find Beez and Amy grinning at me. "So!" Beez began. "I hear you're an absolute genius with microfilm."

Amy gave him a flirty little whack on his arm. "He *is*." She giggled. "He helped me a ton."

"So where'd you learn all that stuff?" Beez asked. "I guess it was your mom who taught you, right? The nutty professor?"

I didn't answer. I knew he was just trying to stir things up, hoping I'd take the bait and say something goofy. I turned back to Delaney, muttering under my breath, "How many football players does it take to thread a microfilm machine?"

"Whoa!" Beez took an exaggerated step backward. "Listen to you! Mr. Comedian!"

Delaney was tugging my sleeve, ready to pull me away, when Mellecker came strolling over. "Hey, what's up?" he asked, casting an uneasy look in my direction. He must have seen me bristling, scowling at his buddy Beez.

"Not much," Beez told him with a chuckle. "Just trying to get some research tips from Mr. Professor Junior here."

"Hey, I could use some tips myself," Mellecker said, quickly smoothing out the prickly conversation. He turned to me. "I don't get it, Crenshaw. With a vault like the one they've got in Oakland, I thought the Ransoms would have been pretty famous in town. But I couldn't find a single word about them on the Web. So what do you think?" he asked. "Where else should I look for clues?"

As soon as Mellecker called me Crenshaw, I could feel Beez turn watchful. Of course he was wondering why his friend would be giving a nerd like me the time of day. So suddenly I was itching to say something impressive—something that would put Beez in his place and prove I was worthy of Mellecker's attention.

My answer flew out before I could think it through. "You could look inside the vault," I said.

Mellecker blinked. "What do you mean? How would I do that?"

"I could get you the key."

"The key?" he repeated.

"Yeah," I told him, trying to keep my voice even. "The key to the Ransom vault. I can get it for you. Don't you want a look inside?"

Mellecker grinned at me in astonishment. He began to nod. "That would be awesome," he said.

Beez hooted. "Crenshaw, my *man!*" he yelled out, and raised his hand for a high five. I reached up to give his palm a hard slap as Amy bounced on her toes beside us and asked if she could come too. But then I glanced over at Delaney, who was observing with her eyes wide, and I felt my palm start to sting. And that's when I thought, *Oh, no, what did I just do?*

J. Edna "Hoover"
THE GREATEST
LITTLE GIRL
TO WALK THIS EARTH
ON TWO OR FOUR LEGS
KEEP WATCHING
OVER ME

HARTSDALE PET CEMETERY,
HARTSDALE, NEW YORK

CHAPTER 12

I ONLY MANAGED TO RUN about a mile with the dogs that afternoon. And the word "run" was an exaggeration. I plodded up and down the blocks in my neighborhood like I was slogging through sand, with C.B. and Spunky dragging me along as I stewed over what in the heck I was going to do about my promise to deliver the Ransom key.

When I came scuffing back to Claiborne Street, Mr. Krasny was exactly where I had left him, sweeping leaves off his front porch. "Back already?" he called out.

"Yep," I said as I slowly climbed the steps to hand over Spunky's leash. "Sorry Spunk didn't get very much exercise today. But I've got an awful lot of homework, and, well . . ." I couldn't hold back my sigh. "It's just been one of those days."

Mr. Krasny leaned on his broom, peering at me through his thick glasses. He nodded sympathetically.

"Understandable. Have days like that myself sometimes."
Then his watery blue eyes turned hopeful with an idea.
"Would you like to come inside and have a Coca-Cola? The
dogs can have a romp together in my backyard. I bet they'd
enjoy that."

I could almost feel C.B. glaring at me through his eyebrows as he sat waiting to be taken home. I didn't want to go
into Mr. Krasny's stuffy little bungalow either. I had always
wanted our house to be cleaner, but Mr. Krasny's house felt
too neat somehow—with the way its knickknacks and doilies
and furniture were locked in their permanent spots, like some
sort of museum or movie set from the 1950s. I glanced down
at C.B. again, trying to think of an excuse, but then Mr. Krasny's doormat caught my eye. BLESS OUR HAPPY HOME, it said.
It must have been lying there for years, since before his wife
died, before their two sons grew up and moved out to the
coasts.

The next thing I knew, poor C.B. was trapped in the
backyard with Spunky, and I was wedged at Mr. Krasny's
kitchen table with a glass of warm Coke in front of me. Mr.
Krasny plunked down a plateful of cookies next to my Coke.
"Here, have one," he ordered. "I made them myself." He told
me what they were called—something that sounded like
"shankies," but I couldn't quite catch the name.

I picked up a cookie, took a bite, and tried not to make a
face. It was so plain, it tasted kind of like chalk dust.

"You need to dip it!" Mr. Krasny instructed from across
the table, where he was settling himself with a cup of coffee.

"Excuse me?"

"Dip it." He lowered a cookie into his cup, waited a beat, and then took a loud, slurpy bite. "Tastes much better this way."

Yuck, I thought, but I shrugged and gave it a try.

He was right. It worked, even with warm Coke. We sat chewing in silence for a while, and I almost cracked up at how funny Mr. Krasny looked, happily munching away. He had floppy earlobes, and his white hair sprang out from his head like dandelion fuzz.

"So you've got a lot of homework, do you?" Mr. Krasny said after a minute or two. "What are you studying in school these days?"

"Oh, nothing too exciting." I stretched back in my chair. "I guess we're doing factoring in prealgebra and . . . a bunch of grammar work sheets in English. You know, the usual stuff." As I shrugged and let out a big breath of air, it occurred to me how much I was sounding like the typical bored adolescent— the kind of kid that Mr. Krasny's generation worried about. "But my class went on a pretty cool field trip to the historical society today," I told him with a little more enthusiasm. "They kind of let us have the run of the place so we could get started on our research projects."

"Oh?" Mr. Krasny perked up. "What kind of projects?"

I quickly ran through the basics of my Adopt-a-Grave assignment, forcing myself not to glance up at the loudly ticking cuckoo clock that hung on the wall by the refrigerator. Then I finished up by telling him a few things I had found out about the Black Angel monument that day. "Supposedly, the people buried there came here in the 1870s, from a place called Bohemia . . . wherever that is," I added under my breath. I reached for another cookie. Maybe if I dunked one more of his shankies, Mr. Krasny would be satisfied and let me go.

But now he was watching me with an amused spark in his eyes. "Don't you know? Those are Bohemian cookies you're eating."

I stopped chewing. "Really?" I mumbled with my mouth full.

"Yes. *Sušenky*," he said, pronouncing the word more clearly this time. "It's an old family recipe. My father was Czech. He came from a village not too far from Theresa Feldevert's."

I coughed in surprise, and a tiny spray of wet crumbs flew out. "You're kidding!" I said with a hard swallow. "Did he know her?"

Mr. Krasny chuckled and handed me a napkin. "Not very well, as I remember. But they were certainly acquainted. Anyone who lived in this neighborhood back then knew about the Widow Feldevert."

Mr. Krasny took a slow sip of coffee, collecting his thoughts, and I felt my leg start to jiggle with impatience. But then, all at once, he was back to his habit of firing out words like bullets. "This side of town used to be full of Czechs, every one of them from that same region in the middle of Europe called Bohemia. You'll have to look at the map, Linc. Look for the Czech Republic, the western part. Germany and Poland on the north, Austria on the south. That's where Theresa Feldevert and my father and all those others came from way back when. Hoping to make a better life in America. By the time I was born, the Widow Feldevert had definitely made a better life for herself. But she was a miserable old lady. Turned into something of a recluse."

I scooted my drink aside and leaned over the table. "Why do you think she was so miserable?"

"Oh, she had a hard life. Lost her loved ones. After her son Eddie died, she disappeared for years. Moved out west somewhere. The other Czechs said she met a rich old German rancher and married him in a heartbeat. That's how come she changed her name from Dolezal to Feldevert. Then what do you know? He died too. Left her all his money, and one day she appeared in town again out of nowhere. Folks said she had come back to dig up her son and bury him, along with her rich husband, in the fine style they deserved. She hired a famous sculptor from Chicago to make the Angel. Paid five thousand dollars! Quite a bundle back then. It was the talk of the town."

Mr. Krasny sat back in his chair and shook his head as if he were finished with his tale. But then he said, "I saw her once."

"You did?"

"Yes, indeed. I couldn't have been more than six years old, but I'll never forget it. My older sister and I, we used to love to pick blackberries on the edge of the cemetery. That's when we saw her. We were heading home. Buckets full. And here she came, the old Widow Feldevert herself, squeaking along the path in her wheelchair."

"Wheelchair?" I interrupted.

"Oh, I forgot to tell you." Mr. Krasny's voice had turned low and mysterious. I felt my heart thump against the wooden edge of the table. "She only had one leg."

"What?" I whispered.

"That's right," Mr. Krasny went on. "People said she had been bitten by a rattlesnake when she was out west living on that ranch with her husband. The infection from the poison was so bad, she had to have her leg cut clean off."

I felt my eyes widening. A rattlesnake? Amputation? How was I supposed to prove my no-curse theory with mishaps like those lurking in Theresa's past?

Mr. Krasny's gaze drifted to the kitchen window and his story slowed down. "Such a long time ago. But I can still hear that sound. That *squeak-squeak* of her wheelchair when she pushed herself along the path."

He squinted his eyes shut for several long seconds, as if he were watching the scene flash across the insides of his lids. "She looked like she was still in mourning. Black bonnet. Long black dress. Black collar buttoned up high. Long cane across her knees. And her face, the picture of sorrow. I'd never seen anyone look so sad."

We both jumped when we heard Spunky scratch at the back door. Mr. Krasny blinked a few times. "Forgive me, Lincoln," he said with a faint smile. "I've been rambling."

"No, this is exactly the kind of stuff I need for my project," I said, hurrying to reassure him. "Do you remember when Theresa died? It's weird—there's a birth date for her on the monument, but no death date."

"That *is* strange," Mr. Krasny agreed. "You know, I can't recall hearing much about her death, and I don't remember any sort of funeral. I wish my father were here. He could tell us. He made it his business to know about all the other Bohemians in town." Mr. Krasny took a last gulp of coffee and hefted himself to his feet.

I had thought he was ready to let the dogs in and say goodbye. But then he told me that he wanted to show me something, and he led me into his shadowy front room to the row of bookshelves next to the fireplace. The shelves were packed with glass figurines and old black-and-white photographs in fancy frames. I braced myself for what must be coming next: a personal introduction to each of the old-timey faces in the hazy photos. But instead, Mr. Krasny reached past the collection of treasures and pulled a book from a row of matching volumes that lined the back of the shelf.

He rubbed his gnarled hand gently across the red leather cover. "My father's newspaper," he announced.

"Huh?" I said, forgetting my manners for a second.

"The *Slovan Americký*." He pointed to the foreign words printed in gold on the spine of the book. "Or in English—the *American Slav*. This was the weekly Czech newspaper. Published for all the immigrants in these parts. My father, he was a jack-of-all-trades, and sometimes he worked as a reporter for the publisher. Very proud of his stories, he was. He kept every issue. Stacked them up in our damp basement next to the potato bin. Foolish! Awful musty down there. To surprise

Tatínek, for his seventieth birthday we had them bound. He spent his last years reading and rereading each and every article. Dreaming of the olden days, I suppose."

Mr. Krasny cracked the book open, and I peered down at the yellowed newsprint, trying to make sense of the words in the dim light. But the page wouldn't seem to come into focus. I cocked my head for a better angle and stared at the mishmash of letters in one of the headlines: *Velký jarní ples.* The words looked . . . they looked a lot like that faded inscription on the Black Angel.

Before I could blurt out my next question, Mr. Krasny traced his finger under another bold headline, and suddenly his voice and accent transformed as he pronounced the words out loud. "*Farma na prodej!* Farm for sale!"

It was too good to be true. "You speak Czech?"

Behind his glasses, Mr. Krasny's milky blue eyes shone with pride. "*Samozřejmě!* Of course. Tatínek always insisted we speak Czech at the dinner table. And when we were little, he sent us to Bohemian school. Held every summer morning in the elementary school down the street. We sang Czech songs, learned the old dances, recited poems—"

I couldn't help cutting in. "Mr. Krasny, do you think you could translate something for me?"

He hesitated. "I don't know, son. My Czech's a little rusty—"

"It's just a few lines. From the inscription on the Black Angel."

His expression darkened. Maybe he was hearing that wheelchair again. That *squeak-squeak* in his head.

"Well, I guess it wouldn't hurt to try," he finally said.

"Great! I don't have the words yet, but I'll get them to you as soon as I can."

I couldn't believe my luck. I was one giant step closer to solving the mystery of the Black Angel. And all it took was sharing a few shankies with Mr. Krasny.

HERE LIES
LESTER MOORE
FOUR SLUGS
FROM A 44
NO LES
NO MORE

TOMBSTONE, ARIZONA

CHAPTER 13

MAYBE MELLECKER THOUGHT it was a joke, I told myself. All that business about getting him the key to the Ransom vault. Or even better, maybe he and Beez would forget I ever proposed the idea in the first place. There was a big football game coming up on Saturday night. They probably hadn't had time to give the Ransom key another thought.

But they didn't forget. I knew it as soon as I filed out of the lunch line with my tray the next day. "Hey, Crenshaw, over here!" Beez shouted across the entire cafeteria. I glanced over at the BattleBots table, where I usually sat. I could see Cliff and his friends observing me as they hunkered over their trays, trying to figure out why the likes of Jake Beasley would be bellowing my name. If only I had been assigned to second lunch with Delaney. There was still more than a week to go before our stakeout at Oakland, but we could have used lunchtime to plan the details. Then the next thirty minutes would have flown by.

Beez was still waving me over like a traffic cop. With one last glance of apology toward the BattleBots, I headed to the opposite side of the cafeteria.

Mellecker's table was packed and a lot rowdier than my usual spot. When I walked up, three guys at the other end were finishing up a milk-chugging contest. They slammed down their cartons and wiped their mouths on the backs of their fists. Amy and some other girls scattered between them broke into giggling fits when one of the guys let out a nasty sound halfway between a burp and a yawn.

Mellecker smiled up at me as I stood there hesitating, clenching the sides of my tray. "Welcome to my office," he said. Beez had already scooted over to make room for me at the end of the bench. Even on the very end, I still felt claustrophobic with half the table giving me the eye and Beez's bulky shoulder brushing up against mine as he dove into his pepperoni pizza.

"How's it going, Crenshaw?" Beez asked with his mouth full. "Any new developments?"

"Nope. Not that I can think of," I answered. I took a bite of my own lunch and chewed very, *very* slowly. Not an easy task when the menu of the day featured something called Chicken Stix.

"Well?" Mellecker's eyebrows lifted. "Did you get it?"

"Get what?" I stalled. *Think,* I pleaded with my brain. *Think.*

Mellecker let out a dry laugh. "The key, buddy, the key!"

"Oh, *that?*" I forced my voice higher with disbelief. "You're kidding, right? You think I can get the Ransom key just like that?" I tried to snap my fingers, but my hands were too sweaty for any noise to come out.

Meanwhile, the gears inside my head were spinning into overdrive. There was no way I could get the Ransom key for Mellecker. A long time ago Jeeter had shown me where the keys to the mausoleums were kept: in the cemetery office . . . in a closet . . . in a wooden case that looked like an old-fashioned medicine cabinet mounted on the wall. No one ever used the keys unless they needed to get inside a vault to add another coffin after a funeral. And now that Kilgore was in charge, he had probably beefed up security with padlocks and alarms, maybe a hidden video camera or two.

Beez was watching me suspiciously. "Hey, dude, *you're* the one who told us you could get the key. What's the deal? Can you get it or not?"

I felt my cheeks catch fire. A few more kids down the row had started to listen, and across the table Mellecker's face had frozen into a queasy expression—like he felt sorry for me. But what was I supposed to do now? Tell him the truth? That I had promised him the key only because I wanted him to like me? No way. Instead, all I could do was lift my shoulders in a pitiful shrug and stare down at the shriveled pile of Chicken Stix on my tray, shaking my head.

"I told you he'd never do it," I heard Beez say under his breath.

"Just forget it, Beez," Mellecker murmured.

The lunchroom racket swelled around me. Somewhere at a nearby table, Sylvie was ranting about a spitball. "Ewww, it touched my sandwich! You're gross, Douglas Spratt! I'm gonna kill you!"

"Oh yeah? How're you gonna do that?"

"I'm gonna hire a hit man!"

Hit man. Sylvie, of all people, had given me an idea.

I lifted my gaze slowly, giving my features time to set into steel. Mellecker and Beez had gone back to eating their lunches. "Listen, you guys," I hissed. They both looked up, disoriented by my sudden change in behavior. "I know I said I could get the key, but there's something I didn't tell you."

The two of them traded wary looks as I motioned for them to lean in closer.

"Did it ever occur to you, Mellecker," I began, "that maybe the reason you can't find any information about the Ransoms is because they might not want people to know about them?"

Mellecker's face went slack. "What are you talking about?"

Easy does it, I told myself. I needed to make each word ooze with warning—just like Dad when he used to do his impression of those guys from Mafia movies.

"Well, I don't want to jump the gun here," I said cautiously. "But living right next to the graveyard, I see a lot, you know. I'm pretty close with the people in the cemetery office. And let's just say . . . something about the Ransom vault is . . . different."

Beez's mouth hung slightly open. I could hear him breathing. "Different?" he asked uneasily. "Different how?"

I wiped my damp palms across my jeans under the table. It was nerve-racking making all this stuff up as I went along. But it was also kind of exhilarating, like a roller-coaster ride that you love and hate all at the same time.

At least I had a lot of good material to work with. "Well, there's this real creepy guy named Kilgore, he's the cemetery warden, and he keeps all the keys to the mausoleums in a steel box in his office. Every key is labeled and hung on a hook inside that box. Every key . . . except one."

"Let me guess," Mellecker said. "The Ransom key."

I nodded ominously. "That's right. Kilgore keeps that one separate, on a brass ring in his pocket, where he can be sure no one, *I mean no one*, can get to it."

"Why?" Beez asked, keeping his voice hushed.

I pressed my lips together and narrowed my eyes. "I'm pretty sure the Ransoms are paying him off. I don't know anything else about those Ransoms except they're private and they're powerful. And they don't want anybody nosing into their business."

I glanced over at Mellecker. He had leaned back from the table with his arms locked over his chest, still looking kind of skeptical. Beez, on the other hand, seemed seriously spooked. "Soooo . . ." I gave a little shrug. "What I mean is I can get you the key. But it won't be easy. And once you have it, what are you going to do with it? I should be straight with you guys. I wouldn't advise any friend of mine to mess with the Ransoms. For all I know, they've got hit men out there, on the lookout for anybody who gets too close."

I focused on Beez, waiting for him to crack a joke, cram his last wedge of pizza into his mouth, and call it quits. But that's not what happened. All of a sudden he sat up, breaking our little huddle, with a knowing gleam in his eye. "That's where they keep it," he said.

Now I was the one looking baffled. "That's where they keep what?"

"The goods!" he said louder, getting more excited by the second. "Cash. Jewels. Whatever! You say there's something funny going on, right? The Ransoms sound just like one of those families in the Mob. And they've got the perfect place to hide all their money. A cemetery vault! Who would ever think of snooping *there*? Right, Mellecker?"

Mellecker's mouth had spread into a slow smile. All at once I could see it. He was too smart to really believe any of this stuff. But he was having fun playing along. "Yeah, but what if the vault's where they hide all the people they knock off?" he asked.

I bobbed my head up and down. "Yeah."

Beez grimaced. "Oh, man. That'd be foul. But still . . . this project could definitely use some spicing up. You gotta get us that key, Crenshaw. We gotta see what's inside." A wicked look flashed across his wide face. "Hey, maybe we can even snag a little cash or a diamond or two."

I felt my mouth opening and closing like I was some kind of beached fish gulping for air. My plan had backfired in a major way. But before I could confess or interrupt with something sensible, the bell rang, and everyone was grabbing their trays, bolting for the door.

Beez pointed his stubby finger at me as he stood up to go. "Do this, Crenshaw," he said. "Get . . . that . . . key!"

Unknown man shot in
The Jennison & Gallup Co.'s
store while in the act of
burglarizing the safe
Oct. 13, 1905.
(Stone bought with money
found on his person.)

SHELDON, VERMONT

CHAPTER 14

No WONDER JEETER WAS SURPRISED to see me stroll into the cemetery office a couple days later. Even though Mr. Oliver's graveyard project had brought us back together, I hadn't set foot in the office for weeks. Jeeter was halfway asleep when I walked in, with his work boots propped up on the old oak desk in the corner and the soft buzz of a baseball game droning on the radio. He almost tipped backward in his swivel chair when he heard the office door creak open.

"Dang it, Linc," he said, his dazed face filling with relief. He clomped his boots to the floor. "I thought you were Kilgore."

"Kilgore?" I asked with a start. "Aren't you the only one here on Saturdays? Mr. Nicknish never used to work on the weekends."

"Well, times have changed," Jeeter said with a forlorn smile. He reached up to scrub one hand across his goatee and then his sleepy eyes. "Kilgore's been known to show up on one or two Saturdays. Thinks he needs to keep tabs on me, I guess."

He craned his neck to check the clock on the wall behind him. "The good news is if he were comin', he would have already made an appearance by now. He likes to keep his Saturday afternoons open for . . ." Jeeter paused, unable to hide a smirk as he filled in the blank. "For his reenactment club."

"*What?*" I dropped my backpack and plopped into the nearest chair. "What's a reenactment club?"

"Oh, you know. A bunch of guys dress up in uniforms and pretend they're living back in Civil War times." A grin crept across Jeeter's face and kept widening until it was ready to burst at the seams. "They march and fight battles. Camp out. Eat salt pork. Drink out of canteens."

"No way," I gasped. "Kilgore pretends he's a soldier?"

"Not just any soldier," Jeeter said. He poked out his chest like a rooster. "Word has it he's worked his way up to field commander."

I let out an amazed laugh. But actually, it wasn't too hard to imagine—Kilgore with a musket slung over his shoulder, snarling orders with his uniform buttoned up tight around that bony Adam's apple of his.

Jeeter leaned forward with his elbows on his desk, observing me. "Hey, I've been getting to see a lot of you lately. What are you up to? More research on that project of yours?"

I shrugged and tried to avoid Jeeter's gaze. "Yep. I just thought I'd stop by before I head over to the Black Angel. I need to copy down all the words in the epitaph."

If Jeeter noticed me acting funny, he didn't let on. He

scrunched his eyebrows together. "Isn't that epitaph written in some kind of foreign language?"

I told him the words were written in Czech. "And guess what. You know Mr. Krasny from down the street? He actually speaks Czech, and he said he'll help me translate the inscription."

Jeeter wiggled his shoulders up and down. "Oh, Lord, Linc. You just gave me the heebie-jeebies. You sure you wanna know what that epitaph says?"

"Of course I do. Those words might be the clue I've been looking for." I decided Jeeter didn't need to know about Theresa's two dead sons. Or her two dead husbands. Or the rattlesnake bite. Or her amputation.

"I'd have a hard time closing my eyes at night if I was you," Jeeter teased. He gave himself a little shake and rose to his feet. "Well, I guess I better be heading down to the workshop. We got a leaf blower on the fritz, and I promised Captain Kilgore I'd get it fixed this weekend."

I stayed rooted in my chair a beat longer. I had stopped by that day intending to take a quick look around the office and convince myself, once and for all, that it would be impossible to swipe the key. But now I could see there wasn't a padlock on the closet door, like I expected, and no security camera hanging in the corner. And here was Jeeter, ready to wander off and leave the office unattended.

I stood up. "Hey, you mind if I use your bathroom before I go?" I asked, trying to keep the false edge out of my voice. I hated the whole idea of tricking Jeeter, but I couldn't seem to help myself.

Jeeter had his hand on the doorknob. "No problem. But make sure to twist the lock on the front door on your way out, okay? I'll be down in the shop."

My heart started to clunk in my chest as soon as Jeeter was gone. I stared at the key closet, barely five steps away. The door stood ajar, almost begging me to investigate. *Just a quick look*, I told myself. *Then I'm out of here.*

With one more glance over my shoulder, I darted toward the closet and slipped inside. The light came on with a pop when I pulled the string hanging next to a bare bulb in the ceiling, and I stood blinking at the nail holes and the blank spot on the wall where the key cabinet used to be. I let out a small sigh of resigned relief. So that's that, I thought. The keys had been moved. Kilgore had probably decided to lock them up in the safe, where they should have been kept all along.

I was ready to go. I even had my hand on the string to the light switch when I spotted it—the old wooden key case. It was on the floor in the corner, propped against a dented set of metal file drawers. The cabinet must have come loose from the wall, and no one had bothered remounting it.

I stood wavering, imagining myself plunking the key down in front of Mellecker at the lunch table. Beez's jaw would drop open, and Amy would realize I wasn't just some dork who could thread microfilm and . . . before I knew it, I had knelt down, lifted the metal latch, and pulled the door back on its squeaky hinges. Inside were several rows of keys on hooks, all different shapes and sizes, each labeled with a small cardboard tag. I leaned forward and squinted at the words. Fuel Pump . . . Lee Street Gate . . . Equipment Shed. Obviously not what I needed.

I figured I had already spent about five minutes on my "bathroom break." If I stayed much longer, Jeeter might notice and get suspicious. I reached out and flicked through more of the tags. *There!* I started to see keys labeled with names of families and the sections where their vaults were located.

Mulholland/Rose Hill . . . Yoder/Forest Lawn.

But the names weren't in any kind of order. A rumble of sound exploded somewhere below. I jerked back in surprise, then realized it was only Jeeter in the workshop next door, trying to coax his machinery back to life. . . . Whittington/Cedar Lane . . . Abernathy/Sunny Slope . . . It was stuffy in the closet. My skin started to prickle with sweat as I listened to the leaf blower growl and sputter, vibrating the floorboards under my knees.

I had fumbled through all the tags and almost decided to give up for good when I noticed one last key resting at the bottom of the cabinet. It was probably four inches long—an old-fashioned key, too big to fit on any of the hooks. I picked it up, and my palm tingled with the heavy weight of the rust-colored metal. A worn paper tag dangled from a string tied to the curlicued top. The cursive was in pencil and fuzzy with age, but I could still make out the name.

My fist closed around the key. The key to my new life in junior high.

She lived with her
husband fifty years
And died in the confident
hope of a better life.

BURLINGTON, VERMONT

CHAPTER 15

THE KEY FELT LIKE SOMETHING alive in the front pocket of my sweatshirt, waiting for its chance to crawl out of hiding. As I hurried through the graveyard, I scanned the distant tombstones for anyone watching and then switched the key to a safer spot, deep in the front pocket of my jeans.

But it wasn't long before the sound of Winslow's cranky voice came drifting toward me from across the cemetery. *Can you believe he just did that, Dobbins? Snatched that key? And now he actually might do it! Trespass on sacred ground!*

I know, I know. It's enough to make you turn over in your grave. Right, York?

Yeah. I've turned over so many times in the last ten minutes, I'm getting dizzy. But you don't think he'll really go through with it, do you, McNutt?

Over my dead body!

You forgettin' something, Nutty? You are *dead.*

Oh, yeah.

I glared into the distance and started walking faster toward the Black Angel. I was grateful to have a mission. It would help take my mind off the key for a while. When I reached the foot of the monument, I went right to work. I unzipped my backpack and pulled out my secret weapon for reading faded epitaphs—a plastic bag full of flour. Lottie had taught me that trick a long time ago. I walked around to the back side of the monument, and with my hand full of flour I reached out and dusted my palm back and forth across the carved words in the inscription. It took a few more scoops from my Ziploc bag, but soon the white flour began to fill in the crevices of the weathered letters as if they had been painted.

I wiped my hands on my sweatshirt and dug in my backpack for my notebook and a pen. The flour had worked like a charm on the first two lines of the epitaph. I could copy down the strange words from several feet away.

PRO MNE SLUNCE MRAKY KRYLY CESTA BYLA TRNITA
BEZ UTECHY UBIHALY DNOVE MEHO ZIVOTA

But the next part was a struggle. I scooped up more flour and dusted and tried reading from different angles. But even after several tries, only a few words in the last line came out completely clear.

STRAST TEBE OCEKAVA

I couldn't wait to show the mysterious phrases to Mr. Krasny. Hopefully, he'd be able to make some sense of it all. I reached into my backpack again for the spray bottle full of water. I had almost left the water at home, but Lottie's lessons, even from a long time ago, had a way of branding themselves on my brain like tattoos. As I sprayed the last traces of flour from the epitaph, I could hear her softly reminding me, "Always leave a stone exactly how you found it."

But suddenly my mother's words were swallowed up by the sound of tires skidding on gravel. I froze with my finger on the trigger of the spray bottle.

It was Kilgore, slamming on the brakes of Jeeter's golf cart. He had come zipping over the ridge, along a little service road that dead-ended at the cemetery driveway. What was he doing here? Apparently he had run out of battles to fight with his Civil War club and decided to come pick a fight at the graveyard instead.

I felt like a small animal in the sights of a rifle as he climbed out of the cart and stalked toward me. "You again," he said. "Well, I'll be. What you got there?"

My heart lurched in my chest. *The key!* Without thinking, I moved my hand toward my pocket.

"Is that spray paint?" he demanded.

"What . . . ?" My voice trailed off. Then I followed his gaze down to the spray bottle still gripped in my other hand. I started to smile with relief. "Oh! You mean this?

This is just water. See, our teacher assigned this class project, and . . ."

I stopped. Kilgore was standing over me now, staring at me like I was some kind of juvenile delinquent.

"Oh, yeah? If that's true, why didn't I hear anything about it?"

"I'm not sure. I—"

Kilgore grabbed my spray bottle, squirted some liquid into his hand, and lifted his palm up to his nose. His eyes narrowed as he sniffed and sniffed again. Then he walked over and inspected the cloudy drips of water still running down the Black Angel's pedestal.

Kilgore slowly turned back to me. "What's your name again, kid? I should know it, seeing as how we keep running into each other."

"It's Linc," I said in a small voice. "Linc Crenshaw."

"Linc," he repeated to himself, testing the word on his tongue. "That's short for Lincoln, right?" He didn't wait for me to answer. "Well, tell me, Lincoln. Did you know defacing a monument like this goes against every cemetery rule in the book?" He shook the spray bottle. "And not only that. Desecrating historical markers is a criminal offense. You can't just waltz in here and start spraying crud wherever you feel like it. We don't even allow people to do gravestone rubbings in here—"

"No, you don't understand," I said in a rush. "I only used a little flour so I could see the inscription better. And I brought that water along to clean it off. Some people use shaving cream to make the epitaphs more clear. But I'd never do that. Shaving cream has acids that can eat away at the stone."

Kilgore had crossed his arms over his chest. After I had finished my explanation, he stood quiet for a few seconds, looking me up and down. "You're not a normal sort of kid, are you, Lincoln?"

I shrugged. "What do you mean?"

He had stepped toward me, so close that I could smell the thick cigarette smoke that hung on his clothes. I felt myself edging backward. "I mean, how old are you?" he went on. "Eleven? Twelve? What's a boy your age doing hanging around a graveyard on a beautiful Saturday afternoon? Why aren't you out throwing the football or doing stuff with your friends?"

"I told you. I'm here for a school proj—"

"You don't play sports, do you, Lincoln?"

I licked my lips and swallowed. He had hit a sore spot. No, I didn't play sports. Because I was a klutz. But I was trying. My running times were getting better and better. Plus, I had bigger dreams than just playing on some dumb team in high school. But knowing Kilgore, he had probably never even heard of the Seven Summits.

"No sports?" Kilgore's lips slid into a knowing smile. "What about friends? Have you got any friends?"

I felt my face flush hot as I stared back at him. "Of course I've got—"

He cut me off again. "My hired hand tells me your pop's buried right here in Oakland Cemetery. You think if your father was still around, he'd approve of you hanging out here all by yourself day after day? No friends. Nothing to do but make trouble in a graveyard?"

I jerked away and rushed over to collect my things.

"Wait a minute," he said as I stuffed my notebook and the bag of flour into my backpack. "We're not done here."

Oh yes we are, I started to say. But I was interrupted by a roar of noise, and we both looked up to see Jeeter ambling along the driveway, aiming his freshly repaired leaf blower at a swirl of oak leaves. I could tell he was only pretending to be surprised when he glanced over. He cut the motor on the blower. "Well, hey there!" he called out. "How goes it?"

Kilgore looked irritated as he rubbed at the back of his skinny neck. "Just fine," he answered, shooting me a dark look. "Me and your old friend Lincoln here are getting reacquainted. Turns out he's got a real knack for breaking cemetery rules. First it's the dogs, and then I catch him right in the middle of defiling a monument."

"Why, that doesn't sound right," Jeeter drawled as he sauntered over to join us beside the Black Angel. "Lincoln's always been a great kid. One of Oakland's best neighbors." He reached out and set his free hand on my shoulder. For a second I was tempted to sink against him, hide my grateful face in his faded blue work shirt.

"Well, maybe you don't know this kid as good as you think," Kilgore said. He lifted the spray bottle and gave it another hard shake, so we could hear the liquid sloshing around inside.

Jeeter didn't even glance at the bottle. He held Kilgore's stare. I could see the muscle in his jaw tighten as he answered, "Oh, I think I know him pretty darn well. How 'bout you let me be responsible for this one?"

Kilgore's nostrils flared as if he had smelled something rotten.

Jeeter paused, carefully calculating his next move. "Okay, boss?" he added.

"Boss" must have been the magic word. The hard light in Kilgore's gaze flickered off, and his whole body loosened as he shoved the spray bottle into Jeeter's hands. "Fine," he snapped. "But you make it clear to your little buddy here, if I catch him breaking one more cemetery rule, he's out. For good."

"Yes, sir," Jeeter said. We studied the ground while Kilgore marched back to the golf cart and climbed in. Once the buzz of the motor had faded into the distance, Jeeter finally looked up at me with his sad Scarecrow grin. "You see what we're dealing with here, right?"

I nodded.

Jeeter handed me the spray bottle. "I don't mind you coming around here anytime you want, Linc," he said. "Heck, it's nice having you back. But you gotta watch your step, okay? It'd be an awful shame if you couldn't stop by whenever you felt like it." He stared meaningfully over my shoulder, toward the direction of Dad's wall.

"Okay, Jeeter," I said quietly. "Thanks." I turned to go.

"Don't be a stranger," Jeeter called after me.

A stab of guilt cut through me as I started across the

graveyard and felt the key, heavy in my pocket, thumping against my leg. What was it Kilgore had said to Jeeter? *Maybe you don't know this kid as good as you think.*

Jeeter was my oldest friend. Even after all of those weeks when I hadn't bothered to stop by the office and say hello, he had welcomed me back like I'd never left. He had fended off Kilgore. And this is the kind of thanks I gave him? All this sneaking around and stealing cemetery property right under his nose?

I reached into my pocket and squeezed my fingers tightly around the key. First chance I got, I'd put it back. Jeeter would never know it had been gone.

THIS AINT BAD—
ONCE YOU GET
USED TO IT

ST. FRANCISVILLE, LOUISIANA

CHAPTER 16

A FEW DAYS LATER Mr. Oliver sent us all to the school library for the last half of American Studies class. "Think outside the box, people!" he ordered before we trooped down the hall. "Some of you've been complaining that you can't find any information about your Adopt-a-Grave picks. So try another approach. Find out what important things were happening around our country when your adoptees were alive. You might get a better picture of the challenges they faced."

In the library I wandered between the shelves, trying to hide from Mellecker and Beez while I stewed over where to go next with my research on Theresa Feldevert. Like a lot of kids in my class, I felt stuck for the time being. When I had shown Mr. Krasny the lines of Czech that I had copied from the Black Angel's inscription, he hadn't opened his eyes wide and cried, "Aha!" like I had hoped. Instead, he had peered at the words in bewilderment and told me it might take a day or two for him to figure out the translation.

I sighed and stood gazing blankly at a row of encyclopedias. I had just pulled the R (for "rattlesnake") volume off the shelf when Delaney walked up beside me. She looked especially pretty that day. Instead of her usual messy ponytail, she was wearing her hair down and a soft green sweater that matched her eyes.

"Hey there," she whispered. "Only five more days till the stakeout."

"So you really think you can still go?" I asked eagerly. I'd been having my doubts the last few days. Like usual, we hadn't had many chances to talk that week, since she was always running off after school to help out at home and make sure her mother was okay.

Delaney nodded. "I asked Mama about it yesterday. She told me of course I should go, and if I don't stop fussing over her, she's gonna send me away to boarding school." Delaney let out a helpless little laugh. "So I guess I better do what she says."

"That's great," I said, my spirits instantly lifting. "I've got the perfect spot for us to watch for the sunflower lady. The gazebo on the hill. The only thing is," I warned, "we'll have to keep our eye out for the warden too. He's new at Oakland, and I'm on his bad list for some reason."

I couldn't explain more because Mellecker suddenly appeared. "Sorry to interrupt," he said, flashing Delaney one of his charmer smiles. He nudged me with his elbow. "Hey, we haven't seen you at lunch lately."

I scratched at a pretend itch on my cheek. "Oh, yeah. I got behind on some labs for science," I told him. "So I've been going to Ms. Sandburg's room during lunch to catch up." Actually, I'd been bringing peanut butter sandwiches from home and spending my lunchtimes in the chilly court-yard, where all the kids who wore black liked to hang out.

"So?" Mellecker asked, getting right down to business. "Any progress with the key?"

Make it short, I told myself. *Straight to the point.* I took a deep breath. "W-e-l-l, as a matter of fact—" But then Beez came sliding around the corner with Amy on his tail. De-laney scooted back a couple of steps as they crowded into the aisle beside us.

"So what's the latest?" Beez demanded.

"I couldn't get it," I blurted out.

"Aww, man," Beez moaned under his breath. "The only good thing about this whole stupid Adopt-a-Grave Project was that key."

"Shhh." Delaney nodded toward the end of the shelves, where Mr. Oliver was patrolling back and forth. She reached around Mellecker to give my sleeve a consoling little tug, and then she drifted away.

"Did you try?" Amy asked once she had checked to see if the coast was clear. "I mean *really* try?"

"Yeah, I did," I insisted. "I went over there on Satur-day and . . ." And in the next instant, I found myself doing it again, inventing a story as I went along. It gave me a little charge of satisfaction to make up ridiculous things about Kilgore. Plus, Mellecker would probably be done with me after this anyway, so why not go out with some flair?

"Remember that Kilgore guy I was telling you about?" I went on in a breathless, whispery voice. "Well, he's real lazy and he's always falling asleep at his desk in the office. So I waited until he was out cold and I had my hand on the key ring. I almost had it. And then—"

"Then *what?*" Amy pressed.

"His darn phone rang, and he *leaped* out of his chair, like this—" I flung my arms in the air and galloped in place. "And I had to drop to the floor like . . . like one of those commando guys."

Amy gasped and started to giggle. Mellecker was laughing now too, shaking his head, and even Beez had stopped pouting for the moment. He gave me one of those get-outta-here punches on my shoulder.

I nodded. "No, really. You should have seen me. Kilgore was yakking on the phone, and I had to crawl behind a bunch of boxes and hide. Man, it was dirty back there. Dust and spiders and stuff. I had to stay there forever, waiting for Kilgore to get off the phone."

Beez barely let me finish my story. "So when do you think you can try again?"

"Hey," I said, holding up my hands in surrender. "Sorry, that's it. I'm done with keys for a while."

Beez sagged like somebody had just let the air out of his tires.

I thumped my knuckles softly on the cover of my encyclopedia. "Well, I better get back to work, you guys. See you later." Then, before one of them could stop me, I took off around the corner and headed for a carrel on the other side of the bookshelf. *At least that's over,* I thought, sinking down into the chair with relief. Now all I had to do was sneak the key back to the cemetery office.

But as I opened my encyclopedia, I realized I could still hear Mellecker and Beez talking. And they were talking about *me.* "Hey, we should ask him to hang out with us this weekend," Mellecker was saying.

"*What?* Are you kidding?" I heard Beez answer. I froze in my seat. "He's kinda weird, don't you think? And what a load of bull about that key."

"Yeah, but you gotta admit, he's pretty entertaining. He always used to crack me up when we were little too."

"Wait. When you were little? You and Crenshaw used to know each other?"

Mellecker paused. "Oh, yeah. I guess I forgot to tell you. We used to go to school together a long time ago."

"But wasn't Crenshaw homeschooled?"

"Yeah, sort of."

"You mean you went to school at Crenshaw's *house?* Who taught you? That freaky mom of his?"

"*No,* you big dope. Listen, it's a long story. Never mind—"

Fortunately I didn't have to listen to more, because Mr.

Oliver swooped in to threaten them with detentions if they didn't get busy.

"Never mind," Mellecker had said, like I was some penny he had dropped, not even worth the trouble of retrieving. With my cheeks still burning, I flipped to the page on rattlesnakes in the encyclopedia. I had wanted to read the good part, all about how the rattlesnake "sends out poison through two long hollow teeth, or fangs, in its upper jaw." But now the words and the pictures kept blurring together as I stared down at the page.

I was still struggling to focus when a folded note flew over the side of my carrel and fluttered down in front of me. I glanced over my shoulder just in time to see Amy toss her hair and disappear around the corner of the shelves. The note was folded up tight, written on a sheet of notebook paper. I smoothed it out on top of my encyclopedia.

> We're all meeting at Guido's on Sat. nite. You
> should come.   Amy

I gazed down at Amy's fat, loopy letters in red ballpoint pen. I didn't even know what Guido's was. But I couldn't help feeling happy and a little smug as I read the note to myself a couple more times. So Mellecker must have decided to overrule Beez and invite me along after all.

Amy appeared at my carrel again right before the bell rang. "Well?" she whispered. "Aren't you going to write back?"

I didn't answer at first. I pretended to be thinking as she stood there, shifting her feet. She was about to flounce off when, finally, I scribbled two letters on the bottom of the note and handed it back to her:

OK.

I Was Somebody.
Who, is no business of yours

STOWE, VERMONT

CHAPTER 17

MY TIMING WAS TERRIBLE. Lottie had made a real Sunday dinner, kind of—spaghetti with cherry tomatoes and cheddar cheese on top—and now I was planning to rush off again.

"But it's a school night," she said as she watched me stuff a huge forkful of noodles into my mouth.

"No, we've got the day off tomorrow," I told her through my paper napkin. "It's a conference day for the teachers."

Lottie looked disappointed. "Oh. I was thinking we could have one of our chess matches. We haven't played for ages."

"Sorry," I said, swallowing hard. "I already told Beez I could come. I guess he's rented some horror movies to get everybody in the mood for Halloween coming up."

"Who's Beez?"

"Just a friend from school," I said. "Friend" was definitely not the right word to describe Beez. But still . . . the two of us were warming up to each other. Last night at Guido's I had

145

beat him at darts. After my second bull's-eye, he whapped me on the back so hard that an ice cube I'd been sucking on flew out of my mouth. Neither one of us could stop laughing until the pizza came.

Lottie was still watching me eat. "Was Beez one of the ones you were with last night?"

"Mm-hmmm."

"You're getting together two nights in a row?"

"Yep."

"Well, what are they like? These new friends of yours."

I took a swig of milk and ordered myself to be patient. Ever since the day of the field trip, when I had begged her to act more like a "normal" mom, Lottie had been trying. Along with asking questions about my social life, she had bought a can of Easy-Off and cleaned years of black gunk out of our oven. She took C.B. to the vet to get his shots and his toenails clipped. She went to her first PTA meeting. She had even noticed that I'd been running with the dogs lately, and offered to take me shopping for proper shoes. "As soon as I can run for a half-hour without stopping to rest," I had told her, "we'll go."

But something about Lottie's efforts still didn't feel right. Most of the time it seemed like she was only going through the motions, checking off the boxes on some kind of a good-mother to-do list in her head.

"Linc?"

"Oh, sorry," I said with a start. Friends. "Well, they're pretty different from me. They're all into sports—football and basketball and cheerleading and stuff."

Lottie's eyebrows lifted. "Really?"

"I know," I said with a laugh. "Kind of surprising, huh? I guess I'm sort of like a mascot. They think I'm really funny. And they like my stories."

"What kind of stories?"

"Oh, whatever pops into my head," I said vaguely.

At Guido's, Mellecker had made me reenact the entire key-stealing scene I had described in the school library. Everybody at the table had been so entertained that I got brave and told them a real story about the time Jeeter had to call the rescue squad to a graveside service. They wanted all the details, and I doled them out like candy. All about how huge the woman was and how much it had rained that week and how she had wobbled up to the edge of the freshly dug plot to throw in a rose, slipped in the mud, and landed—*kaboooom!*— six feet below on top of her husband's coffin. "They needed to call a fire truck with a crane to pull her out," I had revealed in a loud stage whisper, and the whole table had burst out laughing.

"Well, you've always been a wonderful storyteller," Lottie was saying.

"Maybe so," I said, shrugging with wonder. "Mellecker thinks I'm hilarious."

Lottie stopped. "Mellecker? Isn't he the one who . . . ?" Her voice trailed off for a second. "The one who made you so angry on the field trip to Oakland?"

"Oh, yeah." I flinched a little as Mellecker's mean cartoon flashed back in my head. I waved my hand, wiping away the memory. "He apologized for all that stuff."

"That's good," she said softly. Something in Lottie's voice made me glance up—really look at her for the first time that night, sitting on the other side of the table nudging her spaghetti back and forth across her plate with her fork. *She's lonely*, I realized with a pang in my chest. She wasn't used to me breezing out of the house and leaving her behind. Usually it was the other way around.

I knew I should offer to stay home and play chess. But I just couldn't. They were all expecting me. I stood up to clear my plate. "I should really get moving if I want to catch the next bus," I said.

Lottie nodded, trying to smile. Then I turned away, busying myself with rinsing dishes at the sink, thinking about the stakeout with Delaney tomorrow, wondering if I needed to hurry upstairs to brush my teeth—anything to keep my mind off how lonely Lottie looked.

"Well, have a good time," I heard her say as she headed back to her office like a bee returning to its hive. "Make sure to be home by ten."

By the time I fed C.B. and locked the back door behind me, I only had a few minutes to spare before catching the crosstown bus at the end of our street. But halfway down the block, I spotted Mr. Krasny hunched in his winter coat, hobbling toward me on the sidewalk.

"Mr. Krasny?" I called out in surprise. "What are you doing out here? It's almost dark. Is everything okay?"

His face brightened as I hurried closer and he realized it was me. "Linc," he panted, gripping my arm. "I was on my way to your house. Special delivery. I finally finished translating that epitaph for you."

"Wow, that's great," I said. "But you didn't need to worry about that tonight, Mr. Krasny."

"Nonsense," he scolded. "You're only four houses away. And I know how anxious you've been for me to finish. A few words were giving me trouble. But tonight I found my old Czech-English dictionary. Hiding in the back bedroom! Now I think I've got everything right." As he reached into his coat pocket, it seemed to dawn on him that I might be going somewhere. "By the way, where were you headed off to?"

I told him I was hoping to catch the next bus to my friend's house. "Better run along, then," he said. "You can look at this later." He pulled a folded piece of paper from his pocket. "I have to admit the message chilled my blood a bit. But didn't you say some words might be missing?"

"Yeah, some of them were really faded and hard to see."

"Well, perhaps that would explain it," Mr. Krasny murmured, handing me the paper. "Maybe the message isn't quite as bleak as it sounds."

I gulped down a little flutter of dread and stuffed the paper into the pocket of my jacket. Then I baby-stepped Mr. Krasny back to his door. It was a good thing I had started my cross-country training. I could already hear the bus coming as we said goodbye. So I sprinted down the block, imagining I was running in an eighth-grade meet, with an opponent breathing down my neck as we raced for the finish line. I made it to the stop just before the driver could blow past.

On board I dropped into the first empty seat and pulled Mr. Krasny's paper from my pocket. It was a mistake not to catch my breath before I read his translation of the Black Angel's words, scrawled across the page in shaky cursive.

For me, the clouds concealed the sun.
The path was thorny.
The days of my life passed without comfort.
Suffering awaits you.

Ma Dyed Novem
7 Anno 1696

DEERFIELD, MASSACHUSETTS

CHAPTER 18

MY NERVES ALMOST GOT the best of me at Beez's house. It was just my luck that he had rented a horror movie called *The Corpse's Revenge* and that for the next two hours we would sit in his dark basement watching mangled cadavers rise from their graves and hunt down their enemies from the past, one by one. There were eight of us—five guys and three girls—sprawled on couches and the floor. Beez's mom brought down popcorn and drinks, and while the girls ate and squealed and the guys cheered for the corpses and the gushing blood, I stared at the flickering TV screen gnawing my bottom lip.

What did the epitaph mean? It seemed so . . . so personal. "Suffering awaits *you*." Did that mean *me*? Did that mean anyone who dared to dig too deep into the mystery of Theresa Feldevert? Or did suffering await only those who hurt the monument in some way? I racked my brain trying to remember all the stories that Jeeter used to tell me about the

Curse—about those three college students who had cut off the Angel's bronze fingers and ended up maimed for life . . . about all the evil stuff that could happen if you kissed the Angel at midnight or touched her under a full moon.

The Curse seemed to cover a lot of territory. I took a handful of popcorn and then froze with it halfway to my mouth. *What about me?* I had touched the Angel's pedestal—rubbed flour all over her inscription and sprayed it down with water.

Suddenly I realized the room had gone completely quiet. Up on Beez's huge wide-screen TV the star of the movie had just annihilated the last corpse with a torch and a can of gasoline. He stood slumped in the graveyard, heaving with exhaustion, sweat trickling down his bulging biceps. Like everybody else, I knew it was coming—something terrible—and I tensed my whole body in preparation. That still didn't stop me from nearly flipping over the back of the sofa when a moldy hand *shot out of the ground*, grabbed the hero's ankle, and dragged him screaming into a dark hole in the earth. The girls screamed too. My popcorn flew into the air. Even Mellecker jerked back in his seat. Then—*thank you, Thankfull*—it was over.

Once we had all finished laughing and collecting ourselves, Amy said, "Hey, let's tell ghost stories." She bounced up and down in her seat. "You go first, Linc. You're the best storyteller." After feeling so squirmy all evening, I definitely wasn't in the mood to be entertaining. But I didn't have a choice. Beez had fixed me in the beam of the flashlight, and now all the others were listening.

"Hmmm, let me see," I said in a slow, sly voice. I drummed my fingers together and leaned forward, letting the suspense build while I scoured my memory for something scary. All I could think of was Jeeter's story about the three guys who cut off the Angel's fingers. So I told it. But I spiced it up with lots of juicy details. In my version, Paul, Joe, and Nick were college freshmen who had just joined a fraternity and had to bring back the three bronze fingers to pass their initiation.

I have to admit, my version was ten times better than Jeeter's. I even grossed myself out when I got to the parts about Paul's accident at the sawmill and Nick's hand rotting off with gangrene. Sophie, Mellecker's latest girlfriend, hid her face in his shoulder, like she had been doing all night, while Amy and her friend Taylor shrank back into the sofa cushions and held on to each other. The guys helped things along by yelling "Foul!" and "Nasty!" in all the right places.

When I was done, Beez kept the flashlight beam trained on my face. "Pretty good, Crenshaw. But aren't you the one who's supposed to be proving the Curse of the Black Angel is a bunch of bull?"

"Yeah, supposedly," I muttered. "But I may have to change my hypothesis."

Sophie clapped her hands over her ears. "Don't tell us any more! Turn on the lights!"

Of course Beez snapped the flashlight off instead, and the basement went completely black. Mellecker spoke up in the darkness, ignoring Sophie's whimpers. "Hey, I got a great idea. Wouldn't it be cool to go see the Black Angel on Halloween?"

"Yeah!" Beez chimed in. "Let's cut off another one of her fingers and find out what happens."

"Halloween's not the best time to sneak into Oakland," I warned. "You can't get away with anything that night because the staff stays late to keep an eye on things. They start patrolling as soon as it gets dark, and they make rounds all night long, watching out for kids tipping tombstones and stuff like that."

"Tipping tombstones?" I could hear the spark of excitement in Beez's voice, so I was glad when the overhead light suddenly flipped on. Beez's mother was standing in the doorway, shaking her head at all of us squinting into the brightness like moles.

"Okay, everybody," she announced. "Time to break it up and head home. That's enough horror for one night."

I couldn't have agreed more.

To live in the hearts
We left behind
Is not to die.

PROVINCETOWN, MASSACHUSETTS

CHAPTER 19

WINSLOW & COMPANY were up early to greet me the next morning when I looked out my bedroom window to check on the weather.

Morning, Mr. Tomato Head. We hear you got a big date over in our neighborhood today. So why are you looking like the cat who ate the canary? Can't you see it's pouring out here? Take it from me, kid. Ladies hate being out in the rain. Makes their hair frizzy.

Don't you get it, fellas? The warden's been on his trail, and now he thinks just because it's a little wet outside, Captain Kilgore won't be bothering with guard duty today.

Fat chance! The Black Angel summed it up for you, didn't she? Suffering awaits!

And what about the key, son? You think you can keep that thing hidden in your sock drawer forever? You need to put it back where it belongs before it's too late!

Puttin' that key back is gonna be harder than it sounds. I can feel it in my bones. Ha! Get it? Bones?

As it turned out, Winslow was wrong about one thing. The rain didn't seem to bother Delaney a bit. We had planned to meet in the gazebo on the hill overlooking the stretch of cemetery where the Raintree grave stood. She showed up right on time with a red umbrella and wearing a bright yellow slicker, landing like a parrot in the middle of all of those gray clouds and acres of old stone.

"Mama made me bring this," she said as she folded her umbrella and dropped it along with her backpack on the long wooden glider in the gazebo. "She thinks we're crazy for coming out here today."

"How's she doing?" I asked carefully.

"Pretty good. Everything looked fine at her last doctor's appointment," Delaney said, sounding like a mother herself. "At least she's finally being reasonable and trying to stay off her feet some. She even skipped going to church this past Sunday." Delaney rolled her eyes. "*That* sure never happened before."

I wanted to ask more, but Delaney was already glancing down the hill toward the lonely headstone she had adopted. Except for some brown leaves rattling in its branches, the giant oak nearby was practically bare now, giving us a clear view of the gravesite. "So you think the sunflower lady will come?" she asked. "Even in this weather?"

"Jeeter says she's never missed a week as long as he's been working here."

Delaney's face went still. "Whoever's buried there must have been awful special to her."

"Yeah," I agreed, reluctantly tallying in my head how many times I had visited poor Dad. I didn't even need a whole hand to count the number.

I looked out over the graveyard, restlessly scanning the distance for Kilgore. "If she really doesn't come till two o'clock like Jeeter said, we've got some time to kill before she gets here."

"That's good." Delaney nodded shyly at her backpack. "I brought us lunch."

"Really?"

"I thought we might get hungry." Then she paused, hugging her arms across her middle. "Before we eat, though, I've got a favor to ask."

I smiled and crossed my arms too. "What kind of favor?"

"I want you to take me to Babyland."

Her request was so sudden and strange, I almost laughed out loud. But then I saw how serious Delaney had turned, and I remembered the mesmerized expression on her face from the field trip, when Lottie had first told our class about the corner of the cemetery reserved for children.

"Sure," I said. "We can go over there right now. The rain's almost stopped." She nodded, and we stepped into the light drizzle, leaving her backpack and umbrella behind. Delaney didn't say anything else until we were standing inside the low iron fence surrounding Babyland.

"Do you mind if we stay here for a few minutes?" she asked.

"'Course not." I turned in the opposite direction so Delaney could wander on her own. My shoes squelched in the wet grass as I weaved up and down the rows of tiny graves. Back in the old days, I used to follow Jeeter through the creaky front gate of Babyland and wait while he tended the plots, making sure not to disturb the little tokens that visitors had left behind. People left all sorts of things— not only flowers, but seashells and teddy bears and birthday cards . . . sometimes even Barbies and Happy Meal toys. A shivery feeling used to creep into my stomach whenever I bent down for a closer look and read those pitiful inscriptions carved beneath the sculptures of lambs and babies with wings.

I walked a little farther, pausing at a few of the graves I remembered best.

Emma Bennet
Died 1947, Aged 2
So small, so sweet, so soon . . .

TYLER SMITHINGTON III
May 4, 1970–April 28, 1974
Little Boy Blue Has Gone

I remembered Tyler's grave because of the blue balloon that someone always used to leave tied to a rock next to the stone. Blue must have been Tyler's favorite color. Or maybe blue was just a sign for how sad his family felt.

But there was no balloon today. I looked up and down the rows, suddenly realizing there wasn't a single gift left on any of the plots anymore. The graves were completely bare except for some bouquets of flowers here and there. Something about the sight of all that emptiness bothered me, and with an ugly suspicion creeping its way into my head, I went back to check the small sign on the front gate. I hadn't taken the time to stop and read it when we came in. It said:

Only living plants and cut flowers are permitted as grave decoration. The cemetery warden reserves the right to direct the removal of all other inappropriate decorations.

Just what I thought. *Kilgore*. I knew the rule had to be his idea. Mr. Nicknish would never be that coldhearted.

I stepped inside the gate again and looked around for Delaney. At first I thought she might have wandered out the back gate on the other side of Babyland. Then I spotted her, sitting on a marble bench in the far corner, sheltered by a canopy of pine branches. I walked over to join her. Her face was halfway hidden under the hood of her slicker, so it wasn't till I swiped a puddle off the cold bench and sat down beside her that I realized her cheeks weren't wet from just the rain. She'd been crying.

I was glad when she started talking first, since I had no

idea what to say. "You remember a while back when you asked me about that calendar hanging in my locker? The one with the red X's?"

"Uh-huh."

She sniffed and rubbed her nose with her sleeve. "I told you about how we move all the time, and you thought I might be marking off how many days me and my parents have stayed here. Well, you were right. But I've been marking something else too. . . . I've been marking how long Mama's made it without losing the baby."

Delaney kept staring out at the miniature graves scattered in front of us. "I lost a little brother about a year and a half ago." I must have flinched, because she quickly shook her head. "It's nothing like you losing your dad. My brother was only a couple days old. He was born about a month too early, and something was wrong with his heart. But still . . . I think about him all the time."

She heaved a huge sigh. "My parents buried him back in Indiana, where we were before we moved here." She let out a bitter little laugh. "I can't even remember the name of the cemetery. I just know it was ugly-looking, with hardly any trees and a highway running past. And nobody there had tombstones. Instead, they had these little plaques set flat in the ground."

Delaney's quiet voice rose and picked up speed. "I *hate* the way we always have to move for Daddy's job, but I was so glad to leave that house of ours in Indiana. There was this little, tiny office that Mama had turned into a baby's room. She painted it blue, all by herself, and hung up curtains and this real cute wallpaper border with cowboys on it. So after Will died, it made me feel sick to see that empty room of his with the crib and the rocking chair, just waiting at the end of the hall. I tried keeping the door closed, but it didn't help."

I watched another tear slide down Delaney's pale cheek. "The only thing I was sorry to leave back there was that little grave of Will's by the highway, even if it *was* ugly." She wiped her tears off with the heel of her hand, and her voice fell to a whisper. "Who knows when I'll ever get back there to visit."

We sat quiet for a minute, listening to the slow drip in the pine branches. I still didn't know what to say. I kept wishing I had a tissue or a pair of gloves at least. Delaney's hands looked freezing, damp and tinged with blue.

"Here, do this," I finally said. I blew on my hands, then rubbed them back and forth on my jeans.

She tried to smile. After she had rubbed for a while, she started talking again. "We're waiting to pick a name this time, and thank goodness, Mama hasn't tried to fix up the extra bedroom yet or unpack all the baby stuff. But now she's further along than last time, and she and Daddy are getting so excited and thinking it's really going to happen. I want to be happy too, but it's like I can't let myself. I start to get my hopes up, and then I remember how things turned out when I felt that way before. So I thought maybe . . ." She rose from the bench and stood surveying the scene in front of us. "Maybe coming to this place would help me somehow."

"Has it?" I asked from my spot on the bench. "Helped, I mean?"

Delaney tilted her head to one side. Then she started to nod. "Yeah, I'm pretty sure it has," she marveled. "But I'm not exactly sure why."

"It's because you can think here, and the graveyard sort of . . ." I searched the little tombstones around us for the right way to explain. ". . . Sort of gives you permission to remember. You don't have to act all cheerful and pretend like it never happened. That only makes it worse, all that pretending and keeping everything balled up inside."

Delaney turned and looked down at me, her watery eyes widening. "That's right," she said. "You *know*, don't you?"

I gave a sad little shrug. "I'm still trying to figure it out myself."

"Your dad," she said softly. "Is he buried here in Oakland?"

"Yep."

"Will you show me?"

As we walked to the columbarium, Delaney fired out one question after another.

"What kind of father was he?"

"Where did he work?"

"Did you look alike?"

It was surprising how easy it was to answer, how good it felt to walk over to the black granite wall and press my hand against his square after spending so much time trying to avoid it.

"I always wanted him to have a gravestone instead of this wall," I told Delaney.

"A gravestone would be nice," she agreed. Then she added wistfully, "But at least you can visit whenever you feel like it."

She was right. I had more than she did. I stood back and sized up the wall, trying to pretend I was seeing it for the first time. It had finally stopped drizzling for good, and a thin streak of sun was pushing its way through the clouds. Where the light hit, the black granite glinted, and in that minute the size of the wall felt comforting instead of dark and depressing, the way it had before.

After I patted Dad's stone once more to make up for lost time, we headed back to the gazebo and Delaney laid out our lunch on the glider between us. Fried chicken drumsticks and biscuits and applesauce cake. It was the best food I had ever tasted.

Delaney informed me that I was eating "southern comfort food." "They're all my grandma's recipes," she explained. "Mama loves to cook. That's one thing she won't give up doing, even for a few months."

I bit into my second piece of cake, working up the nerve to ask about the baby again. I swallowed. "So how many more days are there to mark off on your calendar? Before the baby's supposed to come?"

"Twenty," Delaney answered in a heartbeat. "Mama's due on November eighteenth. The same day as our Adopt-a-Grave Projects are due." She let out a dry laugh. "Isn't that something? It's a big day."

"That's soon," I exclaimed. "Everything's gonna be fine."

Delaney blinked, as if she couldn't decide whether to

holler with excitement or burst into tears. "I hope so" was all she said.

Then suddenly she stopped, squinting into the distance. "Wait a minute." She jumped to her feet, sending her chicken bones and cake crumbs flying. "There's a car."

I scrambled up to join her. All during lunch we had been keeping an eye on the Raintree grave from our perch on the glider. And with the clouds clearing, I'd been checking over my shoulder for Kilgore. But other than a few squirrels scampering by, there were no signs of life until now.

We stood frozen at the edge of the gazebo watching as an old white station wagon with a noisy muffler chugged slowly along the driveway below. Delaney let out a small gasp when the car pulled to a stop. "That's got to be her," she whispered, squeezing my arm as the car door opened and an older woman climbed out.

The woman had silver hair cropped at her chin, and she wore a tan raincoat that looked way too big for her—the kind a man would wear. Then, just as we had been hoping, the woman reached into the backseat of her car and brought out a bouquet of golden flowers. Delaney gasped again. "What should we do now?"

"Let's give her another minute or two. Then we'll go down and say hello and see if she'll tell us anything." For some reason we were still whispering, although the woman was too far away to hear and she hadn't noticed us watching from the top of the hill. Now she was making her way slowly across the lawn to the Raintree stone. Even with that rumpled raincoat almost touching her ankles, her walk appeared stately somehow. She moved like a queen in a procession, cradling the bouquet in her arms.

Finally she reached the grave. We could see her laying the bouquet against the stone, lifting last week's flowers away, straightening to her full height again. . . .

"A little longer . . . ," I said under my breath. From all my years hanging around cemeteries, I knew that some visitors never left a gravesite without bowing their heads to pray. I didn't want to start things off wrong by interrupting a moment of silence.

"Now?" Delaney asked.

"Okay." We started down the hill, slowly at first. But by the time we crossed the driveway where the station wagon was parked, the woman had finished at the grave and was heading toward us. I saw Delaney lift her chin and square her shoulders, preparing to introduce herself. I decided to hang back and let her do the talking. It was her project, after all.

"Hello, ma'am?" Delaney called as she stepped from the driveway onto the grass. The lady stopped in her tracks. Her arms tightened around her bouquet of faded sunflowers. "I'm sorry to disturb you. But I was wondering if you could help me with something."

The lady raised one hand from her bouquet to nervously finger the collar of her raincoat. When she didn't answer, Delaney charged ahead. "I'm here working on a project for school. My friend and I"—she waved her hand back in my direction—"we go to Plainview Junior High, and for our

American Studies class we've been assigned to pick a grave here and find out all we can about it, and well, I chose your grave." Delaney hurried to correct herself. "I mean, not *your* grave exactly, but the one you just visited."

The woman turned to look over her shoulder in confusion. "You mean Papa's grave?" She pressed her palm to her chest. "My papa? Robert Raintree?"

Delaney's head was bobbing up and down. "Yes, yes. That's the one."

The woman took another careful step closer. She was wearing old-fashioned black galoshes with buckles over her shoes. "But why? How did you come to choose my father's grave?" Her voice was high and clear, and sort of formal like her walk.

"Well, I was just curious," Delaney tried to explain. "It's such a pretty spot under that big tree . . . and the flowers you leave every week are so beautiful."

The lady glanced fondly at the bouquet in her arm. "Yes, these were his favorite. Mother would never tolerate fresh-cut flowers in the house, even though Papa loved them so. She said sunflowers belonged in a field."

"Your mother," Delaney said gently. "She's not buried there, is she?"

Delaney was good at this.

The woman pursed her lips. "Oh, no. Mother didn't want to be buried here. She wanted to go back to her people in New York when she died. But Papa was always content to stay in the Midwest." She swept her arm out at the graveyard.

"He wanted his final resting place to be among his students and his colleagues, his neighbors and friends."

"I read about your father online," Delaney said quickly. "He was a famous professor at the university, wasn't he? Like my friend Linc's mother." She turned and motioned for me to come closer. I bounded forward, glad for the chance to finally join in.

"Hello. I'm Linc," I said, reaching out to shake the woman's hand. I thought she might be the type to expect a young man to shake hands.

I must have been wrong. The woman stiffened. I let my hand fall to my side.

"Lincoln," she breathed.

I nodded, trying to smile. "That's right. But most people just call me Linc."

She cocked her head to one side in astonishment. "Is that . . . is that you?" she whispered.

I faltered for a second, feeling disoriented. Why was she acting like she knew me? I'd never seen her before in my life. But before I could say anything else, she took a tottering step backward.

"Excuse me," I said carefully. "Are you all right?" Her face was trembling. She opened her mouth to speak, but no words came out. The next thing I knew, her old flowers were lying at my feet in the slick grass and she was rushing to her car with the tails of her raincoat flying.

"Ma'am?" Delaney called, trotting after her. "Ma'am?" she called louder.

But the woman wouldn't stop. She was already clambering into her car, gunning the engine. Delaney flopped her arms at her sides as she stood on the curb watching the car drive away. Then she turned back to me with an accusing look. "What did you do?" she cried.

"Nothing!" I yelped. "*I swear.*"

WHY LOOK YE HERE?
I AM WAY UP THERE

BREWSTER, NEW YORK

CHAPTER 20

BACK IN THE GAZEBO we were still trying to figure things out. "She acted like she knew you," Delaney kept insisting.

"I know," I said. "But really, I've never seen that lady before in my life."

Delaney shook her head stubbornly. "Then how'd she know your name? She called you Lincoln."

"She only called me Lincoln after I introduced myself as Linc," I reminded her. "Maybe she had me mixed up with somebody else. Or . . . maybe she's a little crazy. That's what she looked like to me, anyway. Remember how Jeeter said he sees her talking to herself sometimes?"

Delaney's shoulders slumped. "Oh, I guess it's no use getting worked up about why she ran off." She began gathering up the foil wrappers and chicken bones and leftovers from lunch and stuffing them in her backpack. "She's gone now, and I lost my big chance for an interview."

"We could skip school next Monday and try again," I offered.

"Are you kidding? Mama would have a conniption." Delaney hoisted her backpack to her shoulder. "Speaking of Mama, I better get going."

Delaney was supposed to meet her mother in the parking lot at three. Even though I knew it would take longer, I decided we should use a side route through the cemetery instead of following the driveway, where we'd be more likely to run into Kilgore.

"What about *your* project?" Delaney asked as we threaded through the rows of tombstones. "How's it coming?"

I groaned. "Don't ask."

"Why?"

"Well, it's kind of creepy. I started out trying to prove there's no such thing as the Curse. And now I'm actually starting to believe in it myself." Then I gave Delaney my Black Angel update, rattling off the growing list I was collecting of the Widow Feldevert's misfortunes. I told Mr. Krasny's story about his spooky sighting of the widow in Oakland years ago. But Delaney didn't seem too impressed, even when I dropped the zingers about the rattlesnake bite and leg amputation.

"Some folks just run into a streak of bad luck," she replied quietly. "That doesn't mean they're doomed for life."

I nodded. I knew she was probably thinking about her baby brother, Will, and trying to believe that better times were ahead for her family. Suddenly it didn't seem right to tell her about the evil prediction Mr. Krasny had uncovered in the Black Angel's epitaph: "Suffering awaits you."

Delaney slowed down beside me. "Hey," she said, pointing to an old stone tomb that rose over the sprawl of graves in the distance. "Is that the one that Mellecker picked?"

"Yeah, that's it." My heart hiccuped against my ribs. I hadn't ventured anywhere near the Ransom vault since stealing the key.

"Can we go see?" Delaney asked. She didn't wait for my answer. She was already hurrying across the lawn. I caught up and watched while she walked around the tomb. Except for the layer of moss and mildew staining its walls, the building looked like a miniature version of one of those temples in Athens. There were fluted stone columns and carved urns on either side of the entrance. And the name RANSOM was etched in imposing letters over the heavy iron door.

"Now that's what I call a proper burial," Delaney said with her hands on her hips.

I nodded uneasily and let my eyes stray down to the worn knob and the large keyhole in the lock underneath. Delaney must have followed my gaze. "You know, Linc," she confessed, "I didn't think it was right when I first heard y'all talking about getting the key and breaking inside. It doesn't seem respectful somehow. But I have to admit," she added a little guiltily, "now that I'm here, I sure would love to see what it looks like in there."

"I've got the key," I said before I could stop myself.

Delaney's mouth opened. "But—but the other day in the library, I heard you telling Mellecker—"

"I know." I sighed. "But the truth is . . . I have it."

"Where? Here?"

"No. It's at home in my sock drawer. But you can't tell anybody. I have to put it back the first chance I get."

Then I spilled the beans on everything—how hard I had been trying to fit in at Plainview and how bad I felt for stealing the key right under Jeeter's nose and how I wished I had never thought of the idea in the first place. At some point we had started walking again. Delaney let me babble, never interrupting once as we moved along a row of dripping cedar trees. But when I was done, she fired out her opinion just like a judge. "You have to tell Jeeter the truth," she said firmly.

I stopped next to a headstone shaped like a giant tree stump, trying to comprehend. "You mean you think I should come right out with it?" I asked. My voice skipped an octave or two. "Admit to stealing the key?"

"Uh-huh." Her face softened as she turned back to me. "Listen, Linc. There's a good chance you'll get caught if you try to sneak it back into that closet. And Jeeter's your really good friend, isn't he? Tell him what you just told me, and he'll understand."

I sagged against the tree stump for a second, gloomily examining the carved bark and knotholes. She was right, of course. I had to tell Jeeter what I'd done.

Delaney laughed at my dreary expression. "Come on." She grabbed my arm and pulled me forward. "You can think about that later. Right now you need to come meet Mama. She says if I don't introduce you two soon, she's gonna invite herself over to your house for dinner."

"Uh-oh," I grumbled as I fell into step beside her. "I hope she likes Rice Krispies."

Delaney's mother was waiting with the engine running. She rolled the car window down when she saw us coming. I did a quick check of the parking lot. The only other vehicle was Jeeter's old truck, so at least I knew Kilgore was out of the way for now.

Mrs. Baldwin's eyes were the same light green as Delaney's, and she had an accent too, but with twice the twang. "I've heard of a lot of meeting places, y'all," she said as we stood at her window. "The movies. The mall. But never a cemetery. In the rain."

Delaney looked embarrassed. "This isn't a date, Mama," she scolded. "I told you, we're just working on our projects for school."

"I know, honey. I'm only teasing," Mrs. Baldwin said, reaching out to squeeze her daughter's hand. "Get in the car now. You're cold.

"And, Linc," she added, giving the front of her coat a pat where it touched the steering wheel, "once this baby arrives, you'll have to come to our house to eat my applesauce cake. Like I told Del, something's not right about serving dessert in a graveyard."

I smiled and promised to visit whenever she was ready. Mrs. Baldwin must have had her heater running on full blast, because her cheeks were flushed and a cloud of warmth was radiating around her. As she rolled up the window and I watched their car pull away, I could feel the spell break over my long afternoon with Delaney. I stood in the gray light of the parking lot, wishing I was riding off in that snug car too, heading far away from the graveyard and my lonely house on Claiborne Street.

When I came through the door of the cemetery office, Jeeter was sitting at his desk, talking on the phone. Something about a backhoe part he'd ordered that had never arrived. He held up one finger, signaling me that he was almost done. I decided it would be best to break the ice first before dropping my bombshell about the key. So when Jeeter hung up the phone, I began by giving an account of my strange encounter with the sunflower lady. I described it all—how scared she had looked and how she had roared off in her station wagon. I didn't notice Jeeter had barely said a word until I was done. "So what do you think?" I prompted him after a few seconds of quiet had passed. "Why'd she run off like that?"

He gave an uncomfortable little shrug, and I tried to make a joke to get him going. "Maybe she saw Captain Kilgore hiding in the bushes with his musket." But Jeeter didn't laugh. He stared back at me with his eyes as big as bottle caps. Then he blinked a few times and made a weird face.

"What is it, Jeeter? What's wrong?"

Something moved behind me. The sound was barely a rustle. Soft and sneaky. I slowly turned and there was Kilgore, leaning against the doorway of the key closet, where he must have been hiding and listening all along.

Quoth the Raven,
"Nevermore."

EDGAR ALLAN POE
BALTIMORE, MARYLAND

CHAPTER 21

KILGORE WAS HOLDING A SCREWDRIVER. For a long time he
didn't say anything. He just kept smirking at me and whap-
ping the steel blade against his palm, over and over.

"Captain Kilgore, huh?" he said at last. His smirk crept
into an ugly little smile. "So you and Gene over there must
have been having yourselves a real good time making jokes
about the old boss behind his back. That right?"

Gene? I had never heard anyone use that name before.
When I had asked Jeeter about his real name once, he told
me he had been Jeeter ever since his grandmother had come
up with the nickname when he was a little boy and it had
stuck. Kilgore must have known it would rub Jeeter the wrong
way. But of course he needed to show he had complete control, even over his employee's name.

Jeeter wasn't reacting, though. He seemed to have turned
to stone in his swivel chair.

"What's wrong?" Kilgore said to me. "Aren't you gonna answer? You were chatting up a storm a minute ago. And what about you, Gene?" he wheedled. "You're awful quiet over there. What happened? You're not gonna speak up for your little buddy Lincoln this time?"

Kilgore feigned astonishment. "And here I thought you fellas were supposed to be such good friends." He sauntered past me, leaving behind a whiff of stale ashtray. "I mean, what was it you were saying the other day, Gene? Oh, *now* I remember. One of Oakland's best neighbors. Isn't that what you called him?"

Kilgore waited, staring down at the top of Jeeter's head. "Huh?" he taunted. "Isn't that what you said?"

"That's what I said," Jeeter finally replied in a hollow voice.

I closed my eyes for a dizzy second. *Jeeter's biding his time*, I told myself, *waiting for the right moment to fight back*.

Kilgore tapped the blade of the screwdriver against the edge of Jeeter's desk. "And as I recall it, you also called him *a great kid*. Well, let me tell you something, Gene. I'm starting to question your judgment. What kind of *great kid* skips school to harass an old woman just trying to pay her respects in peace?"

"I didn't skip!" I cried out before I could stop myself. "We didn't have school today, and I wasn't trying to bother that lady. We were only—"

"What more convincing do you need, Gene?" Kilgore continued. "Sure, maybe he was harmless enough when he was little. But now he's just plain weird." Jeeter was still sitting there like a zombie.

A foul mixture of shame and outrage bubbled up inside me. Kilgore was calling *me* weird? I was sick of people calling me that. And what about him? He was the one who got his kicks pretending he was living back in the Civil War, patrolling the graveyard like it was Gettysburg.

I took a step toward Kilgore. "Everything was fine in Oakland till you showed up!" I lashed out. "Talk about harassing people! It was your idea to put up that sign in Babyland, wasn't it? You're the one who took all those toys and presents off the graves."

Kilgore made a scoffing sound in his throat as he finally swung around to face me. "Oh, man," he said, wagging his head back and forth. "You're even weirder than I thought." Then, all at once, he was pointing the blade of his screwdriver at me like an accusing finger. "That's it. I want you off this property right now."

"You can't kick me out," I said in a shaky voice. "My dad's buried here."

"So what?" Kilgore spat out the two syllables like wads of tobacco. "You think that gives you special privileges to break the rules? Nuh-uh. I warned you when you brought dogs in here, and then again over at the Angel. Now you got three strikes, you're out."

I sidestepped around Kilgore and leaned over Jeeter's desk, slapping my palms against the wood. "Jeeter?" I pleaded. "What's wrong with you? Why don't you say something?"

He slowly lifted his gaze to meet mine. The sadness in Jeeter's eyes shook me. I had never seen him look this tired, or this helpless. But his words shocked me even more. "Kilgore's right," he said. "Get out of here, Linc. Just go home."

Molly tho pleasant in her day
Was sudd'nly seized
and sent away
How soon shes rip
how soon shes rottin
Sent to her grave &
soon for gottin

MILFORD, CONNECTICUT

CHAPTER 22

PIPE DOWN, MCNUTT. *Can't you see he doesn't want to hear it right now?*

Yeah, Winslow? So what? The boy's gotta toughen up. He needs to stop all that sniveling and take it like a man.

C'mon, Nutty. Have a heart. A weirdo! That's what they called him. Then the guy he trusts most in the world tells him to get lost for good? You'd be crying too.

Bah! You can't trust anybody these days. He should *know. Heck, I don't trust you guys, and I've been lying next to you for thirty-two years. Thank God I got the spot on the end.*

Aww, go back to sleep, you big stiff! Shoot, there he goes. . . .

I slammed the back door on their bickering voices and ran straight upstairs to the bathroom to douse my face with water. Just for a second I forced myself to stare back at my angry reflection in the mirror, my scalded cheeks and glassy eyes. "Stop sniveling," I hissed at myself. "Take it like a man."

179

Looking in the mirror was bad enough. But I felt even worse when I went to my bedroom and stared up at those Seven Summits towering over me. The smallest mountain on my wall was the Vinson Massif, only a couple thousand feet higher than Mount Rainier, the most challenging peak that Dad had climbed. But the Vinson was in Antarctica! What had I been thinking? I'd never get there.

I reached out and yanked my poster of the Vinson down from the wall. Once I had yanked the first one, it was easier to see the other six summits come crashing down. Soon the posters were spread out like tornado wreckage all around me, scattered across the dusty floor of my room. Still breathing hard, I gathered them into a messy pile. Then I shoved the whole stack under my bed.

Half an hour later Lottie came upstairs to tell me I had a telephone call. "Jeeter's on the phone for you," she said as she poked her head through my doorway. "Didn't you hear me calling?" Her gaze flicked from one blank wall to another. "Wait a minute, what happened to your posters?" I could see her eyeing a corner of Mount Kilimanjaro, still sticking out from under my bed.

I looked back down at the French book open on my desk, pretending to be engrossed with studying verb conjugations. "I got tired of them, that's all." I pushed myself up from my desk. "Listen, I can't talk to Jeeter right now."

I couldn't believe it. Did he actually think he could make up for how he had turned on me with a stupid little phone call?

Lottie took a step into my room. "What do you mean, you can't talk? Why not?"

"I don't have time," I said brusquely. "I've got a big French test tomorrow, plus I'm late to pick Spunky up for his run." Then, before she could ask more questions, I swept past her and thumped down the stairs.

But Lottie was still waiting for an explanation when I came home from running the dogs. "Is there something going on with you and Jeeter?" she asked as she stood in the kitchen with one hand on her hip.

I knelt down to unclip C.B.'s leash, avoiding her penetrating gaze. "No, why? What'd he say?"

"He wouldn't tell me anything. He said it was between you two."

"Oh, he must have found out some new stuff about the Black Angel for me," I lied, just the way I had rehearsed as I jogged the dogs back to Claiborne Street. I hung C.B.'s leash on the hook by the door. "I'll go talk to him tomorrow. He probably didn't tell you because he knows how much I want to do this project without asking you for help."

I turned around, pasting an empty smile on my face. Lottie didn't look too convinced. That's when I should have come out with it—the whole pathetic story of how I had been banished from Oakland for good. But I hurried back up to my room instead, to my four blank walls and the dim quiet, where I could keep brooding and stewing in peace.

. . .

I showed up at school the next morning feeling like a pot ready to boil over. When Mellecker called hello, I gave him a curt wave and continued to walk past his locker. But something—all that brewing anger, I suppose—made me wheel around and march back.

Mellecker searched my face in surprise. "Hey, what's up?"

"You still want to look inside the Ransom vault?" I shot out.

"*What?*" His eyes narrowed and he started to smile. "You're kidding, right?"

"I'm not kidding. I've got the key."

"Holy crap, Crenshaw!" Mellecker squawked under his breath. "You really got it? All this time I thought you were bluffing!"

"Nope." I could feel my fists clenching and unclenching at my sides. "So you want to do this or not?"

"Of course I do." He clapped his hand to his forehead with a delighted laugh. "Beez's gonna flip. When can we go?"

My mind raced ahead. Once I set a date, there'd be no turning back.

"The night after Halloween," I told Mellecker.

"Excellent!" he whispered as he banged his locker shut. I could already see him searching the tallest heads in the hallway for Beez. I let out a raggedy sigh. It was done.

DR FRED ROBERTS
Office up stairs

BROOKLAND, ARKANSAS

CHAPTER 23

I FOUND MYSELF climbing up to the attic after school that afternoon. Ours wasn't one of those inviting sorts of attics, packed with family heirlooms, at the top of a sunlit staircase. It was just a shadowy space in the rafters that you could reach only by pulling a folded set of steps from a trapdoor in the ceiling. So I usually limited my annual trips to the attic to two—once to bring down the Christmas ornaments and once more to lug them back up again after New Year's.

Each winter when I made those climbs, I would glance over at the three boxes full of Dad's things and think about stopping to look inside. Then I would always change my mind. I couldn't wait to scurry down the rickety steps and slam the trapdoor behind me. And especially at Christmas, I was never in the mood for being reminded of how much there was to miss about Dad.

But today opening the boxes felt like a mission. I needed

something to take my mind off Kilgore and Jeeter—and what might happen the night after Halloween. And the more I thought about the strange lady in the graveyard, the more I began to think Delaney was right—the lady had recognized me somehow. What if it had something to do with us both being Raintrees? Maybe I could find a clue in the old family Bible. Lottie had said that's where my grandmother first came across the Raintree name, recorded in our family tree. If the Bible was really packed away in the attic like Lottie said, I knew I'd probably find it among Dad's things.

His three boxes were lined up under the tiny window that overlooked our front porch. I sat cross-legged in a patch of sunlight on the splintery floorboards and opened the first one. It didn't take long for me to get sidetracked from my search for the Bible. The first carton was full of photos, piles of them scrambled together in no particular order. I began sorting through the jumble, and soon I was surrounded by small stacks of Lincoln Raintree Crenshaw (the First) at different ages.

As a chubby (make that fat) toddler.

As a boy showing off the whopper (minnow) he had caught.

A geeky teenager (nice glasses!) in a graduation cap, his proud parents on either side.

A college student in a beard (yikes) and hiking boots.

People used to say we looked just alike. I squinted down at each image, trying to see past the bad hair and goofy clothes, searching for a resemblance.

As I studied the stack of photos from the husband-and-father years, I caught myself staring at Lottie instead of Dad. There she was with flowers in her hair on the day they got married in someone's backyard in Wisconsin. There were the three of us on a Ferris wheel. Lottie had her head tipped back laughing as she gazed up at the sky.

It made my heart sink to see how much happier she was back then. With a sigh, I gathered up the piles of photos and put them away in order, from Dad's baby years until our backyard campout right before he died. Then I slid the carton back into its place under the window.

The contents of the second box cheered me up again. I had completely forgotten about most of the things in the weird collection of keepsakes Lottie had chosen to save— Dad's favorite Three Stooges coffee mug, a couple of his best fossil specimens, a hunk of lava rock, and a lopsided clay dog I had made for him during my years of begging for a pet. At the bottom of the box I found a Ziploc bag with my parents' matching wedding bands and my father's old watch tucked inside. The battery on the watch was dead, of course, and the leather band had worn thin, but I tried it on for size anyway and spent a couple minutes checking how it looked from different angles.

I hit the jackpot in the last box. The Bible was buried underneath a mishmash of geology research papers. I grunted as I carefully lifted it onto my lap. It was heavy, with a tattered spine and an ornate cross stamped in peeling gold on the leather cover. My chest tightened as I turned to the family record in the back of the book—line after line of entries, listing the names of my ancestors, along with when and where they were born and when they died, all the way back to the 1800s. Someone—probably my grandmother—had filled out my name and birth date in graceful cursive script at the bottom of the list. I glanced up at the entry for Dad. His death date was missing. My grandmother hadn't been alive to fill it in, and Lottie must not have had the heart.

I scrolled my finger toward the top of the page, scanning each entry. My grandmother had been a Wickham before she got married. "Wickham . . . Bell . . . Hollingsworth," I whispered to myself as I backtracked through the record, whispering each new name I spotted. "Barnes . . . Caldwell . . ."

Where was the Raintree we were supposed to be named after? I combed back through the entries to double-check. But besides Dad and me, I couldn't find a single one. I let out a growl and heaved the Bible back into its box. I should have been studying for my American Studies test tomorrow instead of searching for imaginary ancestors.

As I reached for the papers that went on top of the Bible, I caught sight of Dad's old address book buried in the pile. I quickly skimmed through the worn pages, smiling faintly at his messy scribbles. Dad's handwriting had been worse than mine. A pang went through me when I got to the J's. Jeeter, with his phone number at the cemetery office and his home address, was listed right in the center of the page. Was this some kind of sign that I was supposed to return Jeeter's call and hear what he had to say for himself? *Not a chance,* I thought, with the last words he had said to me still echoing in my head. *Get out of here, Linc. Just go home.*

I was flipping past Jeeter's name when an envelope fluttered from between the next pages. I let out a startled breath of air. The envelope was addressed to my grandmother—Ellen Crenshaw in Verona, Wisconsin. I squinted at the return address. It said 266 Fulton Lane, Iowa City, Iowa. . . . What if this was the mysterious letter that Lottie had told me about? The one Dad had discovered when he was in the midst of cleaning out his parents' house and trying to decide among job offers around the country. I slipped the thin sheet of stationery out of the envelope. Just like my mother had described, the typewritten note was odd in every way—from the stiff apology in the beginning to the curt initials at the end:

```
I apologize for breaking my
promise and writing to you.
But I've been tormented with
worry ever since your letters
stopped coming. Please let me
know if all is well.
                    A.R.
```

My thoughts were still whirling when I heard a loud creak on the stairs.

"Linc?" It was Lottie, standing at the top of the ladder. I jerked up straight.

"What are you doing up here?" she asked.

When I didn't answer at first, she ducked her head under the low rafters and picked her way toward me, past the box of Christmas ornaments and a stack of shutters. I could see her face fill with dismay and something else—was it anger?—as she stood under the peak of the roof surveying the piles of paper, the mug, and Dad's rocks and other treasures spread in a messy circle around me.

"What—" she started to ask again, her voice breathy with disbelief.

I cut her off. "Look what I found, Lottie! It's that letter you told me about! I found it in Dad's old address book." Lottie was still staring at me with a baffled expression, so I kept trying to explain.

"Remember? The one that convinced him to move to Iowa? Whoever wrote this letter signed it 'A.R.' See?" I held up the letter and pointed to the initials with a giddy laugh. "I've got so much to tell you, Lottie! A lot of crazy stuff happened yesterday. But first of all, you know how my friend adopted a grave with the name Raintree on it for our project, and I was joking about finding a long-lost relative in Iowa City? Well, maybe my idea wasn't so far-fetched after all. Maybe this *R* stands for Raintree. And now that we have an address, we can find out for sure." I thrust out the letter so Lottie could see for herself. "If Dad hadn't had his heart attack, he probably would have done the same thing."

Lottie didn't reach out to take the letter like I expected. Instead, she winced and blinked her eyes shut as if she had walked into a spiderweb. "I have no idea what you're talking about, Linc," she said. "And you should have asked me before you came up here and started rummaging through these boxes."

Resentment prickled up inside me. "Why? Dad's stuff belongs to me just as much as it belongs to you."

Her gaze landed on the Ziploc bag lying on the floorboards next to me. "Those are *our* wedding rings. I put them up here for safekeeping because I didn't want them touched," she said in an accusing voice. "Wait, where's your father's watch?"

"Here it is," I said weakly, holding up my wrist for her to see. "I thought that . . . that maybe it would be okay if I wore it once in a while. It's a little too big for me, but I could poke another hole in the wristband."

"No!" Lottie cried out.

"Why?" I asked with shock rising in my throat.

Lottie's eyes were wild. "Because," she stammered, "because he *always* wore that watch, even before I met him, until they took it off and gave it to me when he died . . . and I don't want to be reminded."

I looked down at the Three Stooges mug that had made me smile a few minutes ago, and I thought of how good it had felt when I had taken Delaney to see Dad's grave. "Is that such a bad thing?" I asked in bewilderment. "Being reminded once in a while?"

"Yes," Lottie said in a strangled voice. Her face twisted. "All this"—she flung her arm out at Dad's boxes—"it just hurts too much." She swiped her sweater sleeve across her eyes, fighting back tears. "It's not healthy to keep living in the past, Linc. We have to move on."

I scrambled to my feet, scattering Dad's address book and

papers across the floor. "How can you say you're moving on, Lottie? You're not moving on. You're stuck!" I kicked at one of the papers under my foot in frustration. "I've been stuck too. I mean, no wonder! There wasn't a chance to say good-bye or *anything*. Dad's here one day and then, *poof*, he's gone. We didn't even have a funeral because . . . because . . . I'm not even sure why. I just remember you telling me he would have hated all the fuss. Well, it was *you*, Lottie! You're the one who didn't want the funeral. But you can't keep trying to make things better by pretending Dad never existed."

"Be quiet!" Lottie snapped. "You have no right to talk to me that way. I think I've done a pretty good job of making everything work on my own." She lunged forward and snatched up the Ziploc bag that was lying nearby with the wedding rings inside. When she stood up, her face had frozen into a cold mask. "I want you to put everything back exactly the way you found it," she said. "Right now."

I saw her glance at Dad's watch still hanging on my wrist. I yanked it off and pushed it into her hands. Then I bent down and started shoving things into the open boxes. The letter from A.R. had landed at my feet. I found its envelope nearby.

Lottie was already making her way down the ladder. "Wait!" I called out, holding up the letter. "Didn't you hear anything I said? Don't you want to find out who wrote this?"

Lottie stopped with her hands gripping the highest step. I could barely see her face in the shadowy light, but I didn't need to. I could hear the hollowness in her voice. "I don't see the point, Linc. Finding who wrote that letter won't bring your father back."

Of course he's not coming back! He's dead! I wanted to yell into the dark peak above me as she disappeared through the trapdoor. *But what about you, Lottie? What's your excuse?*

But I bit my tongue. Obviously *nothing* I said, no matter how blunt, could chip through the layer of ice that had grown over my mother like a second skin.

I finished repacking the boxes. In two minutes the bits and pieces left over from Dad's life were closed up again under the cardboard lids—all except for one. I folded up the letter and tucked it into the pocket of my jeans. If Lottie wouldn't go with me, I'd have to find A.R. on my own.

Called Back

EMILY DICKINSON
AMHERST, MASSACHUSETTS

CHAPTER 21

THE NEXT MORNING I told Delaney all about what had happened in the attic. I made her late for science class, but she didn't even seem to care once I showed her the letter I had found. "Wait a minute," she said, ignoring the other kids scurrying into the classroom. "So you think A.R. might be the lady from the graveyard?"

"I guess it's a possibility." I shrugged. "If she never got married, her name would still be Raintree."

"But this note sounds more like something a secret boyfriend would write, doesn't it?" Delaney ran her fingertip under the lines of neat cursive. "'I apologize for *breaking my promise* and writing'? 'I've been *tormented* with worry ever since your letters stopped coming'?"

I found myself nodding. Then I remembered how serious and straightlaced my grandmother had looked in those pictures up in the attic. "I don't know," I said doubtfully. "My grandmother didn't really seem like the type to have an old boyfriend hidden in another state. She was more of the . . ." I floundered for the right description. "More of the farm lady type."

Delaney laughed as she handed back the letter. "Well, there's only one way to find out, right?" she said. "We've got to go to Fulton Lane."

"Really? You'll go with me?" I wanted to fling my arms around her in gratitude. "You think we could go today after school?" I asked in a rush. "I checked the map last night. It's not far and we could catch the city bus."

Delaney thought for a second. "I guess I could call Mama at lunchtime and ask."

Delaney's lab partner poked her head out of the science room. "Hurry up," she said in an urgent voice, reaching for Delaney's arm. "We're dissecting owl pellets today, and we need to get going."

"Oh, Lordy," I heard Delaney say as the girl pulled her around the corner. "I'm not sure I'm ready for an owl pellet first thing in the morning."

I didn't see Delaney again until American Studies class. Since we had a big test that day, there wasn't time to talk, but she gave me a cheerful nod on our way into the classroom and whispered that she'd meet me by my locker after school.

But for some reason Delaney's mood had turned somber by the time we boarded the crosstown bus that would drop us off near Fulton Lane. I knew something had to be wrong. She didn't say thank you when I paid the fare for both of us, and she began staring out the window before the bus had even pulled away from the curb.

I peered around her curtain of blond hair so I could see her expression. "Is everything still okay with your mom?"

She nodded, watching the streets flash by. "She's doing fine."

"Are you worried about leaving her by herself this afternoon?"

"No, Daddy's with her. He's taking her to her checkup at the hospital."

"So nothing's wrong with the baby?"

Delaney shook her head with a small, impatient sigh.

"It's just that you're kind of quiet. I thought maybe something had happened."

She swiveled around to face me. Her eyes were wide, glassy pools. "Why didn't you tell me the truth about the Ransom vault when we were in the cemetery?" she demanded.

I opened my mouth to answer, but no words came out.

"You told me you were gonna tell Jeeter the truth and give the key back," she rushed on. "Then today when I was leaving American Studies, I heard Beez bragging about how y'all are planning to open the vault the night after Halloween. And Amy was asking if she could go too."

I groaned and clapped my hand across my eyes. "Oh, no! I told those guys that they needed to keep this quiet."

"So it's true? You're really going? Then why'd you lie to me the other day? Why'd you say you were taking the key back as soon as you could?"

I glared straight ahead, as if I could bore a hole into the seat in front of me. "That's what I meant to do. Until Kilgore and Jeeter decided they wanted to kick me out of the cemetery. Forever."

"Wait," Delaney said with a muddled shake of her head. "What in the world are you talking about?"

I told her the quick version of what had happened in the cemetery office after she and her mother had left me in the parking lot. Although I'd had two days to mull things over, it still stung to say the details out loud. "He kept saying how weird I was," I muttered.

Delaney's brow furrowed. "And Jeeter didn't stop him?"

"Nope. He didn't even try." I thumped the plastic seat with my fist. "That's why I don't feel bad about using that key. It's not like we're going to damage any property or steal anything. We'll take one look in the vault and lock it up again. Then I'm going to drop the key off on the doorstep." I leaned back against the seat. "My parting gift."

We watched another round of passengers climb on board at Third Street. When Delaney spoke again, her voice was prim. "So is Amy really going with you?"

"Amy?" I scoffed. "Are you kidding? I might as well bring along a couple of reporters and a camera crew." Delaney sniffed and focused on her hands in her lap, trying not to look pleased.

"What about you?" I asked suddenly, remembering how one glimpse of the Ransom vault had piqued her curiosity the other day. "You wanna come? Actually," I added before I could stop myself, "I'd feel a lot better if you were there."

Saying those words would have set my face on fire a week ago. I waited for the blushing to erupt just like Old Faithful, right on cue. But miraculously, nothing happened.

Delaney grew still beside me, thinking. The rumble of the bus almost drowned out her quiet answer, but I saw her start to smile, and it was easy to read her lips. "Okay, I'll come," she said. That's when Old Faithful went into action. But so what? Delaney was blushing too.

I led the way off the bus when it stopped on Grand Avenue. As we stood on the sidewalk getting our bearings, Delaney looked up and down the street in surprise. "A.R. lives *here*?" she asked, surveying the rows of huge old houses on either side. "Our real-estate agent drove us down this street when we first came to town. I remember wondering what kind of folks got to live inside places like this."

The houses weren't mansions, but almost—with white columns and stone walkways and wraparound front porches decorated with pots of fall flowers and pumpkins for Halloween. And even though there were plenty of giant trees in the yards, the front lawns looked like flat green carpets that had been vacuumed clean of all their dead leaves.

"This isn't the street," I told her. "But it's as close as we could get on the bus." I squinted over her shoulder, trying to see how far it was to the south end of Grand. "We need to walk a few blocks this way, I think. Then we take a left."

At first it wasn't so obvious, but after a few minutes of walking, I began to notice the houses starting to change, shrinking in size with each block we passed. And by the time we took a left on Fulton Lane, the neighborhood had turned even scruffier than my side of town. Shoved between the fading two-story houses were dingy apartment buildings and squat little cottages with peeling paint and rusted cars and basketball hoops in the driveways.

"What number did you say it was?" Delaney asked.

"Number two-sixty-six," I told her. "We must be getting close. That was two-fifty-four back there."

She hurried ahead, scanning the next two houses. "I can't find any house numbers," she called. I caught up with her in front of a ramshackle cottage. The porch was strewn with tacky Halloween decorations—fake cobwebs, orange minilights, hanging plastic witches and spiders—and as we stood searching for a house number among all the clutter, a little kid appeared in the narrow alleyway beside the house, dragging an overflowing trash can toward the curb.

"Hey, can you help us?" I called. "We're trying to find number two-sixty-six." The boy stopped, eyeing us from beneath his floppy bangs. "Is this it?" I prodded.

"Naw. We're two-sixty."

He must have seen us glance at the next house in the row. "My friend Brian lives there." He took a few steps toward us and pointed down the street. "Are you looking for that one?"

Delaney and I followed the line of his pointing finger. But all I could see was a tall hedge of scraggly junipers.

"Do you know who lives there?" Delaney asked.

"Uh-uh." The boy shook his head, and his hair flopped further over his eyes. "I deliver papers to lots of houses on our street, but never that one." Then he grinned. "Brian and me dared each other to go trick-or-treating there last year. We rang the doorbell, but nobody answered. We're gonna try again tomorrow night."

"Okay. Well, thanks a lot," I said, trading puzzled looks with Delaney. I gave him a wave, and we started down the sidewalk again. When I checked over my shoulder, the boy was still watching us. We passed the line of junipers dividing the properties and walked along an old-fashioned wrought-iron fence. As the house came into view through the trees, I suddenly understood why it would take a dare for a kid to go trick-or-treating there.

"Golly day," Delaney whispered. "Look at *that*." The tall brick house stood far back from the street—three imposing stories of arched windows and fancy stone trim. With its deep yard and towering evergreen trees, the property seemed like it belonged with all those other estates over on Grand Avenue. Until you looked a little closer and began to notice all the frayed edges—the brown lawn, the missing slate shingles, the clumps of weeds poking through the long, crumbling walkway.

"Think we have time to catch the next bus out of here?" I joked.

Delaney called me a chicken, but she looked nervous too as she lifted the latch on the creaky gate. We took the walkway side by side and approached the tall front doors with our shoulders touching. Then I pushed a black button mounted in the brick and we waited, barely breathing, straining to hear the echo of a doorbell or footsteps behind the thick walls. But there was nothing—only the sound of dry leaves rattling across the stone porch.

"Should we knock?" Delaney asked in a hushed voice after I had tried pushing the button again.

I rapped my knuckles against the dark wood. It was like tapping the side of a ship. "Let's try around back," I suggested.

We cut across the weedy lawn to a rutted driveway that hugged the far side of the property. Delaney noticed the car before I did. "Look!" she cried under her breath. She pointed to the white station wagon parked under a sagging shed at the end of the drive. "That's the lady's car, from the graveyard!"

I hung back for a second, feeling confused. Of course a part of me had suspected that she might be the one who lived here. But now, as I tried to connect the dots, nothing made sense. "But what about that letter to my grandmother?" I wondered out loud. "I thought we decided it was a man who must have written it."

Delaney turned to face me with one eyebrow arched. "Maybe the lady from the graveyard isn't the only one who lives here."

I told her she was starting to sound a lot like Miss Marple. But Delaney didn't hear me. She was already making her way alongside the house again. I ran to catch up, and we peered around the corner, searching for a back entrance. Mossy paving stones led from the driveway to a set of steps and a covered stoop. I had just started to follow Delaney up the path when a flash of movement next to the shed caught my eye. I turned in time to see the same lady we had met in Oakland emerge from a raggedy patch of dried stalks—sunflower stalks. Withered flowers still drooped from a few of the tops, and the woman was cradling one of the old flower heads like an injured bird in her palms.

"Linc?" I heard Delaney call from the back steps. Then she stopped short. She must have spotted the woman too.

The lady tucked the flower head into the front pocket of a faded apron that she had tied around her waist, over her old raincoat. As she slowly came toward us across the overgrown lawn, she didn't seem to notice Delaney scurrying to my side. She was staring at *me*. I tried to ignore the shiver creeping across my scalp. She looked even crazier today than when we had seen her in the cemetery. There was dirt smudged on her cheek, and her silver hair hung lank, as if it hadn't been washed for a while. But what was I worried about? Even if she *was* a little demented, she seemed completely harmless. *She's gotta be at least sixty*, I reasoned in my head. *And raving maniacs don't usually wear aprons, do they?*

The woman paused on the grass a few feet in front of me. She was wringing her hands. "I'm so glad you've come," she began in that proper-sounding voice of hers. "I apologize for running away the other day." She shook her head in wonder. "I thought I had seen a ghost. And then later, when I began to think more clearly, I was so upset with myself. I should have asked you for your full name."

This was getting stranger by the second. "It's Linc Crenshaw," I told her. "But my middle name's Raintree," I added quickly. "That's why I'm here."

The woman took another astonished step toward me, her eyes examining every inch of my face. I had to stop myself from edging away. "You're the spitting image of your father," she breathed. "That's why I thought I was seeing things in the graveyard."

"Ma'am," I began cautiously. "Are you saying we might be . . . related or something?"

Her face went still. "You mean you don't know who I am?"

I shook my head apologetically.

"Then how did you find me?"

I wasn't sure where to begin. And it was hard to think with her practically swallowing me up with her eyes. "Well, it's a long story. . . . Remember my friend who you met in Oakland?" Delaney smiled and moved closer, ready to help. But the woman gave her only the slightest nod before she turned back to me.

I thought for a second and tried again. "You see, this all started when Delaney picked your father's grave for our school project. Remember how we were telling you about that the other day? Well, then *I* got interested because I had never heard of anyone else with the name Raintree before."

I knew I wasn't making much sense, and the whole story seemed too complicated to explain standing in someone's backyard, so I skipped ahead a few steps. "Anyway, I found this address in some of my dad's things, and that's how we ended up coming here today."

"So he's had my address?" The woman pressed her hand

to her chest in disbelief. "And . . . and you and your family live . . . where?"

"Right over on Claiborne Street." I jabbed the air with my thumb as if our house were just through the trees.

Her eyes clouded with bewilderment. "How long? How long have you lived here in town?"

"About five years," I told her. "We moved here from Wisconsin." I crossed my arms and swayed back and forth a little. This Twenty Questions game was making me restless. Wasn't it her turn to start giving some answers?

"*All this time,*" she said. She brought her fist to her mouth, still struggling to understand. "Did you tell your father you were coming here today?"

"My father?" I flinched in surprise. Didn't she know? "I'm really sorry, ma'am, but my father, he—" I stole a glance at Delaney's stricken expression and caught myself before I said the word "died." It sounded so blunt. If this woman was truly related to my grandparents somehow, she might be crushed to find out the young man she once knew had passed away.

But she didn't give me a chance to finish explaining. All at once she was reaching out to grab my hand. "Oh, you mustn't apologize," she said. "I understand. There have been too many secrets kept for too long, and now I can see . . . you have no idea who I am. So we'll start from the beginning, all right?" She was squeezing my hand tighter between her dry palms. "My name is Adeline Raintree."

I blinked back at her as the name settled itself in my brain. *Adeline Raintree . . .*

A.R.!

I wanted to interrupt, to ask a dozen questions. But the woman's voice was so desperate and she wouldn't let go of my hand, and now she was herding Delaney and me toward her back entrance.

"Won't you and your friend come inside for a few minutes?" she pleaded. "Please?"

CHAPTER 25

Accused of Witchcraft
She declared
"I am innocent and God will
clear my innocency"
Once acquitted yet falsely
condemned she suffered
death July 19, 1692

REBECCA NURSE BURYING GROUND,
DANVERS, MASSACHUSETTS

"WHAT'S SHE DOING?" I mouthed. Delaney held her finger to her lips, and I clenched my teeth and went back to gawking at the high ceilings, the peeling strips of wallpaper, and the dusty crystals of the chandelier. Adeline Raintree had seated us in carved chairs at one end of her long, dark dining room table. "I would take you to the front parlor," she said as she pushed back the heavy drapes at the windows, "but one of the pipes in that ceiling seems to have sprung a leak, and it's a bit damp in there."

Now she sat at the head of the table between us, bent over her old sunflower. She pushed her thumbs back and forth across the dry husk until the seeds rattled down into a tarnished silver bowl. I squirmed on my chair, and a cloud of must drifted up from the embroidered cushion. Obviously, no one but us had sat in these chairs for a very long time.

Miss Raintree scooped up a handful of the seeds and slowly let them sift between her fingers. "The birds didn't leave very many this year," she said thoughtfully, "but it should be enough to make a few good bouquets for Papa next summer." My pulse raced with impatience. Why was she jabbering on about seeds instead of explaining what she had meant when we were outside? What was all that stuff about "too many secrets"? I glanced over at Delaney, who hadn't fidgeted once. Were all southern people like that—with their good manners etched into them like that *R* engraved on Miss Raintree's silver bowl?

I cleared my throat, and Miss Raintree finally got the hint. "Forgive me, Lincoln," she said with a start. She wiped her hands on her apron. "Some people have prayer beads. I use seeds. They help me to collect my thoughts . . . and this is a story I've never told before. . . ."

I held my breath as she stared down the table at a skinny beam of light that had pushed through the drapes, and finally she began. "A long time ago, when I was barely twenty years old, I fell in love with one of Papa's students," she said softly. "Our romance was a secret, because my father was the head of the law school and this young man didn't want to risk his position there."

Delaney and I exchanged wide-eyed looks across the table. Miss Raintree didn't seem to notice. She was still staring at that sliver of light. "I dreamed he would ask me to marry him, but the proposal never came." She lifted her chin, and something in her face hardened. "Obviously this fellow wasn't the upstanding gentleman I thought him to be. He graduated from the law school and moved on. Shortly after he left, I found out I was expecting his child."

I shifted uneasily in my seat. "Of course, this was considered quite a scandal back then," Miss Raintree went on. "Especially in a small town, with Papa's position in the community." The wrinkle between her eyebrows deepened. "My mother had always been a very proper woman, all about appearances. She was horrified by the news and immediately decided I would go live with an acquaintance of hers in Wisconsin. She wanted my condition to be kept completely secret . . . and she wanted to find another family to take the child."

She licked her lips and her eyelashes fluttered. "While Papa was hurt and disappointed by my behavior, he didn't agree with Mother. He wanted us to raise the baby as our own. But several months before the child was due to be born, my father died of a heart attack. It came with no warning, out of the blue."

Just like Dad.

I think I must have made some kind of surprised noise that snapped Miss Raintree out of her storytelling trance, because suddenly she was turning to me, her eyes welling up with pain. "Without Papa, I had no choice but to give my son up, to the people I had been living with in Wisconsin—an older couple who were never able to have children of their own. The Crenshaws."

Miss Raintree waited, watching my face for a reaction, but all I could do was stare back at her with my brain scrambling to catch up. *The Crenshaws.* What was she saying? This couldn't be right. This sad lady with her lonely old house, where trick-or-treaters were scared to ring the doorbell, was supposed to be Dad's real mother? No way.

She swallowed and went on. "Our agreement was that I would go back home. I would make no claim on the child. I would never try to contact him. And in return, Mrs. Crenshaw would send me letters periodically about his progress."

So that explained the note from the attic. *I apologize for breaking my promise and writing to you.*

Delaney was watching me too, I could tell. But I couldn't meet her gaze, not even when Miss Raintree rose from the table and went over to an antique sideboard that stood against the wall. On the top of the sideboard was a wooden box, which she brought back to the table and set down in front of me. The lid was fancy, inlaid with flowers and vines made from chips of pearl.

"These letters have become my most treasured possessions," Miss Raintree said as she lifted the lid. I leaned forward and peered inside. It was like peeking over the edge of a cliff.

A stack of fat envelopes, addressed from Verona, Wisconsin, to 266 Fulton Lane, waited for my next move. When I didn't reach for the stack, Miss Raintree did it for me, gently pulling six or seven envelopes from the pile. Then she laid out the pages of stationery on the table—some had flowered borders, some were more formal in ivory, all of them filled with graceful script. There were photos too, one or two in every envelope. A baby with a rattle. A toddler in footie pajamas. A boy in a baseball uniform.

. . . A geeky teenager in a graduation cap, his proud parents on either side.

It was the same picture I had found in our attic. It was Dad. Miss Raintree stepped back as I finally lifted one of the letters and skimmed its opening lines.

March 30, 1966

Dear Adeline,
Lincoln is growing like a little beanstalk. He already has one bottom tooth barely poking through. . . .

My fingers felt numb as I pulled another letter from the pile.

September 15, 1971

Dear Adeline,
Lincoln said the most charming thing today, and I just had to pass it on to you. . . .

Miss Raintree was talking again. I looked up, dazed, from the pages in my hand. She had returned to her spot at the head of the table. "Ellen Crenshaw was the kindest of women," she was saying. "I always knew she felt deeply for my situation. When Mrs. Crenshaw wrote that she had christened my son with the middle name of Raintree, I began to think that someday she would change her mind and tell him the truth. And that he would come and find me. I've never given up hope. Even when Mrs. Crenshaw's letters stopped coming. . . ."

"You wrote to her once," I said. It had been so long since I'd spoken, my voice was hoarse.

"Yes." She hesitated and bit her lip. "I broke our agreement, but I have to admit part of me was praying that your father would find my letter and begin to put the pieces together."

"He did," I told her.

Miss Raintree nodded slowly. "I'm sure it's difficult for your father to make contact after all these years. But all I can do is keep praying that he'll come so that I can ask for his forgiveness . . . and my goodness, Lincoln," she exclaimed. She slid her hand toward me, across the dusty wood of the table. Her eyes shone with a joyful light. "Here you are!"

I knew it was cruel to leave her happiness hanging in the air. I knew I should take her hand or say something, but my mouth had filled with the taste of dust, and I could smell the mildew, sickening and sweet, rising from the worn Oriental carpets, seeping into my skin and my clothes. How was I supposed to tell her Dad was dead? And what did she expect from me? Did she expect me to jump up and give her a big hug and call her Grandma?

I had started to scrape the letters and pictures back into a messy pile. "Thank you," I babbled. "Thanks for showing me these and telling me your story." I rose awkwardly from the table, almost sending my chair toppling backward. Miss

Raintree looked up at me in shocked dismay. "I'm sorry," I blurted out. "I think . . . I think I need a little fresh air." I began edging toward the doorway. Delaney looked startled too. She was getting to her feet uncertainly.

"Will you come again soon?" Miss Raintree pleaded. "Will you talk to your father?"

"I . . ."

I couldn't tell her the truth right now. I had to get out. "I'll come again soon," I said weakly. "I promise." Then I turned and bolted. I could hear Delaney making apologies and saying goodbye behind me as I rushed through the house, trying to remember the way to my grandmother's back door.

My life's been hard
And all things show it;
I always thought so
And now I know it.

GUILFORD, VERMONT

Chapter 26

Delaney almost had to jog to catch up with me on our walk back to the bus stop on Grand Avenue. She must have known that I might start bawling or something if I didn't keep marching forward. She didn't ask me to slow down.

"Linc," she panted as she hurried along, "are you okay?"

I nodded, but I kept staring down at the sidewalk in front of my feet. She stayed quiet for another block before testing my spirits again. "You got yourself a grandma," she said softly.

"Yep. I got a grandma, all right," I finally said, slowing my pace. "Not exactly the model I would have ordered from the catalog, but I'm guessing in this case the no-returns policy applies."

Delaney brushed off my meanness with a flip of her hand. "Oh, you're just overwhelmed right now," she reassured me. "Once you've had time to let this sink in, you'll start to feel better." When I didn't answer, Delaney kept musing on her own. "I *liked* her. She told you the truth, exactly like it happened, instead of trying to sugarcoat things because you're a kid. . . . I even liked her house. All it needs is a good cleaning and a coat of paint or two. . . ."

Delaney ignored my skeptical look. We had made it to the bus stop. I flopped down on the metal bench and let my head loll back. Somehow I was surprised to see that the sky was the same bright blue as it had been an hour ago. To me it seemed like whole seasons had come and gone since we'd arrived on Fulton Lane. "But how am I supposed to go back there and tell her that her long-lost son is *dead*?" I moaned up at the branches overhead.

"It'll be hard," Delaney agreed as she sat down beside me. "That's why you can't wait too long. The longer you wait, the harder it'll be."

I sighed. "I can't even imagine how Lottie's going to react to all this." The ugly scene in the attic flashed into my mind.

"Well, one thing's for sure," Delaney said, reaching down to give my hand a quick squeeze. "With the news you've got, I bet you won't have any problem getting your mother to listen this time."

I couldn't help smiling. Delaney had actually held my hand, even if it lasted only a second or two. And she was right—this discovery about Dad's real mother wasn't the kind of thing Lottie could close up in some box in the attic.

I felt the tiniest ripple of excitement deep down in my chest. I'd always been jealous of kids who lived in the same town with a whole pack of aunts and uncles and cousins and grandparents. Even if Adeline Raintree wasn't the grand-mother I would have ordered, it might be really nice to set a third place at our table now and then.

It was almost dusk by the time I made it back to Claiborne Street. I didn't have a chance to keep worrying about how I would break the news to Lottie. The bus driver had just closed the door behind me when I spotted my mother coming down the block. C.B. and Spunky were with her. I started to call out but then stopped when I saw her expres-sion. There was no mistaking what kind of mood my mother was in. Her lips were pressed into a thin line, and she jerked on the dogs' leashes, trying to yank them out of their tug-of-war game.

Before I could even say hello, she was fussing at me. "Lin-coln! Where have you been?" Her voice crackled with irrita-tion as the dogs dragged her toward me. "C.B. was beside himself when I got home from work, and Mr. Krasny has called three times, wondering why you hadn't come to walk Spunky."

"I'm sorry," I said as I reached down to greet the dogs. "I forgot to tell him I'd be late today."

"Well, where have you been?" she demanded again.

"I went with Delaney to—"

"Delaney? Delaney who?"

I closed my eyes for an instant. I needed to keep calm. "Delaney Baldwin, Mom. I've told you about her. . . .

Anyway," I said with a huff, "you'll never believe what happened this afternoon."

Lottie wasn't listening. Spunky had started barking at some guy who had banged out of the house across the street, dressed head to toe in black leather. I almost had to shout to be heard over all his yapping. "Lottie! I'm trying to tell you something."

Lottie let out an angry grunt as Spunky lunged forward. Now the guy in leather was climbing on a giant motorcycle parked in his driveway. "Listen, Linc," she snapped as she wrestled Spunky away from the curb. "I don't like what's going on here. I'm starting to think that enrolling you at Plainview was a huge mistake. Ever since you started there, you've been different. You're gone all the time with all these new friends I've never met, and you come home acting surly and defiant."

Even with Lottie ranting, I couldn't stop watching the man across the street. He kept stomping on his kick-start pedal. It took him five or six tries to get his Harley to splutter to life. "Like Monday, for instance!" Lottie's voice had turned sharper. "You disappeared for hours. Then you stormed into the house with no explanation. And now this! You're three hours late on a school night and you've forgotten all about your obligations to Mr. Krasny."

"What are you saying, Lottie?" I burst out. "What do you want me to do? You want me to quit Plainview right now? You really think that would be a good idea?"

Lottie cast a look up at the darkening sky in exasperation

as the motorcycle man revved his engine. "I don't know, Linc," she cried out. "All I'm saying is that I might have to consider moving you back to your old school if this unpredictable behavior of yours continues."

My insides clenched. "You wouldn't do that," I said. "You can't!"

Her face turned hard. "Don't push me, Linc," she threatened in a voice I didn't recognize. Spunky gave another lunge toward the curb. "Now will you take this crazy dog before he tears my arm out of the socket?"

I snatched both leashes from her hands. "I can't even talk to you about what's really going on. Every time I try, you don't want to hear it."

At last the man was maneuvering out of his driveway. Lottie waited with her teeth gritted until he had sped off with an obnoxious roar. "What do you mean, what's really going on?" she asked suspiciously. Her question rang out in the sudden quiet. "Tell me. I'm all ears."

I stood staring into her blazing eyes, listening to the whine of the Harley's engine fade into the distance, and I could feel the last traces of electricity from my wild afternoon fizzle away like a blown fuse.

"Well?" Lottie repeated, more impatient than ever. "What do you have to tell me?"

"Nothing," I said as I pulled the dogs in the opposite direction from home. "Never mind."

• • •

When I finally showed up on his doorstep with Spunky, Mr. Krasny was too preoccupied to bother asking where I'd been all afternoon. "Oh, good. You're here," he said. "Come inside for a minute, son. I have to show you what I've found."

Mr. Krasny led me back to his kitchen, pumping his frail little arms as he shuffled along. If I had been in better spirits, I would have smiled at how spry he had suddenly become. But I was still reeling from my fight with Lottie. What if she was serious about making me quit Plainview? I could already imagine the I-told-you-so look on Sebastian's face when I showed up on the Ho-Hos' doorstep.

Mr. Krasny motioned me over to his kitchen table, where six or seven red leather volumes were spread open and scattered across the Formica top. I recognized them from the day he had shown me the bound collection of the *Slovan Americký* in his living room. "I knew Tatínek's old Czech newspapers would come in handy someday," Mr. Krasny said. He smoothed his hand fondly across the yellowed pages of one of the volumes. "My sister tried to talk me into donating them to the Czech museum in Cedar Rapids. But I wouldn't hear of it."

I went to stand beside him and peer down at the hodge-podge of foreign headlines splattered across the page. "So what did you find?" I asked, hoping he would tell me something interesting to take my mind off my crazy afternoon for a while.

Mr. Krasny poked his knobby finger at one of the newspaper articles, which was only a paragraph long—and then traced a path underneath the words in the headline. "What does that say?" he asked me.

I coughed out a laugh. "Sorry, Mr. Krasny. I speak a little French, but that's about it. For all I know, this could be Sanskrit."

He smiled mischievously at me over the top of his glasses. "Take another look."

I bent down until my nose was a few inches from the paper—close enough to get a good whiff of the dry, dusty pages—and then I tried to pronounce a few of the words.

"*Pohovor s . . . Terezií . . . Doležalovou.*" I stuttered over the last string of syllables. "*Terezií,*" I repeated, standing up with a jerk. "Is that Theresa? Theresa Dolezal?"

"Bravo," he said, giving the air a tiny, satisfied punch. I had never seen him so jolly. "The headline says, 'An Interview with Theresa Dolezal.' That was her name, remember, before she married the rich rancher out west."

He had me curious now. I bent down again to check the date on the top of the newspaper page. "This was published in 1880. So this would have been written just a few years after she came to this country. Way before her son Eddie died. So what's the article say?"

"It's quite a coincidence," he started. "I'm sure my *tatínek* wrote this story. He used to do little profiles of the Czechs who had immigrated here. Human-interest stories. It was a way to connect people in the community. He would write about the villages where they came from. And someone would realize, 'Oh, my wife came from the town next door.' And, like magic, friendships would form."

He readjusted his glasses and picked up the red leather

book. "This article says that Theresa came from a village in Bohemia called Strmilov."

"I remember that name," I said. "From Eddie's obituary in the newspaper I found at the historical society."

Mr. Krasny nodded, and his wrinkles seemed to multiply as he brooded over the newspaper page, following the words again with his finger. "Well, I haven't been able to figure out every single phrase. But the piece mainly talks about how much Theresa misses her family back in Bohemia. Her father. Her brothers and sisters . . . *sourozenci*. . . . And how she misses her village. But she needed to leave to make a better life for her son. . . ." Mr. Krasny shook his head in annoyance. "Just a minute," he said as he set the volume on the table and reached for his Czech-English dictionary. "*Požár*," he mumbled to himself as he thumbed through the pages. "Why can't I remember *požár*?"

I crossed my arms restlessly and gnawed my lip.

"Aha!" he finally exclaimed. "*Požár* means 'fire.'" He plunked the dictionary back on the table and hoisted up the book of newspapers again. "So from what I can gather," he went on, frowning down at the newsprint, "the people in her village had been devastated by a huge fire. They lost their church and the school and more than a hundred houses—"

"Whoa," I interrupted with a whoosh of breath. "That does it. She really *is* cursed." Mr. Krasny's eyebrows rose and he blinked back at me, as if he were trying to decide whether I was serious or not.

I was serious, all right. I sat down hard on one of his

kitchen chairs. "Don't you see, Mr. Krasny? How unlucky can a person get? She lost two husbands. She lost two sons. Then a rattlesnake bites her and she loses a leg. And now you're telling me that she lost her village back in Bohemia on top of everything else?

"And what about that epitaph?" I asked with a little flail of my arms. "'Suffering awaits you.' I know it sounds crazy. But when you put all the pieces together, it sort of starts to make sense. Theresa had a horrible life, so she decided to get her revenge on the world by building a statue and trying to put a curse on it."

A smile teased at one corner of Mr. Krasny's lips as he lowered himself into the chair beside me. "Now, Linc," he said, "you're a sensible boy. You honestly believe someone could have the power to put a hex on a statue? To doom anyone who crosses its path?"

I thought for a second. Sure, my theory was a bit farfetched. And sure, I was probably feeling spooked by Halloween coming up and all the unexpected curveballs I'd been thrown that day. But even Mr. Krasny had to admit that Theresa and Bad Luck seemed to go together like fire and brimstone. "I'm not saying Theresa's curse ever worked," I backpedaled, trying to sound more reasonable. "There are tons of stories about what's happened to people who mess with the Black Angel, but I guess I don't have any proof. It just makes you wonder, that's all."

Mr. Krasny gave up on holding back his chuckle. "Well, if I find anything in Tatínek's newspapers about Theresa's black magic, I'll let you know." He reached out to give my shoulder a pat, and in a flash I thought of Adeline Raintree—the way she had slid her hand toward me across the table that afternoon. "Really, Mr. Krasny," I said guiltily, "you don't have to worry about helping me with my project anymore." I gestured at the heap of books on the table. "This is so much work."

"Work?" he fired back. "Nonsense, son. This is the most fun I've had in years." He pushed himself up from the table. "Now you better run along home. Your mother's probably fit to be tied by now."

I mustered up a sad smile before I headed out the door. Mr. Krasny was a very wise man.

Passing stranger, call it not
A place of fear and doom
I love to linger o'er this spot
It is my husband's tomb

BISMARCK, NORTH DAKOTA

CHAPTER 27

DARTH VADER, the Grim Reaper, Abraham Lincoln, a princess, a pirate, a couple of hippies from the 1960s—they all started arriving right after sunset the next evening. Until this year, I had always been away from home too on Halloween night. So I had never quite realized how much kids loved trick-or-treating on my street. I guess they thought it was spooky being so close to the graveyard.

I could hear them coming as I sat on the couch in the living room that night, doing my math homework next to C.B. and a big bowl of Dum Dums. They screeched and yelped and ran squealing in herds, moving closer along the sidewalks. By the time they arrived at our dead end, where the shadowy shapes of the tombstones started to materialize in the distance, most kids had worked themselves into a fever of fright. It took C.B. about an hour to calm down, but after that he barely even twitched his long eyebrows whenever someone new came thudding up the porch steps.

I had almost run out of candy when my old Ho-Ho friends, Sebastian and Vladka, showed up at the door, dressed as ancient Egyptians. "Doth he remember us?" Sebastian asked Vladka as I stood surveying their costumes.

"Yes, I think he doth," Vladka played along with her old sly smile and soft voice. Her eyes were rimmed in heavy black liner, and she had made a headdress out of glittery gold fabric. She could almost have passed for Cleopatra if it hadn't been for her Russian accent and the purple high-tops peeking out from under her gown.

Sebastian, on the other hand? Except for the matching headdress, which Vladka must have made for him, he looked about as far from a pharaoh as you could get. "I didn't know King Tut wore glasses," I said with a laugh, dropping the last of the Dum Dums into Sebastian's pillowcase. "And what's that?" I asked, pointing to the thick yards of ivory material that he had belted around his middle with a bathrobe tie.

Sebastian pushed his glasses up on his nose. "My tunic."

"His mother's tablecloth," Vladka corrected. Her voice slid to a disapproving whisper. "He cut a hole in it, for his head to go through."

I heard a gasp behind me. It was Lottie, standing in the doorway to the living room. "You didn't!" she exclaimed as she came over to join us.

"Hello, Professor Landers," Sebastian said sheepishly.

"It's good to see you two again." Lottie beamed. I stood stiffly beside her. She had come out of her office once earlier that evening to ask if I wanted her to take a turn handing out candy.

"No, thanks," I had said curtly. I could tell she was trying to smooth things over between us. But I wasn't ready. I hated how she kept blaming Plainview for all the troubles between us. And now she had practically forced me into keeping secrets from her. After what she had threatened, how could I tell her the truth about everything—about stealing the key and getting kicked out of the graveyard and hunting down Dad's real mother? I might as well book a one-way trip back to the Ho-Hos right now.

Vladka had finally finished giving my mother an update on her latest math competition. "We came to see if Linc wanted to trick-or-treat with us," she said. "We're going to one last street. They always have the best candy over on Dover."

"Great," Lottie said quickly. "That would be fun, wouldn't it, Linc?"

"I thought you said you didn't like me going out on school nights."

Lottie pursed her lips at my snide crack. "I think we can make an exception for Halloween."

I shrugged and said, "Don't you guys think we're a little too old to be going trick-or-treating?"

Sebastian looked offended. He crossed his arms over his tablecloth tunic. "Oh, is that what they're saying over at the *junior high?*" he asked with a nasty smirk. "It's not cool to go trick-or-treating anymore?"

"No, nobody said that." I hadn't meant to start a fight.

Sebastian turned to go. "Come on, Vladka," he said. "I told you he wouldn't want to come."

"Wait," I called. I stepped out onto the porch as they headed down the steps. "I just . . ." My voice died away. How was I supposed to explain? Halloween felt awful this year. Every time I thought of trick-or-treating, I thought of Fulton Lane—little kids dashing up to the old Raintree house, ringing the doorbell, and running away while Adeline Raintree sat all alone at her dining room table, waiting for the night to be over.

Vladka turned back for a second with her sparkly headdress swinging. "It's all right, Linc," she said kindly. Even with all her black liner, I could see the glimmer of hurt in her eyes. "Maybe another time."

I stood watching them from the porch. "Junior high," I heard Sebastian sneer again out on the sidewalk. "At least we're not sitting at home alone on Halloween."

I glared into the dark. I could have been at a party if I'd wanted. Mellecker had invited me over to his house with Beez and a bunch of other kids. But I had made up some lame excuse not to go. I knew Amy would be there, and supposedly she had thrown a hissy fit when she found out Delaney had been invited to go on the Ransom expedition tomorrow and no one had bothered to include her.

Lottie was still standing in the doorway, looking mystified, when I finally turned to go back inside. "Why didn't you want to go?" she asked. "You used to love hanging out with those guys. You used to love Halloween."

"Too much homework" was all I could manage to say as I pushed the empty candy bowl into her arms.

I owed the world nothing,
it owed me a small amount:
but on the 4th of Mar 1854
we balanced all accounts.

Columbus, Ohio

Chapter 28

I waited, shivering, at the end of my street just outside the cemetery gate. So far my plans had gone even better than I'd expected. The sliver of light under Lottie's door had turned dark a little earlier than usual, and when I had finally tiptoed downstairs and slipped out the back door near midnight, C.B. hadn't even bothered to roust himself out of my bed to follow me. But now at least ten minutes had passed, and there was still no sign of the others. Maybe Beez's older brother had backed out on his promise to provide taxi service and the getaway car for the evening. He'd probably decided it wasn't worth it, even though Beez had supposedly bribed him with a whole month's allowance, plus threatened to spill the beans about some wild party his brother had hosted when their parents were out of town.

A thick veil of clouds drifted past the moon. I tugged the collar of my jacket up around my ears and bounced on the balls of my feet to keep warm. The temperature must have dropped at least ten degrees in the last few hours. I jogged up Claiborne Street a little ways, then jogged back, trying to distract myself by thinking about the next step in my training plan. I wanted to run the trails in Hickory Hill Park, where the terrain would be more like a real cross-country course. The dogs would love it. . . .

Just when I was beginning to feel the first tickle of doubt—*They aren't coming*—a pair of headlights raked their way around the corner and bobbed toward me. As I lifted my arm to block out the glare, I caught a glimpse of four shadowy heads and the flick of a ponytail inside the dark Mustang. *Good.* Delaney had made it.

Beez's brother parked along the curb where the road ran out and cut the engine and the lights, plunging the street into blackness again. After a pause the car doors opened, and Delaney and Beez and Mellecker quietly popped out like some sort of nocturnal animals crawling from their den. I fought back the urge to laugh. "I was starting to think you guys weren't coming," I whispered as I hovered next to the Mustang's ticking hood.

"Sorry," Delaney said, keeping her voice low. "That was my fault. I heard Mama get up to go to the bathroom. I couldn't sneak out till I was sure she had gone back to bed."

"We almost left without her," Beez added. Then he leaned down to peer at his brother through the passenger door. "But don't get any ideas, bro. You're gonna stay here and wait for us, right?"

Through the windshield, I could see his brother crossing

his arms over his chest and sliding farther down into the bucket seat. "Yeah," I heard him answer in a tired mumble. "Might as well catch a few Z's. How long are you guys gonna be, anyway? You're just headed over to the Black Angel, right?"

"Right," Beez said. "We'll be back in a jiffy." He lifted his head for a second and winked at the rest of us. We had all agreed the Black Angel would be our alibi. "I can't tell my brother what we're really doing at Oakland," Beez had told us that morning in the hallway at school. "Are you kidding? He'd love having that kind of ammunition the next time he wants something. At my house, one good blackmail deserves another."

Beez leaned down to give his brother final instructions. "If we don't show up here in half an hour, you'll know something went wrong . . . and you better come looking for us." Delaney told him to hush. Beez grinned and pushed the car door shut.

As we set off into the cemetery, a giddy rush of power welled in my chest. Tonight *I* was in charge for a change— the only one who remembered to bring a flashlight and the only one who knew this territory like my own backyard. I couldn't resist pointing my beam at all the eeriest spots along our path—the tall crooked cross off to the left, the big beech with gnarled branches at the bottom of the hill, an old tomb up ahead with crumbled stone sides. Something scuffled in a clump of bushes nearby. Delaney grabbed the tail of my jacket, and Mellecker and Beez jumped a few feet sideways.

"What's that?" Beez croaked.

I had to bite back another laugh as I aimed my light at the shrubs and then, for good measure, skimmed it across the tops of the pale tombstones in the distance. "Could be a squirrel," I said lightly. "Or maybe a raccoon . . . or a ghost."

"Very funny, Crenshaw," Mellecker said.

Delaney had let go of my jacket almost as soon as she'd grabbed it. When I glanced back to check on her, she pursed her lips and gave me a small, grudging smile.

"Hey, which way's the Black Angel from here?" Mellecker asked excitedly.

I waved my flashlight toward a row of cedars off to our left. "It's over there—through those trees."

Mellecker stopped. "Let's go take a look, you guys. C'mon—we're so close." He turned to Beez. "And your brother's probably going to ask us about it later."

Beez backed up a few steps like a stubborn horse. "Ohhh, no. The Black Angel was only supposed to be our cover story."

"Hey, you were the one who was talking about cutting her fingers off a few nights ago," Mellecker said. "What happened? You gettin' cold feet?"

"Not just cold feet," Beez spluttered from underneath his hood. "Cold feet. Cold hands. Cold everything! If we don't hurry up and get over to the Ransom vault, I'm gonna freeze to death." As if to prove his point, a puff of Beez's icy breath billowed into the air and hung in the middle of our huddle.

"Oh, suck it up, you big baby." Mellecker laughed. "This'll only take a minute." Beez let out a resigned groan.

"Wait a second," I stalled. Half of me wanted to delay heading over to the Ransom vault as long as possible, but the other half didn't want to go anywhere near the Black Angel that night, especially after all the spooky stuff I'd been learning about Theresa Feldevert. I tilted the flashlight toward Delaney, hoping she might give us an excuse not to go. "What do you think, Delaney?" I asked. "You mind making a detour?"

The fabric of her coat rustled as she lifted her shoulders in a little shrug. "I don't mind," she said. I should have known. Ever since the day we'd first met at my locker, Delaney had never once turned down the chance for an adventure—even with all her worries at home.

"Hear that, Beezy?" Mellecker said. He reached out to give Beez a punch. "Delaney will protect you. Lead the way, Crenshaw."

Past the line of cedar trees, the rolling lawn was even more crowded with gravestones. Beez weaved and dodged among the markers like a drunkard, trying to keep up. "Geez!" he complained. "I keep stepping on dead people."

Then he yelped when I switched off the flashlight. "What'd you do that for?" he rasped. Mellecker and Delaney halted in their tracks.

"Sorry," I whispered. I pointed to the dark shape looming at the bottom of a shallow hill in the distance. "The Black Angel is right over there. We just need to make sure nobody's standing guard."

"What do you mean?" Mellecker asked, searching the

darkness down the hill. "I thought you said they never patrol except on Halloween."

"They usually don't," I told him.

Beez took a jittery look back over his shoulder. "Are you saying that Kilgore dude you were telling us about might be out here somewhere?"

Delaney was starting to look nervous too. "Nobody's here but us," I reassured them. "I only want to scout things out a little bit. So wait here a minute, okay? When you see my flashlight go back on, you can come down."

I scampered ahead, ducking behind the largest stones and peeking out, until I had scanned the entire perimeter surrounding the Angel. More than once Jeeter had shown me exactly where he and Old Nick used to park the truck for their stakeouts on Halloween. They'd pick up carryout pizza and sit waiting in the shadows for hours, telling jokes and stories. "Then these kids come along trying to stir up trouble," Jeeter had told me, "and we flip those headlights on high and scare the patooie right out of 'em. You should see 'em scatter. Just like cockroaches!"

I squinted up and down the empty sweep of driveway. *Relax*, I told myself. *Gene* was probably at home snoozing away right now. And even Kilgore wouldn't be paranoid enough to keep up midnight guard duty after the thrill of the Halloween hunt had come and gone. I stepped out of the shadows and stole a quick glance up at the Black Angel. The moon, small and hard as a dime, had slid from behind the clouds again. Its light gleamed against the black bronze of the Angel's face, illuminating cracks and crevices that I had never noticed before.

I fought off a little shudder. If I didn't keep moving, I'd start obsessing over that stupid curse again. I switched on the flashlight and waved it defiantly through the air. Soon the others were scurrying toward me down the hill.

"Whoa," Mellecker breathed as he took the flashlight from me and circled around the statue. "This lady is *not* happy." Beez observed from a safe distance while Delaney stood at the foot of the Angel, gazing up into her moonlit face.

"Okay, guys," I said once another minute had passed. "Ready to go?"

Mellecker's smile flashed in the darkness. "Hey, we can't leave yet. Not without cheering her up first. Somebody's gotta give her a kiss."

My breath caught in my throat as I tried to laugh. "No, come on. Really. We need to get going."

Mellecker wasn't listening. "Go ahead, Beez." He swept his hand up at the Angel. "Climb up there and kiss her."

"No way," Beez said brusquely. "Why don't you do it if you think it's such a great idea?"

"I would, but she's not my type," Mellecker told him.

"What about you, Crenshaw?" Beez asked. He took a couple steps forward, unable to resist the chance for a little goading. "You and the Angel must have gotten pretty close these past few weeks."

I was shaking my head when Delaney suddenly chimed in. "Lift me up," she said. "I'll do it."

"Well, well, well." Beez's voice swooped up in surprise. "Sorry we didn't ask you first, Delaney." He lumbered over to help hoist her up. "I guess we figured she wouldn't be your type either."

"No!" I said, rushing forward. "Don't do it, Delaney. This is stupid. We don't have time."

But Delaney was already gripping the granite edge of the statue's base, stepping into the little hammock Beez had made with his fingers. "What's wrong, Crenshaw?" he grunted as he boosted her higher. "You jealous?"

"I just—" I could hear my voice rising as I floundered for words. "I just don't think this is very smart—"

I watched helplessly as Delaney reached out and clutched the bottom edge of an upraised wing to steady herself. She looked tiny pressed against the massive statue's shrouded skirts. Even on her tiptoes, the top of her head barely reached past the Angel's torso. "Please, Delaney," I said quietly, trying to sound calm. "Come on down."

But it was no use. Beez was shushing me, and Mellecker was training the flashlight on Delaney as if she were some kind of high-wire performer in a circus act. And we all seemed to fall into a trance as she inched along the pedestal's ledge and carefully leaned down and placed a gentle kiss on the Angel's cold bronze hand.

DRED SCOTT
BORN ABOUT 1799
DIED SEPT 17 1858
Freed from slavery
by his friend Taylor Blow

St. Louis, Missouri

Chapter 29

As we all made our way over to the Ransom vault, I couldn't help keeping an ear out for Winslow and his grumpy crew. But their voices were strangely absent tonight—as if what I was about to do had shocked them into silent disapproval.

Mellecker had kept my flashlight, and now that he had his bearings, he was up ahead with Beez, leading the way. Delaney gave me a nudge as we hiked along the driveway behind them.

"What's wrong?" she asked softly.

"I don't know," I waffled. "I was surprised, that's all. . . . You know how spooked I've been about the Black Angel lately. Were you making fun of me back there when you climbed up and kissed her?"

"Of course not," Delaney said, letting out a frosty puff of

air. "I don't know why I did it." She flopped her hands to her sides. "I guess it was mainly because those boys always try to act so tough, but they're such sissies underneath. I wanted to call their bluff for once."

I smiled into the darkness. Then the mischief faded from Delaney's voice. "And I did it 'cause . . . this is gonna sound silly, but when I was looking up at that Angel, I felt so sorry for her. To me she doesn't look evil—she looks sad, with those wings of hers drooping down and her poor fingers chopped off. For a minute it almost felt like she was real." She paused for a second, embarrassed. "Does that sound crazy?"

"Not really," I told her. *Hey*, I was tempted to admit, *that's nothin'. I'm the one who listens to talking tombstones.*

But Beez had turned around to squawk at us. "C'mon, you two! What do you think this is? Some kind of date or something?"

Mellecker veered off the drive, leading us into the heart of the graveyard again. I tried to pick up the pace, but my feet had felt like anchors ever since we'd left the Black Angel. I reached into my jacket pocket and let my fingers curl around the cold shaft of the key, hoping I would feel something— anything to spur me on. But all that burning anger I had been storing up for Kilgore and Jeeter had suddenly sizzled away. Now I just felt empty—and *scared*. Breaking into a vault went against every sacred rule that Jeeter had taught me about respecting the dead. What had possessed me to come this far? What if those stories I had invented were true and there really *was* something horrible hidden inside the Ransom tomb?

But all at once the dim shape of the mausoleum was jutting up in front of us, and the others had stopped, waiting for me to speed up and take charge. I swallowed hard and pulled the key from my pocket, reminding myself to think like Lottie. *Just pretend you're on another research trip, gathering facts, making notes.*

All the way to the vault Mellecker and Beez had been goofing around, sprinting and cutting between the headstones like they were punching through an army of defensive linebackers. But not anymore. No one spoke as I approached the tomb and climbed the three steps to the door. Mellecker followed close behind, grazing the light over the front entrance—the name RANSOM etched in the mossy stone. As he pointed the beam of light at the keyhole with its rusted edges, I looked over my shoulder one more time. Delaney was watching intently from the bottom step, but Beez had planted himself a few yards away. Somehow seeing him act like such a coward made it easier for me to push the key into the weathered slot and give it a turn. I sucked in my breath. At first the key snagged, but then there was a small screech of metal and a clunk as the ancient lock gave way. I stopped, staring down at my hand suspended in the light. "It worked," I whispered in amazement.

I could hear Beez nagging behind us. "What's taking so long? Go on. Open it!"

"Shut up, Beez," Mellecker snapped under his breath. I slowly lowered my hand to the knob.

The smell hit me first when I shoved the door open—a draft of damp earth and age like a whiff from the deepest corner of a root cellar. I reached back for the flashlight, using my toe to push the door open even wider. Then I took a few tiny steps forward and scanned the vault's inner room. Mellecker and Delaney hovered in the doorway, trying to peer in. "What do you see?" Delaney whispered.

"Not much," I answered with a shaky sigh of relief. I edged a few more feet into the icy space, aiming the flashlight to the left, then the right, at the long granite panels lining both sides of the narrow room. I could feel the tension rising from my muscles like steam. The vault looked a lot like the pictures in the books I had sneaked out of Lottie's office last night—nothing more than a simple chamber made entirely of stone, with a built-in granite bench at the far end.

Mellecker ducked under the doorframe. "No bodies?" he asked, sounding surprised.

"Well, sure, corpses are in here, but you can't see them," I said. "See those bronze things on the wall that look like decorations? They're actually bolts, and if you unscrew them, the panels come off and the coffins are stacked behind there on shelves." I used my flashlight as a pointer, underlining the names and dates carved across the panels. "Looks like six people were buried in here."

Delaney shuffled along the wall, reading the inscriptions out loud. "Letitia Halsey Ransom . . . Born 1862. Died 1920. . . . William Michael Ransom . . ."

Beez appeared in the doorway, still looking skittish. His gaze darted around the murky corners of the burial chamber.

"You mean to tell me this is it?" He pushed his hood off his head in disbelief. "There's nothing here?"

Mellecker had crossed his arms over his chest. "Nada."

Beez's eyes popped open wide. "Unbelievable, Crenshaw," he burst out, full of bluster all of a sudden. "You dragged us out here in the freezing cold, in the middle of the night, for *this?*" He waved his arm at the barren space.

"Give me a break, Beez," I scoffed. "A minute ago you were shaking in your shoes. And now you're gonna stand there and—"

"Y'all be quiet," Delaney broke in excitedly. I whirled around with the flashlight. At some point she had wandered over to inspect the far end of the tomb. "There *is* something here. Look at this!"

Delaney's discovery sat in the recess of the stone bench, tucked so far back in the shadows that none of us had noticed it before—a small wooden trunk with metal straps and a curved lid, the kind you would find in an antique shop. Even more amazing, there was no sign of a lock on the latch.

The three of us hurried across the chamber to cluster around Delaney. "Hey, it's just like one of those pirate chests," Beez exclaimed in a rush of breath. "Sorry, Crenshaw. Looks like I owe you an apology."

Mellecker was already reaching down to lift the metal clasp on the trunk. "Remember, Beez," he said with a crafty grin. "I'm the one who picked the Ransom vault, so don't be getting any ideas about splitting things evenly." I raised the flashlight higher as he hoisted the lid and we all leaned forward to peer down inside.

Delaney shrank back.

"What in the—?" Mellecker croaked, and Beez stumbled away, covering his nose. "It's bones!" Beez cried. "And they stink!" I stood cemented to my spot, too confused to move. They were bones all right—piled like crazy Pick-Up Sticks at the bottom of the trunk. But something was different about them. I pushed the flashlight closer. Then all at once I realized where I'd seen bones like that before. In a field near one of those roadside cemeteries Lottie had dragged me to years ago, we had stumbled across a bleached rib cage hidden in the tall grass . . . a long, slender skull exactly like the one lodged in the corner of the chest. I still remembered my mother putting her arm around my shoulders and bending down to explain.

"Wait a second, you guys!" I cried. "These are just deer bones! See?" But Beez and Mellecker had already run outside.

". . . so foul!" I could hear Beez ranting out on the steps. "I mean, geez! Let's get out of here."

"Crenshaw!" Mellecker barked. "What are you doing in there?"

"C'mon, man," I overheard Beez shout from the distance. "Who cares if they're coming or not? Just leave 'em. Let's go!"

"Can you believe that?" I said to Delaney. She had stopped halfway to the door. "They ditched us. What cowards!" I wasn't a bit surprised that Beez would run off like that, but Mellecker too? *Talk about lello!*

But Delaney wasn't paying the slightest bit of attention to my tirade. "You're sure those bones aren't . . . human?" she asked in a thin voice.

"I'm sure," I told her as I turned to shine the light on the chest of bones again. "But I still don't get it. Why would there be deer bones in here?" Delaney edged closer. She had just started to peer over my shoulder when we heard the noise. We both froze in place, listening. It sounded almost like a laugh, low and muffled, coming from somewhere across the chamber . . . no . . . from behind the open door. Then we heard it again, and Delaney gasped and grabbed my arm. She must have knocked me off balance—who knows? It all happened in a blur, like we were in the middle of a fun house, but somehow the flashlight flew out of my hand. It smacked against the floor and clattered away, and we both went rigid as the light flickered off . . . back on . . . then off for good.

"What was that?" Delaney whispered, still clutching my arm.

"I don't know," I said. I braced myself for another laugh to come creeping from the far corner. All I could hear, though, was my own breathing, heavy with fear, echoing against the stone walls.

"Beez, you jerk!" I shouted into the blackness. "Mellecker? This isn't funny! Is that you?"

No answer.

I started to pull Delaney toward the entrance. That's when something sprang to life in the corner and the door swung shut with a rusty creak. Delaney let out a small scream, and both of us staggered back.

"Beez!" I shouted again, loud enough to scrape my throat raw. I was straining to hear his reply when a tiny burst of flame lit up the form blocking the entrance to the tomb.

"Boo," Kilgore said, holding his cigarette lighter high.

STEEL TRUE
BLADE STRAIGHT

Sir Arthur Conan Doyle
Hampshire, England

Chapter 30

I know we were in trouble when I saw what he was wearing. A blue uniform jacket like the ones the Union soldiers used to wear in the Civil War. He had unfastened the row of buttons, and the jacket hung open, showing a plain white T-shirt underneath.

Kilgore leaned against the door to the vault, sizing us up as he took another long drag from his cigarette. At first I had been relieved when he had reached down and held his lighter to the small propane lantern at his feet. But now the flickering light had carved his sharp face into shadows, into sunken cheeks and hollowed eyes like a cadaver's, and he looked as though he could lounge that way—blocking our only exit— for hours.

Delaney stood shivering beside me. Even though she had never seen him before, I could tell she knew right away—this was the nasty cemetery warden I had told her about.

Kilgore slowly blew out a plume of smoke. "Well, I gotta admit, kid," he said, pointing his cigarette butt at my chest, "I'm impressed. I didn't figure you'd know the difference between a pile of deer bones and a pile of human ones. But you caught on right away. Unlike those yellow-bellied friends of yours." He picked a piece of tobacco off his tongue, and his wiry frame shook with a quiet chuckle. "So that's who you brought along to protect you?"

Kilgore dropped his cigarette butt on the floor. I stared down, barely breathing, at his boot twisting back and forth, grinding the ember into the stone. Experience had taught me it was better to keep my mouth shut. Trying to defend yourself with Kilgore only made things worse.

"And who's this?" he asked, exploring his luck with Delaney. "Wait a minute. Don't tell me you're his girlfriend?"

Don't answer, I pleaded in my head. *Don't answer.* Delaney stayed silent. But then Kilgore took a step toward her. "You might as well start talking now, darlin'. The police will be asking you all sorts of questions for their report."

Delaney stiffened beside me. "The police?" she repeated, her voice barely above a whisper.

It was like throwing gas on a flame. I could see Kilgore's face light up. "You're dang right, the police. I'm the warden here. You think I'm not gonna report a case of grave robbing?"

"But we weren't planning to steal anything," Delaney said in a breathless rush. Her eyes glistened in the light from the lantern. "We only came here to look, to find out more about the Ransoms for a project at school."

Kilgore sneered. "You'd almost have me convinced with that sweet little accent of yours . . . that is, if I hadn't been standing right there behind that door the whole time. I heard everything, honey. I heard how disappointed your boyfriends were when they thought this vault was empty, and I heard 'em talking about splitting up whatever was in that treasure trunk over there."

Delaney's mouth opened in dismay.

"And if all you wanted was a little look inside, why didn't your ringleader here just ask his good friend Gene to give you a tour?" Kilgore demanded. "Why'd he have to steal the key and sneak in here in the dead of night?"

His gaze raked over me with disgust. "You think you're so smart, but I knew it was you. I knew as soon as I realized the key to Vault Number Four was missing. Gene wouldn't believe it. 'No, sir,' he kept saying." Kilgore's face contorted as he mimicked Jeeter in a sugary falsetto. "'Lincoln would never do such a thing. He's a fine kid, that Lincoln.'

"That's when he crossed the line," Kilgore said, dropping his voice back to its husky pitch. "That's when he told me if I wanted to go after you, I'd have to go through him first."

Something lurched inside me. Jeeter had said *that*?

Kilgore must have noticed me flinch. He leaned closer, and I couldn't help wrinkling my nose. *What was that smell?*

"How did that feel?" Kilgore needled. "Getting your old friend fired from the job he's had for fifteen years?"

I felt my jaw go loose. "You fired Jeeter?" I asked in astonishment.

Kilgore drew back in mock surprise. "He didn't tell you? Awww, isn't that sweet? He probably didn't want to make you feel guilty."

"When?" I asked weakly. "When did you fire him?"

"Same day I got rid of *you*. I was taking one more inventory of the keys that afternoon just to be sure nothing else was missing when, lo and behold, who comes wandering into the office? After you left, Gene wouldn't back down, so I gave him his marching orders too, right there on the spot. Haven't seen him since."

Kilgore nodded to himself. "But I knew you'd show up here eventually. . . . Good thing we keep duplicates of all our keys," he rambled. "I thought I'd give you a scare if you ever came sniffing around Number Four. I planted those bones from my last hunting trip, but I never figured I'd be lucky enough to catch you in the act."

He let out a scornful snort. "Not too smart, coming in here on a Friday night with your buddies, right after Halloween. You might as well have set off a flare gun over by the Angel, the way you were waving your flashlight around, blabbing about the Ransom vault. . . ." Usually every movement of Kilgore's was tight as a spring, but now he swung his arm in the air like a rodeo rider, imitating me with the flashlight, and that's when it all started to make sense—the smell on his breath, the mushy endings to his words.

I sneaked an urgent look at Delaney. We had to find a way to escape soon, especially if he'd been drinking. *But how?* Even though Kilgore had stepped away from the door, I knew he was too riled up to let us get past him without a fight. I glanced around, searching the dim corners of the tomb for some sort of solution.

"You know what they used to do to soldiers caught for stealing in the Civil War?" Kilgore leered. He made a chopping motion at one of his wrists. "They used to cut—"

"Listen," I said, "if you're going to call the police, go ahead and do it. Call now and tell them to come and get us."

Kilgore narrowed his eyes and smiled as he scratched at the stubble on his chin. I could tell I had caught him off guard. He wasn't ready to let us go. He wouldn't be done until he had watched us turn desperate, like flies batting against a windowpane.

My mouth was so dry, I could barely talk. "If you don't have a cell phone, you can leave us locked up in here while you go to the office and call. I just need to get my flashlight. . . ." I started angling toward the spot where the flashlight had landed in the corner. "Here it is, right here," I said, keeping up my nervous chatter while I bent down to pick it up. Something in the shadows had caught my eye. I crouched for an extra second, trying to make sense of the round shape on the floor and the wet stain spreading out on the stone.

"Wait," Kilgore said, moving toward me. "What are you doing over there?"

I scrabbled sideways and snatched up the strap. Kilgore stopped cold as I raised the old army canteen and took a deep sniff from the open spout. My head flooded with boozy fumes. I winced and made a sour face. "What's this?" I asked, pretending to be shocked. "Sure doesn't smell like water."

"Give me that," Kilgore growled.

I took a step backward into the gloom. "I don't know," I said. "The police might need this for that report of theirs."

"Listen, you little smart-mouth—" Kilgore lunged at me, grabbing for the canteen. Before he could rip the strap from my hands, I hurled the canteen at his face and sidestepped around him. Delaney was already racing for the door, yanking it open.

"Go ahead!" Kilgore yelled behind us, his voice thick with rage. "Run! I know where to find you!"

CHAPTER 31

Peaceable and Quiet,
a friend to his
Father and mother,
and respected
By all who knew him, and went
To the world where
horses don't kick,
Where sorrow and weeping
is no more.

WILLIAMSPORT, PENNSYLVANIA

Two days later I was standing at the sink full of dirty dishes, looking out at the graveyard, when Winslow, Dobbins, York & McNutt finally decided to break their silence. They weren't bickering this time. They were singing, all together in their gruff, scratchy voices.

> *If you ever laugh when a hearse goes by,*
> *then you may be the next to die—*

I wheeled away from the window, rolling my eyes, and went over to the phone to dial Delaney's number again. I stood there listening for ten rings, then ten more—longer than I had listened yesterday afternoon or last night or early this morning. Why wouldn't Delaney pick up the phone? And why didn't the Baldwins have an answering machine?

Even Lottie had broken down a couple years ago and signed us up for voice mail.

I banged the receiver back on the hook. Delaney had to know I wanted to talk to her. We hadn't spoken since Friday night, when we'd run out of the graveyard, wild-eyed and gasping for breath. Beez and Mellecker were sitting on the hood of the Mustang, and Beez's brother was still zonked out inside. "Where have you guys been?" Beez had screeched, throwing his hands up in exasperation. "We thought you were right behind us."

I had let Delaney do the explaining. I was too rattled, and too angry with them, to get the words out. But now, in the safe light of day, all I wanted to do was talk to Delaney, to go over every crazy detail of what had happened with Kilgore in the tomb.

Maybe *I* was the one Delaney was mad at—for getting her into such a big mess. She didn't know Kilgore like I did. I had a feeling he was bluffing about calling the police, especially since I had stumbled upon that canteen of his. But Delaney was probably petrified right now, thinking Kilgore might be trying to hunt us down at this very minute.

I stormed back over to the sink and ran the water full blast over the dishes, hoping I could drown out the background noise. The old men were still singing.

> *They put you in a wooden box*
> *and cover you up with dirt and rocks. . . .*

I must have jumped when Lottie blew into the kitchen, carrying a clinking tower of dirty coffee mugs from her office. "Sorry," she said as she unloaded the stack of cups on the counter. "Didn't mean to scare you." Out of the corner of my eye, I could see Lottie crossing her arms and leaning one hip against the counter. I busied myself fishing for a sponge at the bottom of the sink while she stood there assessing me, as if she were still gathering information for her "Linc's Abnormal Behavior Since Junior High Started" file.

"Listen, Linc," she finally said. "This is getting ridiculous. You can't keep up this silent treatment forever."

I stopped fishing for the sponge and stood with my hands submerged in the soapy water, trying to decide how to respond.

The worms crawl in, the worms crawl out.
The worms play pinochle in your snout. . . .

Lottie took a little step toward me, her face softening with concern. "Look at those huge circles under your eyes. Do you think you could be coming down with something?" She reached out to feel my forehead. Before I could catch myself, I dodged her hand, splashing us both with dishwater in the process.

Lottie dropped her arm to her side with a wounded look.

"Sorry," I said, reaching for a dish towel. "But . . . I know I don't have a fever. I feel fine. Really."

"All right, Linc," Lottie answered in a clipped voice. "I give up." Her expression had already gone cold as she brushed past me and went over to sort through the pile of mail on the kitchen table.

I give up too, I thought as I gazed blankly out the window over the sink.

CUT! CUT THE MUSIC! Did you hear that, fellas? He said he's giving up!

Yeah, we heard. Dumb. He's not even a teenager yet, and he sounds like he's ready to move in with us.

Good grief. Wouldn't you think he'd see the resemblance?

What resemblance is that, Winslow?

Well, look at him! Standing there with his mouth zipped, trying to pretend nothing's wrong. Just like his mom.

You gotta hand it to her. She taught him well.

"Okay! Okay!" I said out loud.

Watch it, Tomato Head! You don't have to get huffy. We'll go back to playing dead anytime you're ready. . . .

Lottie was staring at me, a piece of junk mail still clutched in her hand. "Okay, what?" she asked.

I shrugged and gave her a shaky smile. "Okay, I know how much you hate doing dishes. . . . I'll wash," I offered, "if you dry."

We never got done with cleaning the kitchen that afternoon. I decided to unload my biggest secret first—Adeline Raintree—and then work my way around to the rest of my confessions from there. While I scrubbed and rinsed and began to tell about my trip four days earlier to Fulton Lane, Lottie dried and stacked, listening in startled concentration.

But when I got to the part about the box full of letters in the Raintree dining room, my mother dropped her dish towel and went over to the kitchen table to sit down. She leaned over the table in stunned silence, staring at the crumbs scattered between her forearms while I told about the photos tucked in each envelope—Dad's baby pictures, snapshots from his first communion, and graduation day.

Lottie shook her head. "How could Ellen have kept such a secret from your father?" she asked, her voice weak with disbelief. "Even after he was a grown man and completely capable of understanding."

"I guess that was the agreement between the Crenshaws and the Raintrees," I said. "Since Adeline Raintree never wrote back until it was too late, Dad's parents probably didn't know how awful she felt all those years. They probably thought she got married and had more kids of her own . . . and lived happily ever after."

"Looking back now, I should have suspected something," Lottie said, more to herself than to me. "There were little clues here and there. Maybe that's why your father was so intrigued by finding that letter. Maybe he had a feeling."

I nodded. Then I bit my lip. "Lottie, that's not all."

Lottie looked up at me. "What?" she said. "What else could there be?"

"Adeline Raintree thinks Dad's still alive."

Lottie closed her eyes. "You didn't tell her?"

"I couldn't, Lottie. I was kind of . . . in shock, you know? Things just got all mixed up, and she seemed so overjoyed about finally getting to meet us."

"Oh, no," Lottie breathed. "Are you telling me she's over there in that big old house, all by herself, waiting for him to come?" When I nodded again, Lottie sprang up from her chair and began to pace back and forth across the kitchen floor. C.B., who had been sleeping on his dog bed for the last hour, hopped up too and zigzagged across the kitchen, hoping it was time to go outside.

Lottie stopped and frowned down at C.B. panting at her feet. "I don't know if we can take this on right now," she flung out. "I mean, from the sounds of it, she has no other family. And you said there might be some dementia going on?"

"I didn't say she was demented, Lottie. I said she was kind of . . . different."

"I just need to think for a while, Linc," she said, pressing the heels of her hands against her eyelids. "Before we do anything else, I need to think."

After Lottie had retreated back to her office, I stayed at the kitchen table, trying to figure out what to do next. Relief and then worry crept over me like the shivers. I felt ten pounds lighter without the story of Adeline Raintree balled up inside. Lottie had taken the news much better than I'd expected. But now she was starting to get that caged-bird look in her eyes. And I hadn't even begun to tell her the rest of my troubles.

The rest of my troubles. . . . I grabbed C.B.'s leash, and we hurried out the door.

Here Rests in
Honored Glory
An American
Soldier
Known But to God

UNKNOWN SOLDIER
ARLINGTON NATIONAL
CEMETERY, VIRGINIA

CHAPTER 32

JEETER'S LITTLE SHOE BOX of a house was only a couple of miles from ours. I had never been there before, never known where he lived until I had spotted his name and address in Dad's book in the attic. But I could tell I was at the right place as soon as I saw the front yard. His small patch of grass was groomed with the same golf-course precision that he used when he mowed around the tombstones at Oakland. And I had heard all about the cast-off slab of granite perched beside his front stoop. Etched with a picture of a bass and the words GONE FISHIN', it was originally intended to be sitting on top of a grave at Oakland instead of in Jeeter's flower bed. According to Jeeter, the man who commissioned it for his father's plot refused to pay when he realized the fish was a bass instead of a walleye, like he'd ordered. When Jeeter saw the half-finished monument, he shook his head and called it a thing of beauty, and his stone-carver buddy decided to give him the slab right there on the spot.

C.B. pulled on the leash and sniffed at the grass around the Chicago Cubs mailbox—another surefire sign that I had come to the right place. The only hitch was that Jeeter's battered old truck was missing from the gravel parking space. He probably wasn't even home. I let C.B. sniff along the curb for a minute more as I tried to decide whether it was even worth it to go up and knock on the door. Soon we had edged past Jeeter's house, and that's when I heard the sound of hammering drifting through the alleyway.

I found Jeeter in his backyard, inside an old wooden outbuilding. The rickety double doors were propped open, and he was bent over a rough length of board stretched between two sawhorses. Maybe if he hadn't had three nails pressed between his lips, Jeeter would have shown more of a reaction to my unexpected visit. Instead, when he glanced up to find me standing in his doorway, he had a few seconds to compose himself while he slowly reached up to retrieve the nails. "Well, what do you know?" he drawled. "If it isn't the two famous outlaws—Lincoln Log and his canine sidekick, C.B."

"Hey, Jeeter," I said softly. "I didn't think you were here at first. Your truck's not out front."

He reached for the tape measure hanging on his belt and bent over the board again. "I sold it."

"You sold it?" I was shocked. Jeeter had always loved that old truck.

"I got to eat, don't I?" he asked as he scratched a mark on his board with a carpenter's pencil.

I blinked down at the top of his head in dismay, wringing the end of C.B.'s leash until I couldn't hold back anymore. "I'm sorry, Jeeter," I said in a gush of emotion. I could feel the hot sting of tears building up behind my eyes. "I know I'm the one who got you fired. You stuck up for me when Kilgore said I stole that key to the vault. So I wanted to come see you and apologize for everything." Jeeter wasn't looking at me. Without taking his eyes off the pencil mark on his piece of wood, he lifted a circular saw from its perch on a nearby stool. "And I wanted to tell you the truth," I rushed on. "The truth is I didn't deserve you taking up for me. Kilgore was right. I *did* steal that key."

The saw roared to life, making me jump and C.B.'s tail disappear between his legs. The blade bit into the chunk of wood with a hungry shriek. Then, just as quickly, it was quiet again. My ears were still pulsing from the blast of noise when Jeeter said, "I knew you took the key before Kilgore did."

"*You knew?* But how?"

"Didn't exactly take a detective to figure it out, Linc." Jeeter blew the sawdust off his fresh cut of wood and finally raised his gaze to meet mine. "You were in the office an awful long time for somebody who supposedly only needed to use the bathroom real quick. And then when you left, you forgot to switch off the light in the closet where we keep the keys."

I squeezed my eyes shut and slid my hand down the front of my face in embarrassment. "What a heehaw," I said under my breath. "So why didn't you say anything, Jeeter? Why'd you tell Kilgore it wasn't me?"

"I figure everybody's got to make their own mistakes," he said after he had thought for a second. "And I wanted to buy you a little time. I kept thinking the guilt would force you into doing the right thing. Any day now, I thought, Linc's gonna stop by to see me and come clean. But nope, the days kept passing by." He shook his head and stepped around the sawhorses. "I tried giving you a call after Kilgore kicked you out that afternoon, but your mom said you wouldn't come to the phone." He shrugged. "So I decided you'd have to learn your lesson the hard way—from Kilgore, not me."

My shoulders sagged. "I learned the hard way, all right," I said glumly.

Jeeter led me outside to his little quilt square of grass and the crisp afternoon. With C.B. flopped at our feet, we sat in a pair of low wooden chairs next to his barbecue grill, and I told him about my wild night in the tomb—everything from Kilgore planting those deer bones and lying in wait to me sniffing out his secret canteen. "It made him madder than anything when I found it," I said. "You think he's gonna call the police like he threatened?"

"Naw." Jeeter swiped his hand at the air. "He won't report you. He'd be too scared you'd tattle on him for hitting the bottle on cemetery property." Jeeter's jaw tightened as he fixed me with a grave look. "But that doesn't mean you're off the hook."

"What do you mean?"

"I mean you've got to make amends." He pointed his finger at me like a schoolteacher. "This is what you're gonna do. You're gonna let him settle down for a couple more days. Then you're gonna march in there and apologize and offer to do your time working on the grounds. He's shorthanded now and he won't be able to say no . . . that is, till he finds some other poor heehaw to take my place." The beginnings of a chuckle crept into Jeeter's voice. "Plus, he'll *love* playing drill sergeant and bossing you around. Maybe he'll even let you borrow one of his Civil War uniforms." He leaned back in his chair, laughing.

I cut my eyes at Jeeter. Then I leaned back too, accepting my fate with a gloomy nod. He was right. I had messed up and now I had to do my time, even if it meant following orders from Captain Kilgore for a few days. Then another idea popped into my head. "If I work really hard and get him to like me, maybe I'll be able to talk him into giving you your job back."

Jeeter shook his head. All of a sudden I realized his goatee was gone. Without it his chin looked raw, like a Band-Aid had just been ripped away. "Look, Linc," he said, "I been haunting that old cemetery since Old Nicknish gave me my first job straight out of high school. This needed to happen ten years ago. You just helped things along."

"But what will you do instead?"

Jeeter drew himself up, pretending to be offended. "What do you mean, what will I do instead? Didn't you see me working my wonders in that wood shop over there? I'm gonna make furniture."

I glanced over at the sagging toolshed. "Furniture?" I asked, trying not to sound skeptical.

"Yeah. Furniture for the outdoors." Jeeter sat up straight and started talking faster, as if he'd been zapped by a bolt of enthusiasm out of the blue. "I'm real good at hunting down old scrap wood. Then I use it to make stuff that's comfortable and looks like it's been around forever and stands up in any kind of weather. People love it. I just filled my first order."

"Really?"

"Yep, a guy named Gene ordered two chairs for his backyard about a week ago. Now he's telling all his friends."

I smiled and looked down at the wide armrests of my chair, at the traces of barn-red paint buried in the grain. "Wow," I said, letting my body go loose against the sturdy, sunbaked wood. "That Gene, whoever he is, sounds like a real good guy."

The Stone the Builders
Rejected

JACK LONDON
GLEN ELLEN, CALIFORNIA

CHAPTER 33

DELANEY WASN'T AT HER LOCKER the next morning. Before the bell rang for first period, I scanned the clogged hallways, anxiously hoping to catch sight of her. Then I rushed back to my own locker, thinking she might show up there. I found Mellecker waiting for me instead. He was leaning against the door to the janitor's closet nearby with his hands shoved in his pockets in his usual relaxed way, but I could tell he felt out of place. He wasn't used to waiting around for people.

"Hey," he said as he ambled over. "How's it goin'?"

I didn't answer. "Have you seen Delaney?"

"Not yet." He pulled his hands from his pockets. "I haven't seen her since Friday night, when we dropped her off." He started to grin a little. "Man, on the way home she was telling us more about that Kilgore creep. How he was boozing it up in the vault, waiting for you. That must have been intense."

I opened my locker and reached for my French book. "Yeah, it was. It would have been a lot *less* intense if there had been four of us instead of two."

Mellecker's gaze slid away. "I know." He sighed. "I should have gone back to check on you two as soon as I realized you weren't right behind us." He shrugged with an uneasy little chuckle. "But you know how Beez is. I told him we should go back, but he kept saying you and Delaney probably just wanted to be alone."

From the disgusted look on my face, Mellecker must have known I wasn't buying it. But I couldn't resist making sure. "Oh, yeah?" I said as I banged my locker shut. "Since when did you start taking orders from Beez?"

I started to walk away, but Mellecker snagged my arm. "You know, I remembered something this weekend," he said when I turned around. "About when we were both at that Ho-Ho school." He hesitated, a bashful look creeping over his face. "You were always in the lead back then. Even when we would tie ourselves together and climb up that stupid dirt pile, you always went first. And then there was that time we pretended I fell in a crevasse, and I started dragging you down, and I remember asking you if you would ever cut the rope. You know what you said?"

I nodded. "Yep. I remember. I said I'd never do that to anybody."

"Yeah, that was it," Mellecker said. "I wish I had thought of that earlier, when we were in the graveyard."

Then he went off down the hallway before I could think of what to say. I didn't see him again until lunchtime, when

Beez nabbed me in the sloppy joe line and dragged me over to their table. Mellecker was in his usual spot. When I glanced down the table, I noticed a few other kids were looking up at me with expectant faces. Beez must have been bragging about our exploits in Oakland Cemetery, and now I was supposed to entertain everybody with more stories.

Beez slid along the bench and nodded to the space beside him. "Have a seat, Crenshaw. Everybody wants to hear what happened on Friday night." He was already digging into his sloppy joe.

I stood there holding my tray with a snide answer lodged in my throat like gristle. *Oh, which part do they want to hear? The part where you screamed like a baby when you saw a pile of old deer bones? Or the part where you ran off like a rat and deserted us?*

I looked down at Mellecker. Our eyes met for a quick second, and that's all it took to make me hold my tongue.

"Has anybody seen Delaney Baldwin today?" I asked in a loud voice. The kids at the other end of the table looked up and shrugged.

Amy was sitting a few spots away. Apparently she was still offended because she hadn't been invited to come along Friday night. "Delaney's not here today," she snapped. "Taylor lives next door to her, and she said Delaney's mom went in the hospital this weekend."

"*What?*" I asked. My voice rose above the drone of the cafeteria. "What happened?"

Amy was reaching inside her purse, fishing for something. "I guess she was supposed to have a baby in a couple weeks, but something went wrong." She turned to the girl beside her. "Ewww, I'd be totally grossed out if my mom got pregnant now, wouldn't you?"

The noisy cafeteria tilted, then shifted out of focus for a second. I set my tray next to Beez and hurried over to Amy so I could hear. Amy had pulled a tube of lip gloss out of her purse. "What do you mean, something went wrong?" I demanded. "Are they okay? I mean, Delaney's mom . . . and the baby?"

Amy stopped with the lip gloss halfway to her mouth. She stared up at me, her expression as blank as a china doll's. "I don't know," she said. "Taylor didn't say."

I spun around and veered toward the exit door.

"Hey, Crenshaw. You're leaving already?" Beez yelled after me. "Can I have your sloppy joe?"

Oh, little Lavina she has gone
To James and Charles
and Eliza Ann.
Arm in arm they walk above
Singing the Redeemer's love.

NEWFANE, VERMONT

CHAPTER 34

LOTTIE WAS RUNNING OUT OF PATIENCE. "Linc, you're not making sense," she insisted. "How could it be your fault that your friend's mother might lose her baby?"

I closed my eyes in frustration. I had finally poured out the whole story about Friday night—*all of it!*—and Lottie still didn't understand. "Don't you see?" I asked. "I let Delaney do it. I just stood there and watched while she climbed up and kissed the Black Angel's hand. With everything I know about the statue now, and that weird epitaph—'Suffering awaits you'—why didn't I stop her? Why'd I ever let her come with us in the first place?"

I flopped back, miserable, in my mother's chair. Lottie had come home from work to find me hunched over the phone at the desk in her office. I had already tried calling the maternity ward at the university hospital twice, but the crabby nurse on the other end wouldn't tell me anything. She said if I wasn't related to Mrs. Baldwin, she couldn't give me any specific information.

"Well, if you see her daughter," I had pleaded, "can you tell her to call Linc? I'm a really good friend of hers."

The nurse had sighed into the phone. "I have no idea who you're referring to, young man. And we're awfully short-handed here today. It won't do your friend a bit of good for you to keep calling and taking up our time."

Now Lottie was sitting in my usual spot, the old swivel chair, and it squeaked as she rolled closer. "Linc, I understand how concerned you must be," she said, carefully choosing each word. "But it's *you* I'm worried about. You're not sounding too rational at the moment. Actually, from everything you've told me, it sounds like you went off the deep end about two weeks ago. I mean, you *stole* a key right under Jeeter's nose and broke into a vault? And then you get caught by the warden, who sounds like a complete maniac? Really, Linc. How did this get so out of hand?" Somehow Lottie had managed to keep her voice calm as she spoke, but her gray eyes were wide and frightened.

I slumped lower, shaking my head. "I know. I know," I said hoarsely. "It sounds crazy. And I know you think junior high's the reason I've done all of this stuff. And sure, maybe I did some of it to try to fit in. But I'm smarter now. I've learned a lot. . . . More than I ever would have learned if I had stayed with the Ho-Hos."

"Maybe so," Lottie murmured. But then her brow furrowed

again. "But what are we going to do about this Kilgore person? He's threatened you more than once, and he may be drinking on the job. I feel like I should call the police, or at the very least go over there and have a talk with him."

I sat up in alarm. "No, Mom, you can't! I'm the one who has to fix this. Jeeter told me what I have to do to make things right with Kilgore. And I'm going to do it . . . but first I have to find out if Delaney's okay."

I stared over Lottie's shoulder at her wall full of gravestone rubbings—all those hazy rows of epitaphs—and suddenly another awful thought popped into my head. "What if . . . what if Mrs. Baldwin woke up that night and realized Delaney was gone and got scared?" I said out loud. "What if that's what caused her to lose the baby?"

Lottie's face turned stern. "Stop it, Linc."

"I can't help it," I said weakly. "If something bad happens, I'll always feel like it was my fault." I leaned my elbows on Lottie's cluttered desk and dropped my face into my hands. I didn't look up, even when I heard the *click-click* of C.B.'s toenails on the hardwood floor.

"Oh, brother," Lottie said in a tired voice. "The dogs. You haven't been over to Mr. Krasny's to walk Spunky yet, have you?"

I shook my head with my face still buried in my hands. I needed to stay by the phone in case Delaney called.

"I'll go," I heard Lottie say.

I spread my fingers like fence pickets and peeked through. "You will?"

"Yes." She rocked up to her feet. "Come on, C.B."

After they were gone, I folded my arms into a bony pillow and laid my head down, right on top of all of Lottie's papers and sticky notes and eraser dust. If I closed my eyes, just for a little while, maybe the phone would ring.

"Tomorrow to fresh woods, and pastures new"

RICHMOND, VIRGINIA

CHAPTER 35

WHEN DELANEY WASN'T AT SCHOOL the next day either, I decided my worst fears had come true. I couldn't imagine how I would ever face her again. How could I have done it—talked her into sneaking out of her house in the middle of the night, even when I knew it was such a risky time for her mom? The afternoon dragged on, and I moved through the crowded hallways like a ghost, feeling haunted and invisible. I had to keep passing Delaney's locker on my way to class, but I didn't even bother glancing in that direction anymore. I kept my eyes on the clock at the end of the hall, watching the little hand slowly inch its way to the magic number three.

At first I thought I was imagining things after seventh period, when I heard her call out my name. But nobody else said my name that way—Lanc instead of Linc—and when I whipped around, there she was, standing by her locker with a stack of books in her arms. I dodged around a huddle of kids and pushed my way toward her. "You're here!" was the only thing I could manage to say. Then my heart dropped. She looked terrible. Her skin was as pale as chalk, except for the dark shadows under her eyes.

"I came to get my homework," Delaney said. "I called your house this morning and talked to your mother, but you'd already left for school."

I swallowed, trying to loosen the knot of worry in my throat. "Is . . . everything okay?" I asked, bracing myself for the answer.

Delaney nudged the door of her locker open wider with her elbow and stepped out of the way so I could see her calendar hanging inside. It was flipped to November, and in the clean square of space under Saturday the second, Delaney had written in black pen:

Eleanor Marie Baldwin

Born 8:35 p.m., 5 lbs., 5 oz.

"So the baby's fine?" I blurted out. "It's a girl?"

Delaney nodded, and her tired face began to glow with a smile. "We're going to call her Ellie. Isn't that sweet? Even though she's tiny, she's awful strong." Delaney took one more look at the second of November's square before she pushed the locker shut.

"Mama's the one we've had to worry about," she told me as we started down the hall. "I've never been so scared. She fainted in the kitchen on Saturday afternoon, and we had to call an ambulance. The doctors were real worried about her blood pressure, and they had her hooked up to all sorts of monitors and kept calling in different specialists.

Then finally they decided to operate and deliver Ellie that night."

Delaney said her mother had started feeling better this afternoon, feisty enough to order her and her dad to go take showers at home and bring her back some chocolate pudding and gossip magazines.

I walked Delaney out to the front entrance of Plainview. "My imagination sort of ran away with me when you didn't call or show up at school," I admitted as we pushed through the heavy front doors. I tried to laugh. "I kept thinking about that curse, and how if anything bad happened, it would be all my fault."

Delaney stopped underneath the flagpole. "I'm sorry," she said, her eyes welling up with sympathy. "I should have called you sooner. I completely lost track of time." Then she started to smile. "But see? I had a feeling about that statue the first minute I laid eyes on her. I thought . . . this is just a guardian angel in disguise. And now with Ellie, you've got living proof."

I nodded, even though I felt a twist of doubt deep in my chest. The Black Angel's epitaph still bothered me, but there was no way I could share my worries about its frightening prophecy with Delaney anytime soon.

"There's Daddy," Delaney said, waving at a man who sat in the blue Ford idling by the curb. "I would introduce you, but we better be getting back to the hospital."

There were at least five more things I wanted to say swirling around in my head—mainly how much I was hoping the new baby meant her parents wouldn't want to move for a while. But I decided to keep it short. "I'm really happy for you," I told her. Delaney looked like she wanted to hug me. But since her arms were full of books, she kissed me on the cheek instead, right there with her dad watching. I was so surprised, I didn't even remember to say goodbye.

I was still thinking about that kiss when I walked to the bus stop a few minutes later. I didn't even notice Lottie's car until she had rattled up next to me and honked the horn. It took her a few extra seconds to crank the stubborn window down. "Hi there," she said brightly.

I squinted at her in confusion. "What are you doing here? You never pick me up at school."

"Get in," she said. "There's somebody we've got to go see."

"Who?" I asked warily.

Lottie paused and drew in a shaky breath.

"Listen, Lottie," I said. "I already told you I can handle Kilgore on my own."

"Not Kilgore, Linc. We're going to see your grandmother."

... If I take the wings
of morning
and
dwell in the uttermost
parts of the sea ...

ANNE AND CHARLES LINDBERGH
KIPAHULU, MAUI, HAWAII

CHAPTER 36

I ONLY HAD TO PUSH the buzzer once this time before Adeline Raintree opened her tall front door. I blinked in surprise. She was wearing a dress today—belted around her thin middle and printed with old-fashioned sprigs of flowers—and she had tucked her limp hair behind her ears with bobby pins. It was as if she had been waiting there, just inside the shadowy entrance hall, ever since I had hurried off nearly a week ago, promising to return soon. Her face lit up when she saw me, making me realize this was the first time I had seen her smile. It was a little kid's smile, nothing but happy and innocent. Then it faded as she glanced uncertainly at Lottie and peered past our shoulders, searching the long walkway for Dad.

Lottie reached out to shake her hand. "I'm Linc's mother, Charlotte Landers."

Miss Raintree's fingers were trembling as she slowly lifted her hand to grasp Lottie's. "You're my son's wife?" she asked.

Lottie faltered. "Yes, I am. . . . I mean, I *was*, but—"

Miss Raintree didn't let her finish. "Lincoln, why don't you take your mother around back to the garden?" she said in a rush. "I wanted to serve tea there. This might be our last fine day before the cold sets in."

I hesitated. She wanted to serve us *tea*? *Right now*? But Lottie was quick to fill up the silence. "That sounds lovely," she said. "May I help you?"

"Oh, no," Miss Raintree told her. "Everything's ready. I only have to put the kettle on. I'll meet you in the garden in a few minutes."

As she disappeared inside, Lottie and I made our way to the so-called garden and found seats at an old wrought-iron table next to the dried-out sunflower patch. The sun was shining, but a cold breeze rattled through the stalks, and we perched on our rusted chairs hunching our shoulders against the chill. I followed Lottie's gaze around the remnants of the flower beds. An old rose arbor nearby leaned sideways under a brown tangle of vines. You could tell the yard must have been pretty once, before the years of neglect had taken hold.

"Doesn't this seem like kind of a weird time to have a tea party?" I half whispered. "I mean, she can see Dad's not coming. And it's freezing out here."

"She must have been planning this reunion for years," Lottie said sadly. Her gaze drifted up to the top stories of the house and down again. "She probably imagined herself sitting out here with her son, sorting out the past over cups of tea."

I squirmed on the edge of my chair. "We've got to tell her right away."

Lottie nodded. "I'll do it," she said firmly. "As soon as she comes out." We both stared across the overgrown lawn toward the back stoop, nervously waiting. When a few minutes more had passed and Miss Raintree still didn't appear, Lottie pushed herself to her feet. "I'm getting worried," she said. "We'd better go see if everything's all right."

We could hear the shrill whistle of a teakettle even before we stepped through the back door. It was boiling away on a huge iron stove in the dingy kitchen, steam hissing and screaming from its spout, and there was a tall silver teapot waiting on a polished tray next to the stove. But Miss Raintree was nowhere in sight.

Lottie shot me a frightened look. "Hello?" she called out. "Miss Raintree?" Lottie found a frayed dishcloth amid the clutter. She pulled the noisy kettle from the burner and turned off the flame. Then we stood like statues for a few seconds, listening for clues in the sudden flood of silence.

"We should go look for her," Lottie whispered. I nodded and led the way through the narrow pantry that connected the kitchen to the rest of the house. We didn't have to search very far. We found Miss Raintree sitting at the head of the long dining room table, bent over her wooden box full of letters. She barely looked up when we entered the room.

"Miss Raintree?" Lottie said softly. "Adeline? Are you all right?"

She slowly raised her head. A dusty shaft of sun from the far window lit up the sorrow in her face. "He's not coming, is he?" she said. "My son."

"No, he's not," Lottie told her.

I wanted to move, to help somehow. But all I could do was watch, rooted like a stump, as my mother went over to sit at the table. I saw the sad lines in Miss Raintree's face deepen as Lottie carefully explained what had happened five years ago.

"Just like Papa," Miss Raintree whispered. Her eyes shimmered, and as the tears began to spill down her cheeks, I was wishing for an excuse to turn away. Maybe I could go get her that cup of tea from the kitchen . . . or a box of Kleenex . . . anything.

But there was something that held me there, something haunting and familiar about the way she bowed her head. Then all at once I remembered where I had seen that exact same expression before—frozen in bronze on the Black Angel. And I thought of Delaney hoisting herself up to kiss the Angel's broken hand with hardly a second of doubt. She—and her mother too—had decided to take a chance and stare sadness straight in the eye. And now they had a new member of their family to show for it.

I found myself walking toward the table. As I slid into the chair across from Lottie, Miss Raintree looked up at me in a fog. "I'm sorry," I began. "I'm sorry I ran off the other day without telling you what happened to Dad."

I could see her face starting to crumple again. "I guess I got overwhelmed," I tried to explain. "It was so hard to believe—that you might be my real grandmother, and all this time you've been living just a few miles away." I stole a look at Lottie. She gave me a tiny nod, urging me on.

"But now that I've had time to think," I said, leaning

across the table, "I was wondering . . . I mean . . . do you think we could start where we left off? With the letters? I've always wanted to know what Dad was like when he was my age."

As Miss Raintree carefully reached for the box, like she must have done a hundred times over the last forty-five years, I thought I saw the haze begin to clear from her eyes. We spent the rest of the afternoon poring over Ellen Crenshaw's letters and snapshots, passing them around our small triangle. Every so often I would read an interesting line or two out loud. "Lincoln came down with a terrible case of chicken pox this week, and today he insisted that we count them," I read, making a face. "Now he's feeling quite proud of himself. Fifty-seven spots in all."

Lottie nodded knowingly. "That must have been when he got that little scar on his forehead." Out of the corner of my eye, I could see Miss Raintree listening, hoarding each new detail we mentioned like gold.

She even noticed a smile flit across my face when I read a letter about company coming to the Crenshaws' for Sunday dinner and Dad getting into trouble for hiding food in his napkin. "What is it?" she asked eagerly. "What's funny?"

"Dad hated broccoli just as much as I do," I told her, feeling strangely satisfied.

A dozen letters later Lottie was exclaiming, "*What?* Lincoln was voted prom king? He never told me that!"

"Yes," Miss Raintree confirmed with a proud lift of her chin. "Prom King of Verona High School, 1982."

Lottie and I couldn't help snickering a little. But the next time I looked over, my mother had started to cry. "What's wrong?" I whispered. She didn't answer. I glanced at the neat cursive script on the piece of stationery in her hand. Then I understood. She was reading the letter I had just finished— one Ellen Crenshaw had sent right after Dad left for college. It described how much she missed him, how any minute she expected to hear him come clomping up the front porch stairs.

"Shall we put the letters away for now?" Miss Raintree suggested in a small voice.

"Oh, no," Lottie said through her tears. "Not yet." She blinked at the two of us in astonishment. "I almost forgot what a relief it is to cry."

I KNEW THIS
WOULD HAPPEN

TEMPLE, TEXAS

CHAPTER 37

LOTTIE INSISTED ON COMING WITH ME after school the next day to face Kilgore. She stood silently near the doorway with her arms crossed while I babbled out an apology and offered to serve my time working on the cemetery grounds.

Kilgore never smirked or interrupted once as he sat behind his desk hearing me out. He waited for me to finish, his pointer fingers propped like a church steeple under his sharp chin. Obviously my mother's presence had startled him into acting professional for a change. He must have known I had told her about the canteen in the vault. His gaze kept darting in her direction as he decided how to respond to my proposal.

"Well, I sure appreciate you and your mother coming by to set things straight," he said, his voice as slick as oil. Lottie didn't make a sound behind me. "How many hours are you offering to work?"

I clenched my arms tight to my sides. I had known this was coming. "That's up to you, I guess," I said guardedly. "Whatever you think is fair."

He tapped his fingertips together. "Let's see," he considered, plainly beginning to enjoy himself. "I'd say eighty hours would about do it."

Eighty? I almost choked. It would take weeks to work off all that time. As if he could read my mind, Kilgore added, "If the snow starts falling early like last year, there might not be as much work for you to do around here. But that's okay." He allowed himself a hard little smile. "Whatever time you don't finish this fall, you can make up in the spring."

Already I felt weary at the thought of spending all those hours under Kilgore's thumb—whole seasons of following his orders, waiting for him to snap like a rubber band pulled too tight.

"When do you want to start?" Kilgore asked.

I let out a deep sigh. "Tomorrow?"

"Fine." Kilgore scrubbed his hand across his mouth as if he were trying to wipe off another smile.

Then I heard the swish of Lottie's long patchwork skirt, and suddenly she was there beside me. "I'll make sure that Linc keeps a time sheet of his hours," she said. "And since we live right next to the graveyard and I work from home quite a bit"—she seemed to be lingering over each syllable, carefully enunciating, until somehow her words of reassurance shifted into a warning—"it will be very easy for me to keep a close watch on *exactly* what he's up to over here."

A long second passed. I could almost hear what Kilgore

was thinking as he sat there measuring up my tiny mom with her mop of streaky hair and secondhand-shop clothes. *What a kook.* But something in the way Lottie raised one eyebrow and fixed Kilgore in her steely stare must have made him decide to watch his step.

"Yes, ma'am," he finally said.

That's what got me through those cold November afternoons working in the cemetery. Whenever my hands turned numb on the rake and Kilgore zoomed up in his golf cart to point out another tiny pile of oak leaves I had missed in the fading light, I would smile to myself, remembering how scared he had sounded as my mother stared him down. "Yes, ma'am," he had practically mumbled, like a kid in the principal's office.

Meanwhile, our Adopt-a-Grave Projects were due in the middle of November. I took two days off Kilgore duty so I could rush to the historical society after school and search for more clues about the Black Angel. It was always dark by the time I finally got around to taking the dogs for a quick run. But Mr. Krasny seemed to understand. One night he even invited me to stay for dinner. He made us something called *lívance*—Czech pancakes—and after dinner I showed him what I had found on my latest trip to the society. We didn't even realize another hour had passed until Lottie came to rap on Mr. Krasny's front door and order me home to bed.

I was so tired those afternoons working in the cemetery. Some days I did my own version of Civil War reenacting, pretending I was a downtrodden soldier in the winter campaign of 1863 as I swept out the toolshed or pushed wheelbarrows full of mulch. When Kilgore showed up to fire out more orders, I pretended he was an evil army captain all the troops hated, and I made up mean nicknames for him under my breath. Killer Kilgore. Hatchet Face. Old Smokey. Captain Killjoy.

But the main thing that kept me content as I whittled away at my eighty hours was the thought that from now on I could wander into the cemetery and visit Dad's grave whenever I felt like it, without worrying about Kilgore or anything else keeping me out. I had earned the right.

THE BEST IS
YET TO COME

FRANK SINATRA
CATHEDRAL CITY, CALIFORNIA

CHAPTER 38

ON A BRIGHT SATURDAY, just before our Adopt-a-Grave Projects were due, I organized my very own field trip to Oakland so Delaney and I could practice our reports in front of a handpicked audience. Kilgore happened to be standing outside the workshop when we drove into the parking lot. He watched our weird little flock with narrowed eyes—me, Lottie, Delaney, Mr. Krasny, and Adeline Raintree, bundled in coats and hats, gloves and boots and galoshes, pouring out of my mother's old car. I was wearing my brand-new running shoes. I was only supposed to use them for training, but I hadn't been able to resist putting them on that morning. They were bright red and white—Plainview's colors—and they made me feel like I had springs in my feet.

Kilgore took a few steps into the parking lot as I hurried around to open Lottie's trunk. We had brought along Mr.

Krasny's wheelchair so he wouldn't get too tired on our expedition. "What's going on?" Kilgore called out. "You coming to work today?"

"Not today," I called back cheerfully. "We're just here to pay our respects." I hoisted the wheelchair out and slammed the trunk closed, trying not to laugh as I caught Delaney's eye. The gravel crunched behind me, and I turned around to find Jeeter rattling up on a rusted bicycle. Looking over Jeeter's shoulder, I could see Kilgore gawking in disbelief, deliberating whether he should come over to investigate.

"You made it." I grinned.

"'Course I did," Jeeter huffed as he lodged his front tire in the bike rack nearby. "You think I'd miss a chance to hear the real story of the Black Angel?" He turned to greet the others gathered beside the car. "Ladies," he said with a gentlemanly nod. "Nice to see you again, sir," he said to Mr. Krasny. Then he lifted his arm to wave at Kilgore. "Mornin'. How you been?"

Kilgore didn't answer. He clamped his jaw shut and, with a disgusted shake of his head, retreated into the office. Jeeter let out a satisfied little chuckle. After he had given Lottie a hug, I introduced Jeeter to Adeline Raintree. He cocked his head in surprise when he heard me say "grandmother." The word still felt foreign on my tongue.

"You're Linc's grandmother?" Jeeter repeated in confusion. His gaze raked over her old wool coat with its missing buttons, and he glanced at me for an uncertain second. But something in my expression must have made him know he didn't need to ask any more questions. His shoulders lifted in a tiny shrug. "Well, it's real good to meet you, Miz Raintree," he said, reaching out to clasp her hand.

She honored him with one of her rare, delighted smiles. "Addie," she said, looking around at the rest of us. "Please. I'd like you all to call me Addie. That was Papa's pet name for me and I've always preferred it to Adeline."

Everyone nodded. I helped Mr. Krasny get settled in his wheelchair with a blanket over his knees. Then we set out under the cold sunshine, slowly making our way in what was probably the most ragtag procession to ever wander through Oakland Cemetery.

As it turned out, we had a lot of stops to make. Mr. Krasny wanted to show us his wife's grave. I rolled him right across the browning grass so he could kiss his fingertips and rest them on top of the headstone for a minute.

Then Delaney wanted to pay a quick visit to Babyland.

"This won't take long," she said, opening the squeaky gate and slipping inside. We all gathered along the wrought-iron fence to watch as she unzipped the top of her large satchel and, like a magician, pulled out a huge store-bought bunch of miniature daisies. Once she had worked the rubber band off the stems, she quickly filed along the rows, leaning down to leave a single daisy on each small grave until the bouquet was almost gone.

"Thank goodness," Delaney breathed, hurrying back to us with a relieved smile. She tucked the last of her daisies into her satchel. "I was afraid I'd run out."

"A flower for each one," Addie marveled, looking over those bright flashes of white scattered across the dry ground.

"I have a new baby sister," Delaney explained. "I just wanted to do something special in her honor."

Addie seemed curious to hear more, so Delaney told her every last detail about Ellie on our way to Robert Raintree's grave—down to how many times she had smiled so far. It was funny. Even though we were making rounds through a grave-yard, everyone's mood couldn't help but stay light with all that talk about how often babies need to eat and burp and have their diapers changed.

Under the giant oak we gathered around Professor Rain-tree's tombstone. Delaney took out her notes and launched into her report, and I had to keep reminding myself, *This is my great-grandfather she's talking about.* As Delaney described the highlights of Robert Raintree's law career, I couldn't resist glancing over at Addie. She was mesmerized, savoring every word.

When Delaney was finished, we gave her a round of ap-plause. "Thanks, y'all," she said. Then she turned shyly to Addie. "But did I leave anything out?"

Addie clasped her hands together. "It would be impossible to tell everything about Papa in a single report. I've often thought someone should write a book about him." Then it was her turn to dive into details. Jeeter rocked on his heels and exchanged a patient smile with Lottie as Addie described how my great-grandfather had worked his way through col-lege delivering milk from the back of a horse-drawn wagon, how he had given only two A's during his entire time teaching at the law school, how he had sung baritone in the university's faculty choir. . . . Delaney pulled a pencil from her satchel and took notes.

"And," Addie concluded as she stepped closer to his headstone, "he adored sunflowers." She stared at the blank patch of ground where her bouquets usually sat. "If only my garden could bloom all winter long."

"Here," Delaney said, reaching into her satchel again. "If you'd like, I have a few daisies left."

Addie paused. Then she accepted the limp flowers with a grateful nod. "Thank you," she said as she bent down to arrange them carefully at the base of the headstone. "Come to think of it, Papa would probably appreciate a little variety now and then."

Lottie crouched next to her to examine the stone. "This carving of a torch," she said. "It's quite unusual. Do you remember anything about how your family chose this particular design?" I pressed my lips together to keep from looking smug. I'd been wondering how long Lottie could last without reverting to her professor mode.

Addie frowned as she stood up, as if the memory still pained her. "It was Mother who chose it. Since I was the only child in the family and a daughter, she wanted an upside-down torch for Papa's memorial to symbolize his death and the end of the Raintree line." She paused. "But I refused to accept that idea."

We all blinked at the sudden rise in Addie's voice. Jeeter stopped fidgeting. Then Addie turned to look at me, her eyes shiny with determination. "Even after I had given in and agreed to let the Crenshaws take my son, I knew it wouldn't be the end of the Raintrees. I went to see the stonemason myself and tried to convince him to make a few changes. In the end, he compromised and carved the torch lying on its side."

"With the flame still burning," I murmured.

A triumphant smile crept over Addie's face. "Exactly," she said.

I had always felt kind of embarrassed about my middle name. I mean, who wants a weird middle name like Raintree? But finally it made sense and felt right—just like it felt right for all of us to move on to Dad's wall. I let Jeeter push Mr. Krasny's wheelchair, and I felt a calm seep over me as I led the way. Once we were there, Lottie guided Addie closer to see the spot where Dad's name was etched in the black granite. Addie didn't cry. She just stared for a long, peaceful minute, leaning on Lottie's arm.

When no one was looking, Lottie pressed something into my hand. It was Dad's watch, ticking away with an extra hole in the strap. "Thank you, Lottie," I whispered as I fastened the watch around my wrist. It fit me perfectly now.

Jeeter was standing with his hands on his hips, squinting up at the names on Dad's wall. "Your father's got some great next-door neighbors," he blurted out.

"Excuse me?" I said, wondering if I had heard him right.

"Well, I knew a few of these folks from around town." Jeeter walked farther down the wall. "And so far I don't see a single one I didn't like."

I shook my head. "You're crazy, Jeeter."

"Good neighbors are important," Mr. Krasny chimed in, and I smiled to myself, thinking of the grumpy old men in their plots under my bedroom window, resting in peace at last.

The Black Angel was the last stop on our graveyard tour. I hadn't exactly planned for my report to be the grand finale of our field trip, so I felt a little unsteady as everybody assembled around the statue, watching me fumble for the pages of notes folded in my coat pocket.

Of course, having Lottie there made me extra nervous. I knew she had been biting her tongue for the past month, resisting the urge to ask too many questions about my research or dole out directions whenever she saw me floundering. But now I could see how eager she was to hear my results. She stood off to the side, smiling with anticipation.

I smoothed the creases from my sheets of paper and let out a jittery breath of air. "Today I'd like to tell you the *true* story of the Black Angel," I announced. "The story begins with a mysterious woman named Theresa Dolezal Feldevert."

Jeeter was watching me with his eyes wide, like a kid at the movies. All he needed was a bucket of popcorn.

"Theresa was born in 1836 in the small village of Strmilov, Bohemia. But like the date of her death missing from this stone," I continued, turning to point at the dates carved on the front of the statue's pedestal, "her life has always been shrouded in sadness and superstition—*until now*." I paused for effect, just like I had planned.

"I started this project thinking the superstitions were ridiculous. How could a silly statue be a messenger of doom? But I have to admit, the more I learned about Theresa Feldevert, the more I couldn't help believing there might really be a curse linked to her name."

To prove my point, I spilled out the list of tragic events in Theresa's life, beginning with the fire that destroyed her family's village and ending with the death of her rancher husband in Oregon. "She returned to Iowa, frail and crippled," I said dramatically, "but determined to build a magnificent memorial to honor those she had lost."

I glanced over at Mr. Krasny, who was hunched in his wheelchair, listening intently. He looked like a wise old gnome with his stocking cap perched on the top of his mostly bald head. "I might still be convinced that the Curse was real," I confessed with a smile, "if it hadn't been for my neighbor, Mr. Martin Krasny. Mr. Krasny actually remembers seeing old Widow Feldevert near this very spot when he was a little boy."

When the others turned surprised looks in Mr. Krasny's direction, he elbowed himself up in his wheelchair. "It's true," he murmured.

"But the real key to solving the mystery," I announced, "is the fact that Mr. Krasny also happens to speak Czech— Theresa's native language."

"Only a little," Mr. Krasny corrected, trying to brush away the attention with a swipe of his crooked hand.

"Enough to help me figure out what Theresa was really like," I said flatly. "See, Mr. Krasny's father was Czech too, and he wrote articles for a Czech newspaper that used to be published for all the Czech immigrants in town. Turns out Mr. Krasny still has copies of those old newspapers, and when he found out about the project I was working on, he started combing through the pages, looking for clues. Just like Sherlock Holmes."

The sun glinted off Mr. Krasny's glasses as he chuckled and shook his head.

"No, really," I went on. "He searched every inch of those papers—even the advertisements. And that's where he found the answer to one of the main questions that had been bugging me about Theresa from the beginning. I kept wondering how she earned a living before she met her second husband. She and her son Eddie were all alone when they first came to this country. So how'd she get money to buy food and pay rent all those years?"

I waited an extra beat, stretching out the suspense for as long as possible.

"Well?" Delaney said with an exasperated laugh rising in her throat. "Tell us."

I looked down at my page of notes. "I'll read you the translation of the advertisement that Mr. Krasny found: 'Terezií Dolezal, an experienced midwife from the Vienna Clinic, has settled in Iowa City and will assist everyone perfectly with deliveries and asks for the favor of all in town as well as in the countryside.'"

Delaney let out a gasp. "She was a midwife? That's amazing." Her gaze drifted up to the Angel over my shoulder, and I knew she was thinking back to our night in the cemetery, when she had followed her crazy urge to climb up and kiss the statue's hand. Ellie was born the very next evening.

Suddenly Lottie was chiming in, her voice cool and analytical. "Interesting. But is that the only piece of information that persuaded you to give up on the idea of a curse? In the old days, midwifery was often associated with witchcraft, you know."

Lottie lifted one eyebrow. I could tell she was teasing but testing me at the same time, as if I were one of her students at the university. Jeeter was waiting to hear my answer, looking more spooked than ever.

"The ad's just the beginning," I said in a rush. "Remember how I said Mr. Krasny ran into the widow once, here in the cemetery, when he was little? He thinks he was about six years old when that happened, so it must have been sometime around 1923. From her birth date listed on the monument, I figured Theresa would have been about eighty-seven then—close to the end of her life. So I used that date to help narrow down my search for her obituary in the old newspapers at the historical society."

Lottie was nodding her approval, and I found myself talking faster, gesturing with my hands. "I started with the 1923 papers on microfilm," I breezed on excitedly, "and worked from there. It didn't take too long for me to find a newspaper story about Theresa's death in 1924. The article said that Theresa had ordered the statue to go up in Oakland several years earlier, and she had arranged to have the ashes of her son Eddie and her husband Nicholas moved to this location. And the obituary said she was going to be cremated and buried beside them, right here in the shadow of the Angel." I tapped the hard ground with my toe.

Jeeter interrupted me. "Then why isn't her death date carved on the stone?"

I shrugged. "I think the stonemason must have forgotten. He had a bigger carving job to worry about. But I'll get to that in a second."

I pulled my shoulders back and kept going. "So once I had a death date, Ms. Beckett at the society helped me track down a copy of Theresa's will in the old records. That's how I found out what she did with all the money she inherited from her husband out in Oregon."

I looked around at everyone's expectant faces. "Theresa left most of her money to her village back in Bohemia. She wanted it to be used for building a children's hospital."

Delaney gave a little hop in place. *"See?"*

"Yep," I said to Delaney. "You were right all along. Theresa wasn't evil. She was only heartbroken. I guess she probably wanted to build a children's hospital because of the way she lost her two sons when they were so young."

I could see Addie's eyes turning misty with understanding. Until that minute I hadn't really thought about how much they had in common. Just like Theresa, Addie had spent her whole life grieving over the loss of a son, waiting for the day when she could make things right somehow.

"And there was one last thing in the will," I revealed.

"I found the Czech epitaph that Theresa wanted the stonecutter to engrave on the base of the Angel when she died."

I paused and added sheepishly, "Turns out the inscription was a little different from what I copied off the statue when I started this whole thing. Some of the words had faded over the years, so the first version I gave to Mr. Krasny to translate was missing some important phrases."

I glanced over at Lottie, expecting to see an I-told-you-so smirk stamped across her face. But she wasn't gloating in the least. She actually looked kind of impressed.

Then I walked toward Mr. Krasny, handing him my page full of notes, where I had carefully copied down his most recent translation. "Will you read the real inscription out loud for us, Mr. Krasny? Since you're the one who did most of the work?"

With a satisfied nod, Mr. Krasny carefully adjusted his glasses and cleared his throat. I had never heard him speak in such a slow, solemn voice:

> *For me, the clouds concealed the sun. The path*
> *was thorny.*
> *The days of my life passed without comfort.*
> *I always accomplished my work for the good of*
> *the world.*
> *I fold my arms and bow my head, but my spirit*
> *flies away into the distance.*
> *Suffering is over. An eternal reward awaits you.*

There was a small moment of quiet as everyone stared up at the Angel and let the meaning of the words settle in. Lottie was the first one to break the silence. "Well, in that case . . . ," she said, stepping over to join me at the base of the statue. At first I thought she wanted to give me a big hug of congratulations. But she just smiled and brushed past me, and then, standing on her tiptoes, Professor Charlotte Landers, *of all people*, reached up to press her palm against the Black Angel's skirt.

"Heck," Jeeter blurted out. "Why not?" He loped over and gave another fold in the Angel's skirt a good rub.

Then Mr. Krasny was pushing himself out of his wheelchair, and Addie and Delaney were coming up to take a turn. I squeezed in between them and laughed as I laid my hand next to theirs, soaking up the warmth of the bronze in the sun.

Author's Note

My first trip into Oakland Cemetery came about by accident. My family had recently moved to Iowa, where we were lucky enough to find a house near the largest public park in Iowa City. Whenever I had time, I would take a jog through Hickory Hill Park, exploring the rambling network of wooded trails. One morning I followed a small dirt path off the main route. I could see some sort of clearing through the thick trees up ahead. I emerged from the shadowy woods and found myself on the edge of a sprawling graveyard.

I had always been fascinated by cemeteries, and this one pulled me back again and again over the next month or so. I would jog along the pathways past the graves—old and new, plain and ornate—and think about all the poignant stories hidden behind the simple names and dates etched in the stones. It was a crisp fall evening, right at dusk, when I first encountered the Black Angel. I had been determined to run five miles that day without stopping (a little farther than Linc's goal), but as soon as I saw the forbidding statue rising up in the heart of the cemetery, my feet slowed to a skittish walk. I circled round the pedestal and tried to make out the strange foreign words in the inscription. *Who could be buried here?* I wondered.

As the next several years passed, I kept my ears tuned for historical facts about the Black Angel. But no one seemed to know any more details beyond the dark warnings associated with the monument. Soon even my own three daughters, ready for an added thrill after trick-or-treating each Halloween, were begging me to drive them over to Oakland Cemetery to visit the Angel. One Halloween we arrived to find votive candles burning around the base of the statue. My kids and their friends dared each other to sprint over and touch the Angel's candlelit skirts, but eventually they agreed they were perfectly satisfied to stay in the car and look.

When I finally decided that I wanted to write a novel about a boy who grows up next to Oakland Cemetery, I spent days in the State Historical Society of Iowa, digging for more information about the family whose names appear in the Black Angel's epitaph. But the few clues I could find in the archives about the Feldeverts were sketchy and disjointed— certainly not interesting enough to provide a gripping plot for my novel.

I had almost resigned myself to the idea of demoting the Black Angel, pushing her to the background of my story, where her only role would be to add a little mystery and atmosphere, when one of the librarians at the historical society asked me, "Haven't you met Tim Parrott? He's writing a book about the Black Angel too."

A wave of surprise and worry rippled through me. *Some-*

one had beat me to it! Once I contacted Tim Parrott, however, I couldn't believe my luck. After years of meticulous research and detective work, Tim had unlocked the secrets of the Black Angel and recently published a small, carefully foot-noted booklet about his findings. His connections to the statue run deep. His grandfather worked as a superintendent of Oakland Cemetery from 1947 to 1964, and Tim grew up listening to stories about the cemetery's residents. And not only is he descended from a long line of Czechs, but he also has a working knowledge of Czech, along with seventeen other languages (!), which he puts to use in his part-time em-ployment as a translator.

Tim quickly became the inspiration for the much older character of Mr. Krasny. Like the fictional Mr. Krasny, Tim first began to hunt for clues about Theresa Dolezal Feldevert in the *Slovan Americký*—a Czech-language newspaper pub-lished in Iowa City from 1873 until 1891, when its offices were moved to Cedar Rapids. Looking back at these old issues on microfilm, I'm amazed that he could find any scraps of in-formation in the cramped rows of splotchy foreign print. But with stubborn perseverance, he uncovered a treasure trove of leads—advertisements for Theresa Dolezal's midwife skills, an obituary for her beloved son Edward, and short bulletins notifying her fellow Czech immigrants of comings and goings.

Tim used these clues to trace Theresa's path from her native village in Eastern Europe and then back and forth across the United States. With the help of genealogical researchers around the world, he unearthed copies of birth, marriage, and death records documenting the family's tragic history. He also found confirmation that Theresa had completed her midwife training at the University of Vienna's Clinic of Obstetrics in 1869 and, eight years later, boarded a steamship, the SS *Mosel*, with four-year-old Edward, to make her way to America.

Along with providing an interesting account of Theresa's rather mysterious marriages, Tim's booklet also clears up a long history of confusion surrounding her commissioning of the Black Angel statue. Based on the recommendation of a friend, Theresa hired a well-known Czech sculptor, Josef Mario Korbel of Chicago, to create a fitting memorial for her family. She paid Korbel an astounding $5,000 for his work—the equivalent of $237,500 today—and the nine-and-a-half-foot-tall statue was cast in bronze and shipped to Iowa City by rail in 1912. According to an article published in the *Iowa City Press-Citizen* in 1922, Mrs. Feldevert "was disappointed at the blackness of the angel, but the artist argued that a 'shiny' bronze statue would be a foolish monument."

While most of the newspaper stories covering the raising of the Black Angel in Iowa City were sensationalized and based on questionable secondhand accounts, one article that appeared in the *Des Moines Register* in 1925 provides a rare peek at Theresa Feldevert's true spirit. In an interview at her home with a reporter named Blanche Robertson, Theresa looked back on her life and mourned in snatches of Czech and broken English. Robertson describes the scene in heartbreaking detail:

She suddenly gave her chair an energetic push and sailed across the room. Manipulating her chair with great skill, she wheeled up to a closet door, opened it, rummaged around, poking bundles with her cane, and finally brought out a huge package wrapped in newspaper. With a triumphant little smile she wheeled back across the room, and with trembling fingers untied the strings and removed the papers.

She drew forth an immense photograph of a handsome young boy. "This is my son—my boy—my Edward." She touched the life-sized features affectionately and gazed for a long time at her dead son. Then came another picture of a man, I should judge to be about 45 years old. "My husband," she murmured proudly. "This other picture is of me," she said. In the photograph she appeared to be of middle age, altogether different from the poor, withered old woman before me. For a long time she looked at the pictures in silence, then she said, "My boy—he get sick and die. My husband, he get sick and die. Now I am sick and soon I, too, shall die." Then carefully wrapping the photographs she replaced them in the closet.

Nor was she far wrong in her predictions, for she died not more than a week after our conversation.

While many details related to the Black Angel in this book are based on historical facts, I also want to remind readers that *Here Lies Linc* is a creative work of fiction. Several characteristics of the statue, as well as historical records, were invented or slightly modified in hopes of keeping the story lively and the pages turning. For example, the fading of the inscription on the base of the Black Angel has been exaggerated in the story, and small bits of phrasing in the English translation have been rearranged for clarity.

I have also taken a bit of creative leeway with the Feldevert name. In the course of my research, I was surprised to learn that the original surname of Theresa's German husband, Nicholas, was actually Feldewert, with a *w*. And to make matters more complex, a shorter version of this name—Feldwert—appears in several legal documents pertaining to the couple. So why did Theresa choose yet another variation—Feldevert—to be etched on her family monument? Her decision might have been related to pronunciation issues. Because there is no *w* sound in German, the original name would have been pronounced "Fel-da-vairt." So perhaps Theresa chose this spelling to ensure that future visitors to her gravesite would pronounce the name properly, once and for all. Whatever the reason, I decided to honor Theresa's last wishes and use the name Feldevert.

Names of streets and places in Iowa City and elements of Oakland Cemetery have also been fictionalized. Jim Wonick, the former superintendent of Oakland, and his successor, Bob Deatsch, whom I interviewed for this book, have nothing in common with the cantankerous Kilgore. They cheerfully answered a long list of unusual questions, took me on a tour of their workshop, and even showed me the small back-room cabinet where the keys to the mausoleums are kept. I only wish I could have convinced them to let me peek into one of the tombs, but professionalism kept them from granting this one request.

Finally, I'd like readers to know that the epitaphs at the opening of each chapter are real, excerpted from actual headstones scattered throughout the United States and beyond. To me they capture the vast range of emotions and experiences represented in our graveyards. Sadness, but also humor and joy. Accomplishments, both humble and grand. I hope you have a chance to wander through an old cemetery soon, just the way you might browse through a good book, waiting for the hidden stories to come alive.

Delia Ray
August 2011

Acknowledgments

I HAVE MANY PEOPLE to thank for lighting the way during my months of wandering through cemeteries. My deepest appreciation goes to:

Loren Horton, my very first cemetery consultant, for teaching me to recognize symbols on headstones.

Tim Parrott for laying the groundwork for this novel with his painstaking research on the life of Theresa Feldevert. I could never have brought the mystery of the Black Angel to life without Tim's willingness to share his Czech-translating skills and his precious "black book"—a gold mine of primary-source information.

Jim Wonick and Bob Deatsch, superintendents of Oakland Cemetery, for patiently answering my questions on every behind-the-scenes subject from grave digging to tombstone tipping.

Michael Lensing of Lensing Funeral Home, who cheerfully contributed his ideas on cemetery trivia and the funeral industry.

My test-readers, Ana Hollander and Sam Buatti, and to the helpful threesome from Horace Mann Elementary—Alex

Moen, Zach Williamson, and Colin Donnelly—for sharing secrets about what it's like to grow up with a cemetery for a backyard.

My faithful writing group members—Dori Butler, Terri Gullickson, and Jennifer Reinhardt—for their critiques and inspiration.

I'm also immensely grateful to the best-agent-ever Laura Langlie for making sure this book found its proper home and to my wonderful new editor, Nancy Hinkel. Thank you, Nancy, for all those "Hah!" and "Nice!" scribbles in the margins, for asking the wisest questions, and for helping Linc and his crew find their footing.

And as always, I owe a special thanks to Matt for being my biggest booster, and to my lovely mother, Bobby, a rare friend, who happily listens to entire chapters read over the phone.

Selected Sources

Carmack, Sharon DeBartolo. *Your Guide to Cemetery Research*. Cincinnati, Ohio: Betterway Books, 2002.

Colman, Penny. *Corpses, Coffins, and Crypts: A History of Burial*. New York: Henry Holt, 1997.

Greene, Janet. *Epitaphs to Remember: Remarkable Inscriptions from New England Gravestones*. Chambersburg, Pennsylvania: Alan C. Hood, 2005.

Keister, Douglas. *Stories in Stone: The Complete Guide to Cemetery Symbolism*. Layton, Utah: Gibbs Smith, 2004.

Parrott, Timothy, C. *The Enigma of Theresa Dolezal Feldwert and the Black Angel*. 2nd ed. Iowa City, Iowa: Timothy Parrott, 2010. Additional copies available from the author at timoshka@aol.com.

Yalom, Marilyn. *The American Resting Place: Four Hundred Years of History Through Our Cemeteries and Burial Grounds*. Boston: Houghton Mifflin, 2008.

Online resources

Cemetery Culture: City of the Silent at alsirat.com/silence

The Epitaph Browser at alsirat.com/epitaphs

findagrave.com

Links to resources on cemetery history and cemetery preservation at potifos.com/cemeteries.html

thegraveyardrabbit.com

About the Author

WHEN DELIA RAY WAS LITTLE, she and her sister and their cousin invented the Brave Girls Club as a way to make the long, hot summers in Tidewater, Virginia, a little more exciting. They dared each other to perform all sorts of daunting challenges—swims across an algae-covered, snake-infested pond, for example, or solo trips to the second story of an old, abandoned farmhouse hidden deep in the woods. Delia still uses her Brave Girl training today whenever she's conducting research for her books, which have taken her on adventures from the Yukon Territory in Canada to cemeteries spread across the state of Iowa. Between adventures, Delia lives in a house overlooking the Iowa River with her husband, three daughters, and a strange-looking mutt named Griff, who came from the animal shelter and provided the inspiration for C.B. in this book. *Here Lies Linc* is Delia's third novel for young readers. To find out more about her, visit deliaray.com.

AVON PUBLIC LIBRARY
BOX 977 / 200 BENCHMARK RD.
AVON, COLORADO 81620